By Kim

Published by Dreamspinner Press
www.dreamspinnerpress.com

By Venona Keyes

Coming of Age
Don't Try This at Home (Dreamspinner Anthology)
With Shira Anthony: Prelude
With Kim Fielding: Running Blind
With Shira Anthony: The Trust

Published by DREAMSPINNER PRESS
www.dreamspinnerpress.com

Running Blind

KIM FIELDING   VENONA KEYES

DREAMSPINNER PRESS

Published by
DREAMSPINNER PRESS

5032 Capital Circle SW, Suite 2, PMB# 279, Tallahassee, FL 32305-7886 USA
www.dreamspinnerpress.com

Running Blind
© 2016 Kim Fielding, Venona Keyes.

Cover Art
© 2016 Anna Sikorska.
Cover content is for illustrative purposes only and any person depicted on the cover is a model.

ISBN: 978-1-63477-891-6
Digital ISBN: 978-1-63477-892-3
Library of Congress Control Number: 2016913017
Published November 2016
v. 1.0

Printed in the United States of America
∞
This paper meets the requirements of
ANSI/NISO Z39.48-1992 (Permanence of Paper).

To K.C., Joel, Nick, Max, Greg, and a host of other narrators. You bring us joy when you bring our books alive.
—K.F.

To the beautiful men of adventure everywhere—especially FVK, wherever he may be. And to my wonderful cowriter, coconspirator, and fellow NPR listener Kim Fielding, to whom I am ever grateful for asking me to write a story with her.

—Venona Keyes

Acknowledgments

NPR. DREAMSPINNER Press. Elizabeth North. Greg Tremblay. Without these ingredients, this story would not have been made.

The spark of this story came from a shared love of listening to NPR, and Elizabeth North's 2014 Dreamspinner Press Writers' Conference in Portland. Kim heard about Peter Sagal and his stint as a running guide in the Chicago Marathon. Venona had heard the story about Riddoch Syndrome. Voilà! A story is born. After two years of juggling schedules, weekly phone calls, back-and-forth writing, research, laughs, deadlines, interviewing voice-over artist and narrator Greg Tremblay, interrogating Greg Tremblay, and questioning Greg Tremblay excessively (and only having to buy him one drink), we finally wrote "The End." We are grateful to Greg, who is really a saint for putting up with us, and we're glad to call him not only a colleague, but a friend. And to Elizabeth, who encourages all the writers, thank you for your faith in us and our story.

Along the way, we had a few others that were invaluable to this story: Thea Nishimori for knowledge of all things Japanese, Harry Bogart for firsthand accounts of living with a blind sibling, Constance Guardi for schooling in the area of Chicago architecture of greystones and bungalows, KC Kelly for another VOA point of view, Mary Calmes for patient feedback on our story, Karen Witzke for polishing the rough edges of our writing, and last but not least, Peter Sagal, for his touching account of being a guide that started this story.

CHAPTER ONE

WHILE KYLE bustled around the house, gathering his things and getting ready to leave, Matt leaned on the doorjamb between the kitchen and the living room, cup of coffee in hand, and watched him, amusement clear on his face. "You always get so nervous before a recording session," Matt said. "You should be used to it by now; it's day twenty!"

"I am used to it. But we're wrapping things up today, and I just want to make sure I get everything right. The long days take a toll, and I want to be up to par. This season has been a tough one for Ecos."

Matt pushed off from the doorway, put down his coffee cup, and gently grasped Kyle's shoulders. "You'll get everything right. Even if you make a mistake, the world won't end. You'll do a retake. And your fans will remain as adoring as ever. Besides, it's in English this time, not Japanese. You've got this."

Although Kyle knew he was good at his job, and although he appreciated Matt's undying support, he made a face. "It's not easy. I know it looks like I'm just getting paid to talk, but—"

"But I just get paid to take pretty pictures. I *get* it, Kye." Matt squeezed Kyle's shoulders. "Go break a leg."

Kyle smiled. "That's for the stage."

"Good point. And with a broken leg, you couldn't come with me to Belize either. Then I just might be tempted to chase after a cabana boy or something."

Kyle rolled his eyes. It was an old joke between them. Each of them was confident the other would never cheat, so it was something they could tease comfortably about. Sometimes, though, Kyle secretly thought it might be better if Matt *did* fall for some cute guy. He and Matt loved each other as friends, not passionately like lovers. That ship really sailed many years ago. Something essential was missing between them, and Kyle wondered if they weren't holding each other back.

Well, that was definitely a conversation for another time. Kyle tiptoed so he could land a kiss on Matt's cheek. "I'm going to be late.

Remember the wrap party. It'll probably start about eight, though you can get there sooner. You can watch as we finish up."

Matt let go of him. "Okay. I'll get there about seven. Hope the recording goes well today."

"Thanks." Kyle grabbed his jacket from the stand near the door and put it on. He checked once more to make sure the script was in his bag, then waved at Matt, who'd collected his coffee and was making his way down to the basement to complete a montage for the week in photos. "You have a good day too. See you later."

"DON, CAN I try that again? I think my timing was a bit off on that last sequence."

"Sure, Kyle. Rewinding."

Kyle watched the screen, heard the familiar beep cue in his ear, and then synced his voice to the animation. "Nooo! It's poison!"

A momentary pause came before Don Perry, the director in the Chicago voice-over studio, switched on the speaker. "Great take! That's a wrap for you." Kyle took off his headphones and rubbed his temples. "Kyle, are you okay? You're looking kind of tired and pale."

"Yeah, Don. It's just a headache. I think it might be eyestrain, or maybe the headphones were too tight. Aspirin should take care of it."

"You've been going at this for nearly ten hours. Why don't you rest, and we'll get you when we start the wrap party. Michelle, David, you're on deck next. Let's see if we can knock this out in less than an hour."

A nap sounded like heaven at the moment.

Both the Japanese and American studios were pushing the English dub for the new episodes of *Ecos*, the wildly popular Japanese manga that was now an anime. For the past three weeks, the voice-over teams had been putting in twelve-hour days to get the dub up at the same time as the Japanese version. Then there would be a nine-month hiatus while the animation studios started work on the next two arcs. Kyle Green had been the Japanese and English voices of the character Ecos for the past five years, and damn, this current story arc was one of the best, but it was challenging the heck out of him.

The headache had been plaguing Kyle all day. Aspirin first, nap second. The first-aid cabinet had the two-per-packet aspirins. Maybe four tablets instead of his normal three? Kyle washed them down with a slug from his water bottle, a constant companion in the studio. He checked the studio's rest and restore room for an available sleep pod. Kyle and some of the other VOAs occasionally napped between takes or until they were needed back in the studio. He could use a quick fifteen-minute snooze to help the aspirin take hold. He lay down in the pod, pulled the cover around, and went to sleep.

THE INCESSANT beeping! Why can't they cue up the damn machine correctly? Where's the script?

"Mr. Green, can you hear me?"

Kyle was groggy. Why was someone trying to wake him? Damn! Had he overslept?

"Hey, Kye, don't try to get up. Just lie back down."

Matt? Why is he here?

"Hey, Kye, didn't catch that. Could you repeat it?"

I didn't say anything, did I? I must be dreaming. God, I don't feel well. I just need to open my eyes—

"Hey, doc! He's throwing up!"

Kyle couldn't seem to get out of the dream. And it felt so real. That was what he got for working too many hours. He was just so tired....

FABRIC RUSTLED next to the bed and woke Kyle. He turned toward the noise.

"Mr. Green?" A soft female voice. "I'm Sheanne, your nurse. How are you feeling? Do you have any pain?"

A big bass drum played in his head. "I ache all over. And my head is pounding."

More rustling of fabric. "On this pain chart, which best describes your pain?"

"I can't see the chart with the eye coverings. You need to remove those first."

Kyle thought he heard a hitch in Sheanne's breathing.

"Mr. Green, you don't have anything on your eyes. They are open."

He ignored a flare of panic. "I can't see anything."

"It's okay, Mr. Green. Sight is sometimes the last thing to come back. On a scale from one to ten, one being no pain and ten unbearable, how is your pain?"

"About a seven." A number was good. It was something tangible, something to hold on to.

"Do you want something for that?"

"Yeah. Please."

He heard taps on a screen, then what he assumed was the flick of a syringe being filled from a vial. A pause, and within thirty seconds, the headache seemed to abate. He was very tired again.

Where am I? he wondered as he drifted off.

"You're at Northwestern Memorial Hospital, Mr. Green."

Huh. Evidently he was talking instead of thinking to himself.

"Is he up? Kye! Kye!" Matt called for him down a long tunnel as Kyle drifted back into the deep dark of sleep.

KYLE AWOKE from his nightmare and sat up suddenly. He waited for his eyes to adjust. Why was it so dark? He should've been able to see the lights from the blasted beeping hospital machines or even lights under the door. He should at least have been able to see the television where a newscaster droned at low volume.

"Kyle? Are you awake?"

Matthew Labrecque, Kyle's partner of ten years, was trying to soothe him by rubbing circles on his back. Kyle loved the touch.

"Matt? What's going on? Why can't I see?"

Matt took in a big breath and let it go, as he did when the news wasn't good. "Kyle, you had a stroke during your rest time at the studio."

Didn't strokes leave people unable to talk or move? Kyle frantically worked his legs, hands, feet. They all felt fine. "I had a stroke?"

"Kyle, calm down. The only thing not working seems to be your eyesight, babe."

The words didn't even make sense at first, as if Matt had spoken another language. Even once Kyle translated them into something that made sense, he couldn't apply them to himself. Strokes were for *other* people. Old people, sick people. And Jesus—his *eyes*!

"What's wrong with my eyes?" It was hard to get the words past his tight throat.

"Your eyes are fine. But the stroke…. The doctors aren't sure yet what's going on."

Not sure. That meant there was hope. Some small mistake, maybe. They'd give him some pills and he'd see again. But now the darkness was so heavy. When Kyle tried to speak again, nothing came out but a distressed moan.

Metal slid over metal as Matt lowered the bed railing. The linens crinkled and the bed dipped as he sat on the mattress and hugged Kyle tightly. Kyle sobbed into his partner's shoulder and, a while later, slipped back into sleep.

"MATT?" SOMETHING had awakened him. Footsteps, maybe.

"Nope. You got me, Kyebye." His sister's familiar voice sounded more hushed than usual.

"Lily? Why are you here?"

"I'm here because I sent your partner home to take a shower and get a decent night's sleep in his own bed. He's been camped out with you for five weeks."

His breath caught slightly. "Five weeks? Shit!"

"Yes, baby bro, five weeks. You've been a resident of the Rehabilitation Institute of Chicago for the last two of them. I've been here. Matt, Mom, and Dad too. Paul is still deployed, and Evan is in baby-watch mode. We've been keeping vigil."

"The trip…."

"Your travel adventure to Belize has passed. Sorry, sweetie. I know how much you and Matt wanted to go."

Fuck! I've lost time. This must be a nightmare.

"You don't understand." If he spoke calmly, the disaster wouldn't be real, right? "It was Matt's assignment to do *National Geographic* photography. The deadline was really tight."

Lily rubbed his arm and sighed. "I know, Kyebye. He called his editors and told them the situation. They sent out someone else."

Before he could process that disaster, the next one hit him. "Wait—I have gigs for dubbing. What day is it?"

"Kye, I had to reassign your books and your immediate VOs. The ones that are a few months out are still on your calendar, depending on whether you get your sight back." Her voice faltered.

Kyle didn't know what to do. If he couldn't see, he couldn't read books for audio, or match his voice to the animation screen or the movie he was supposed to dub. If this was permanent, he'd lost his livelihood. It meant the one thing he loved doing was now out of reach.

"Kye, I don't know what to say. The docs don't know if this is temporary or permanent. You have to be awake enough for them to do an EEG. They did an MRI, but that was inconclusive. You need to be awake for the tests to see what's what."

Kyle's chest was too tight, his stomach tied in knots. He was lost.

"Kye, oh Kye. Come here."

And there he was, once again sobbing.

CHAPTER TWO

MATT AND Kyle had met eighteen years before, over their junior summer in college. Kyle had subleased off-campus housing for the summer semester from a few guys he knew from his media arts classes. Kyle was the only person in the house for the first month. He had no idea who his three other roommates were, as they had moved in their belongings while Kyle was working at the radio station and the recording studios on campus. He also didn't know when they would be back, and after three weeks, he fell into a complacency of being alone in the large house. One morning, clad only in his wash-day thong underwear, Kyle hummed as he started the rice cooker and turned to go to the bathroom to take his shower. A tall, brown-skinned man with thick dark hair and cowlicks that circled his head like a helmet was leaning against the doorframe with a big grin on his face. Kyle jumped as if he were electrocuted.

"Hi! I betcha you thought this place was all yours." The guy pushed off the doorframe and held out his hand. "I'm one of your phantom roommates, Matthew Labrecque. The other guys are going to be here in a minute or two, after they ditch our last dig crew member off at her house. I won the straw draw for who got to shower first, so they dropped me off. I sure hope there's a fifty-gallon hot-water heater, 'cause we haven't showered in three days."

Kyle glanced down at his barely clad body and felt his face light on fire. "There's a twenty-five-gallon heater for each bathroom."

"Great, thanks. Though really"—Matt smirked and gestured generally at Kyle—"you might want to get some more clothes on, unless you're comfortable in your skimpy Speedo or you're one of those models…."

Kyle thought his face would melt off completely as he walked into the bathroom. He called it a success when he closed the door gently.

Once Kyle was clothed and back in the kitchen cooking, his introduction to his remaining housemates was by the sound of their stomachs growling from across the room. Kyle turned, and he saw drool seeping out from the corner of his roomies' mouths over the smell of food cooking. "Are you two hungry, by any chance?"

Kyle only got nods. "Go shower and get dressed. Breakfast will be ready in fifteen minutes."

The scramble to get out of the kitchen was something like an old-time slapstick movie, and Kyle just shook his head and brought out more eggs. Fortunately he'd gone grocery shopping the day before.

As soon as the food hit the table, the feeding frenzy began. Every single morsel of food Kyle had in the house was gone before the food had a chance to cool.

"This is great food! You're a great cook, dude. What's for dinner?" asked Matt.

"Tofu casserole."

Kyle swore he could hear his roommates' brains breaking. Matt barked out a laugh. "We so deserved that," Matt said. "We'll pay for the next round of groceries."

Grocery list made, Matt volunteered to drive Kyle to the grocery store. It was still early enough to get there before the real heat set in and the humidity parboiled everyone who braved the outdoors. Kyle opened the door to the battered and dusty Jeep, and the smell hit him like a brick wall. Eyes watering and hand over his mouth, he stepped back and closed the door.

"What? What's wrong?" Matt looked perplexed.

"I'm getting my car keys."

"Why? My car not good enough for you?"

Kyle shook his head. "It smells like a whole circus of sweat and farts lives in there."

"You're exaggerating. It's not that bad."

Kyle opened the door and made a sweeping gesture.

Matt made a face and took a step backward. "Ah, it didn't smell that bad when we were in it. Maybe the heat and humidity made it bad."

"It needs a wash *and* a fumigation," Kyle called over his shoulder as he walked back into the house.

"Hey, Kye, you drifted off there. Are you okay?"

"Yeah, Lily, just sleepy."

Lily had a weird mental telepathy thing going and could sense when he wasn't telling the truth. She seemed to let it go as she continued to soothingly rub his arm until he did fall asleep.

ON THEIR grocery shopping expedition, Kyle found out Matt was the first in his Lakota Sioux family to go to a four-year university and had a double major in anthropology and photography. "Yeah, I want to be an anthropological photographer."

Kyle blinked a bit. "That's an impressive-sounding career goal." He wanted to be a voice actor—way less impressive.

Matt smiled. "My dream is to document all the petroglyphs of the First Nations of the Americas. My mother is Lakota, my father is French Canadian. We have a ranch out on the South Dakota plains. With all the interest in digging around for oil and expanding population growths, petroglyphs are getting lost to graffiti and new developments.

"That's a good idea having a cooler in the trunk of the car," Matt commented. "I was wondering if we'd have to make a trip back to the house with the milk and ice cream before we finished shopping."

"Military brat. My parents always moved around. With four kids in tow and military pay, you learned to pack for eternally hungry children when driving across the states or countries."

Matt cocked his head slightly as if the topic truly interested him. "Didn't the government pay to move your family around?"

"Yeah, but they didn't necessarily pay for the plane tickets where we could drive. It was fine, though. Mom and Dad made it into an educational vacation. We got to see the sights in a lot of states, Europe, and Asia."

"Really? What's your favorite place?"

"Japan. My dad was stationed there for five years when I was really little, and again when I was an early teen. I picked up the language easily."

"That explains the fish, soup, and rice for breakfast."

Kyle shrugged. "My mom made whatever the locals made for breakfast. Cold cereal was expensive and didn't hold active kids very long. My mom found that out fast when we went through two weeks of cereal in two days."

"My mother said that liquor and cereal made indigenous people diabetic, so she refused to have either in our house. She actually said we were allergic to it. She fed us traditional Lakota food—wasna, which is like a beef jerky made from bison, tallow, and berries, and fry bread—for breakfast." Matt smiled. Not the smirk Kyle saw as Kyle was parading about in his wash-day clothes, but a smile that warmed his face. "What?" Matt asked.

"Good memories of wasna?"

"Yeah. We would make it as kids, pounding it, having fun with our cousins, grandparents, aunts, and uncles. It's one of the only times that everyone got together and old stories were told. The process would go on for a few days." His smile never dimmed as he recounted the happy memory. "It was stored so we'd have food for the winter. Now my mother and grandmother use a food processor to grind it all up and put it into a food dehydrator or a low oven."

"You're actually allergic to cereal and booze?" Most kids lived on both in college.

"That's the only thing you picked up on?" Matt's smirky smile was back. "Nah, she said that so we'd stay away from that stuff. She didn't need to, though. We saw the toll booze and diabetes took on the young and the old on the reservations."

"You didn't go to school on the reservation?"

"No. My family lived in the big city—well, Sioux Falls big, anyway—and went to the public school. After school, our elders taught us the old ways. The reservation school we would've gone to was too far away from where we lived."

"So you're a citified native?" Kyle had his own smirk for Matt.

"Kind of. Family ranch was our weekend and summer home."

"So a little bit country, and a little rock-and-roll?"

Matt burst forth with a strong, hearty laugh. "Kyle Green, I wondered if you were gay, and the Donny and Marie reference clinched it."

A little wiggle began in Kyle's stomach. Matt was flirting with him. "Hey, I would have you know it's part of pop culture. I need to be up on all things, being in radio, television, and theater."

"You keep on telling yourself that."

"Does my sexuality bother you?"

"Not in the least. I'm attracted to it." The wink Kyle received was a nice touch.

A BRIEF fling followed that day but didn't really go anywhere. Instead they became close friends. They roomed together for the rest of their college days, and after graduation, they went their separate ways, keeping in touch for the next six years.

Happenstance brought them together at Pride Fest weekend in Chicago. Kyle had a benefit fundraiser reading gig for the Center on Halstead; Matt was a freelance photographer for the Associated Press. Both still single, they rekindled their friendship and romance. They fell into a comfortable relationship pattern, and Matt moved into Kyle's inherited greystone the next year, making Chicago their base. They found in each other a friend, a lover, and a traveling companion, and together, they saw the world as their respective jobs carried them to the far corners of the planet.

KYLE WOKE up to the Lakota drumbeat of Matt's ringtone. Matt answered quickly. "Hello? ... Dr. Walker? ... Yes?"

Kyle faintly heard the high-tenor Southern drawl of Professor Walker from Southern Illinois University, their alma mater. "We got the grant? Yes! Fantastic!" Kyle could see Matt in his mind's eye, rocking back and forth on his feet as he did when he was excited. Then Matt hesitated. "As great as the news is, I have to let you know that—"

Kyle knew he had to say something before Matt made a big mistake. He waved his hand to get his attention. "Matt?"

"Dr. Walker? Can I phone you back in a few minutes?" A beep ended the call. "Hey, Kye. How are you feeling?"

"Can you come here?" Kyle patted a nearby space on the bed. Matt walked over and lowered the bed railing. Kyle felt the bed dip. Matt must have been at the hospital awhile, as the scent of Matt's High Country cologne was faded, like after a long day. Kyle saw a flash of green as Matt brushed Kyle's hair from his eyes. Weird, but not important at the moment. Probably a random zap of some neglected neuron.

"What's up?" Matt asked softly.

"You should go."

"What?"

"Congratulations on the grant."

"Thanks, Kye, but—"

"Stop. Don't say anything else just yet." Kyle was determined this time to do what he should have done a while back. No more being chickenshit. "I know this is the grant you've been waiting for as long as I can remember. Heck, I remember you telling me about it in college, on that grocery run nearly twenty years ago. This is your dream, your passion. You need to follow that dream."

"What are you saying?" Confusion made Matt's voice waver a bit.

"I love you."

"I love you too, Kyle. What kind of partner would I be if I left you here to recover alone?"

Kyle grabbed Matt's hand. "Hear me out, and don't interrupt me, okay?" Matt didn't move or respond. "Okay?" Kyle asked again.

"Why do I have the feeling I'm not going to like this?"

"Will you promise to listen and not interrupt?"

Matt sighed. "Sure, Kye, I'll listen."

For the first time in this gut-wrenching and mind-bending trip down this rabbit hole of his new normal, calm washed over Kyle as he let the words flow. "You and I are more brothers than lovers."

Matt gripped his hand tighter but didn't argue.

"It's true, Matt. When was the last time we made love? Had sex? Even a blow job? Sure, we could pass it off as a phase or being too busy or getting older. But face it—we aren't meant to be lovers. We're meant to be friends. I know this in my heart, and I think you do too." God, he wished he could look at Matt during this conversation, could see the expressions flitting across his friend's face. Matt as his friend. That felt so right in his head and his heart. "For a long time we've just been too comfortable with each other and too afraid to leave our comfort zone. I want you to be happy, to pursue your dream. I've pursued mine, and I had a great time. I'm happy you finally got that grant you and your team have been working on forever. You should go out to the plains and work on your petroglyph project. I will not be the weight to drag you down. I have a good network of family to help me here."

"Kyle, you don't have to be brave about this. I can spend time—"

"No, you can't. The grant is a full-time gig. I'm not going to have you miss this opportunity. Go. Explore your passion. Tell me about it. I'll still be your friend and confidant. Your partner in crime, maybe. Just not your partner and lover."

Kyle could feel Matt begin to shake, and he opened his arms to hug him. "Come here, big guy." They clung to each other, and Kyle breathed in the faint smoky scent of Matt's redolence and committed it to memory. He would keep it with the face he once knew. Kyle spoke into Matt's ear. "Create a great adventure. Make it a fantastic story like I know you can. And I would be proud to narrate it, my friend." Matt gripped Kyle tightly until Kyle broke the embrace. "Call me and tell me how awesome the project is. Find a good guy who will love you as a lover should, not just as a friend. Now I think you have a call to make. Don't keep Professor Walker waiting."

With one last hug and a familiar sigh that Kyle knew he was going to miss, Matt got up and left the room.

A few minutes later, Lily entered. "Sorry. I eavesdropped. That was a very brave and unselfish thing to do." She sat on the bed.

He leaned into her embrace and started to cry. "It hurts like hell, Lily. It hurts like hell."

"I know, Kyebye. I know."

KYLE HEARD voices. Very faint, but voices. No, just a single voice.

"Lily?"

The voice stopped and Lily moved closer. "Evening, bro!" She sounded awfully perky.

Wait… evening? "Physical and occupational therapy must have really knocked me out. This never-ending labyrinth of learning to live without sight is tougher than I thought."

"Slacker. Thirsty?"

"Yes. No straw."

Lily harrumphed as she poured water into the plastic sippy cup. After placing it in his outstretched hand, she hovered like he was riding a bike for the first time, perhaps in case he couldn't find his mouth. Kyle put the kibosh on straws because he'd nearly poked his eye out last week as he attempted to down a smoothie. He might be blind, but he was *not* going to end up with an eye patch.

"You know you can learn to find the straw if you use both hands, Kye."

"Yeah, well, you didn't almost lose an eye to one."

Lily sighed. "I suppose it's a worthy target for frustration about losing your sight."

Kyle didn't want to argue, so he changed the subject. "Who were you editing?"

"Max Sheppard. He's doing a series for a homeschool program."

"That reminds me, who did you get for all of my gigs?"

Lily moved the chair a bit closer to Kyle's bed, and the light, perfumed scent of peaches and honey waved over him as she sat down. "I got Greg to read that new series of gay-romance books you signed up for. The author was disappointed it wasn't you, but she was happy that Greg took it on. He's in demand right now in the gay-romance circles. He said thanks, and to give him a call when you feel up to it."

"Who took the anime for *Werewolf PTA in Space*?"

Lily laughed. "I had a hard time with that one. You were so iconic as the bad boy in the original *Werewolf PTA* that few others wanted to take it on."

Kyle doubted that very much. "I'm guessing no one wanted to ruin their career with that one. Why would the studio even consider a part two?"

"Because, little brother, that wacky, stupid anime made beaucoup bucks, that's why. The Japanese love that stuff—especially the Japanese women, since it was yaoi."

He racked his brain for his other obligations. "*Star Skaters on Ice*?"

"Max Sheppard did. He thought it was a nice break from the homeschool programming."

Kyle snorted. "If those homeschooler moms and dads find out he did that, his career in education is down the drain."

"Well, Max doesn't seem to care, because just after doing the entire season of *Skaters*, he got a gig doing readings of some evangelical books."

"You mean the religious right didn't know about his character in a yaoi anime?"

"They figured that *Star Skaters on Ice* was the traveling skaters from last year's Winter Olympics." Lily and Kyle laughed. "Besides, they paid a fuck-ton of money for him and his Charlton Heston Moses-like voice to read their books. They said, and I quote, 'His voice has a godlike quality to it.'"

"They don't know he's black and gay, either, I suppose."

"Nope," she said smugly. "His voice just mesmerized them."

"And I thought people would google their potential voice-over readers. Besides, if they'd really done their homework, Aaron did all the talking because Moses, despite all of the pharaoh's teachers, was still a stutterer."

"And you would know since you read the Bible for Books on Tape."

"King James Version, NIV, and Revised Standard Version Catholic Edition. *And* they were tedious to read." All those *begats* and impossible names. Ugh.

"Yeah, wild times in the Bible, yet no call for wild sounds for the Bible."

And for some reason, that struck Kyle as hilarious, and he laughed until his sides ached.

HIS BASIC rehab continued, and parts of it were an adventure. It turned out that loss of eyesight affected balance, so he initially lurched around with his arms out in front of him like Frankenstein's monster every time the therapist left. And since he was uncertain how to stand and aim for the toilet bowl without making a mess, he sat on the toilet to piss. One of the occupational therapists said it was easiest to do exactly that, but he'd assured Kyle that he'd get better with time.

Today Kyle had counted his steps wrong and walked into Marilyn Jones's room. Again. "If you keep coming in here, boy, I'll take it as an invitation that you want to come snuggle with me. I can show you a real good time—I don't have my dentures in!" She smacked her lips and cackled.

Kyle might be blind, but he wasn't *that* blind. Evidently Mrs. Jones was hard up for male companionship, and any old blind man would do. Lily said Mrs. Jones had led a very colorful and full life before a broken hip felled her. He could only imagine.

He put on his best smile, tried not to visibly shudder, turned around, and went back into the hallway.

As he neared his room, he heard Lily talking. "Yes, Daniel, he should be back from therapy soon, and I'll let him know you called. Wait, I think he's back; please hold on."

Lily's voice was excited. "Kyle! It's Daniel Beck and Kurokuma-sensei on the line for you!"

Daniel Beck and Aero Kurokuma wrote and produced the *Ecos* manga. Though Kyle rarely saw them since they lived in Japan, he considered them friends. Neither Daniel nor Aero-sensei had ever said or done anything obvious, but Kyle had always suspected they were a couple. Good for them. "On the line... for me?"

"Yes! They've been trying to reach you. Here, I'll put the phone on speaker and close the door."

Kyle felt around for the chair and nearly stumbled into it. "Daniel?"

"Hello, Kyle! How are you? Did you enjoy the treats basket we sent to you?"

"Yes, thank you and your mother and Aero-sensei for the kind generosity." Matt and the family had enjoyed the elaborate fruit basket the *Ecos* mangaka sent to Kyle. He hadn't been awake to enjoy the gift, but he heard all about it. When Daniel's mother later came to visit and found out Kyle hadn't been able to appreciate the first basket, and noted the awful hospital food, she returned the next day with another basket containing all of Kyle's favorite Japanese treats and some homemade *kake udon*.

"Kyle, I won't keep you long. Aero and I just wanted to let you know that you're still the voice of Ecos. And in this next story arc, Ecos will be silent. He will continue to be silent until you can once again be his voice."

Kyle was overwhelmed by the gesture. Surely they had to know that he was in no position to be a VOA for the foreseeable future.

"Kyle?"

He cleared his throat. Lily put her hand on his shoulder. "I'm still here, Daniel. I'm very grateful for your support."

Then Aero-sensei himself got on the line, and in Japanese he said, "No, you honor us by being what we dream our character embodies. We will wait for as long as it takes. Get better, my friend."

Kyle choked up a bit. "*Arigatō gozaimasu*, Aero-sensei, Daniel-san." He bowed his head.

"Get better, buddy," Daniel said. "We'll see you when we come in for Anime Midwest in July."

"You convinced Aero-sensei to come to the States?"

"We're coming to see you and my family. So I convinced Aero to be the featured guest at the con."

Holy shit! Kyle knew that Aero Kurokuma hated going anywhere and was considered a recluse in manga circles. Now Daniel had him leaving Japan and taking the world by storm. "I'm looking forward to seeing you both when you get here."

After a few more pleasantries, the call ended. Kyle was a mix of emotions, overcome by the confidence the mangaka had in him. They had become friends after he was cast as Ecos in the anime, but to wait for him? And what if he could never come back?

Lily tapped his hand. "Somehow that great news isn't making you feel better."

"I just don't want to disappoint them."

"Kyle, don't you realize how much you touch other people with your work? Your website nearly came down with all the well-wishes once your status was posted. Even the updates nearly take the site down. Good thing Dad is a social-media god and we have the website update your social media, or I would have to hire someone to take it over."

His dad was a social-media guru? Truly the world was spinning on a different axis. Kyle opened his mouth to interrupt, but Lily cut him off before he could get a word out.

"I don't think you've grasped the massive number of food baskets, flowers, toys, and cards that flooded into the hospital, not only from Japan but from around the world. You're rock-star status in Japan, for Pete's sake. The hospital administration decided you were some huge celebrity, based on the barrage of gifts during the weeks you were comatose." Lily touched his hand, grounding him. "You don't understand how grateful the hospital patients and outside charities were when they received your goodies. It was like Christmas for the entire children's ward at the hospital and the rehab center. Those cards I've been reading to you? I barely scratched the surface. There are at least five Bankers Boxes full of them. And that doesn't even include cards that came with the gift baskets."

"B-but Lil—"

"No buts, Kye. We'll figure this out somehow. You're not alone."

All those people were celebrating a person who no longer existed. Damn it! Why did this have to happen?

Lily's voice turned playful. "Hey, Kye, some of the best cards you got were from girls who sent pictures of gorgeous naked men to help inspire you to heal. Who knew there were cards like this for the blind! There's even raised ridge outlines on this guy's pecs, six pack, and penis...."

"You're shitting me, aren't you?"

"Would I lie to you?" She paused. "Don't answer that. Here, feel."

Kyle touched the card. "Hmmm. Seems the outlines are a bit worn down. Is this *your* favorite card, Lily?"

Kyle grinned as his sister blustered. "I was breaking it in for you. Saving you from getting calluses."

"Uh-huh. Inspecting it for my own safety, you little perv?"

He could feel the heat coming off of Lily—she was blushing!

"Oh shut it!" she said and effectively closed the topic.

CHAPTER THREE

IT WAS easy being brave when you were lying in a hospital bed with family and nurses nearby. And Kyle had meant what he said to Matt—although they loved each other, the passion had long since cooled. Way before the stroke, they'd settled into that comfortable, tepid zone where they enjoyed hanging out together but no longer got excited about the physical part. Kyle had been giving some thought to breaking things off, but he hadn't wanted to hurt Matt and, to be honest, was chickenshit about facing the dating world. He hadn't been single since a few years after college, for Christ's sake, and now he was sliding toward middle age. With the recent drastic changes, the last thing he wanted was to hold Matt back. So he'd done the right thing, done what he had to do.

Someone give him a goddamn medal.

Now, though, facing discharge from the rehab hospital and an uncertain future, Kyle wished he'd been selfish. He'd been through occupational and physical therapy to get his bearings, but this new way of life sucked big-time. Although the therapists had helped him come to grips with being sightless, they'd done so in the rehab center's fake apartment. He could chop an onion without taking off his fingers, and he could make a decent stew—all in a kitchen that was not his own. He could negotiate the stairs, and he could now use the cane without too much damage to the nursing staff. With some assistance, he exercised at the gym, and he'd finally conquered drinking with a straw. The doctors had said a lot of things, but few of their words sank in. The recording function on his phone and the text-to-speech app helped. He hoped Lily had been paying attention.

Lily, his mom, and his dad, with assistance from the Bridge Center, had affixed braille labels onto the kitchen and laundry appliances in his house to give him a head start when he arrived home. Someone from the center would meet him at the house to help him adjust to that environment. But once he settled in, how was he going to make a living without vision? Sure, he could still record audiobooks once he got better at braille. But how long that would be, he didn't know. Animation voice-overs were out because he needed sight to sync the voice with the character.

He sat on the edge of his hospital bed, terrified, and startled slightly when the door opened. The ambient hallway sounds drifted in and then suddenly stopped as the door swung closed. "Hi, tiger," said the familiar voice of Fernando, one of the night-shift nurses. "You know it's only 4:00 a.m., right?"

Kyle sighed. "Yeah, Siri told me." A smartphone had turned out to be extremely handy for a blind man. "But I'm still wide-awake. My sleep cycle's off."

"Could be nerves, and hospitals are noisy places even at night. When you settle back into your life at home, you'll probably sleep better."

Settle into life—right. Like that was going to happen. Kyle didn't say anything, but his face must have registered skepticism, and the mattress dipped as Fernando sat next to him.

"Give yourself time, tiger." Fernando had a nice voice, warm and slightly rumbly. Kyle wondered if he was handsome, then quickly realized it didn't matter. Fernando could have had green skin and three noses for all the difference it made to Kyle. Maybe it was a good thing he could no longer judge people based on their looks. He'd have to think about that.

"It's disorienting. I have no sense of whether it's day or night unless I ask my phone or someone comes to take me to my lessons or therapy."

"A routine will probably help, as the OT told you. But look, if you keep having problems with sleeping, talk to your doctor about Non-24."

"Huh?"

Fernando chuckled slightly. "Sounds mysterious, doesn't it? Sort of sci-fi. It just means some people have a body clock that's naturally set longer or shorter than twenty-four hours. Like a watch that's off, right? But for most of those people, when they see daylight, the clock gets reset automatically to the right time, so they're cool. The resetting doesn't happen for all sighted people, though, and if your eyes can't register the light to begin with, well...."

"Great. Another lovely side benefit of blindness that I hadn't even known about." Because at first he'd been focused on the obvious—no more driving, no more reading printed material, no more admiring pretty sunsets or mountain views. He was gradually learning that he'd lost much more than those things.

"Hey, you may not be Non-24. And even if you are, there are treatments like melatonin."

Kyle nodded but couldn't help another noisy sigh. They sat next to each other for several minutes, the muffled sounds of voices and footsteps coming and going in the hallway. Even in the wee hours, the rehab hospital was a hopping place. Kyle knew that Fernando had a busy workload, so he was grateful for the time lavished on him.

"Your sister going to pick you up?" Fernando finally asked.

"Yeah."

"What time?"

"Nine, she said. But she's always late."

"Ah. One of those." Fernando shifted a little on the bed. "You need help packing?"

"No, thanks. I think I got most of it." He gestured to his duffel bag, which sat out of the way and tight against the wall. Not that he had many personal effects to deal with. He'd asked Lily to bring him only the basics—toiletries, a phone charger, and a couple changes of clothing, which he learned to tag for color in one of the rehab classes.

More silence between them. Then Kyle realized he was jiggling his leg and made an effort to still it. His entire body felt wound tight, a spring ready to release at any moment. "God, I miss running," he mumbled. "And before you say anything, running on a treadmill is not running."

But that led to another thought, one he'd been worrying about almost since he regained full consciousness. "It's not fair. Christ, I know I'm whining, but it's *not*. I'm only forty. And I take good care of myself! I eat right—even pay extra for the organic stuff. I run—*ran*— four days a week and lifted on my off days. I took vitamins. I always used a condom!"

Fernando was a good man. He didn't tell Kyle to lower his voice or stop bitching, and he didn't point out that practicing safe sex had little to do with avoiding a stroke. All he did was pat Kyle's arm. "You're right, man. It's not fair. I have a relative—let's see... second cousin twice removed? Anyway, he's a mean old bastard who has beer for breakfast and booze for dinner. Never met a deep-fried anything he didn't like. About the only exercise he gets is clicking the remote and yelling at his wife. And the son of a bitch is in his eighties and healthy as a horse. And here you are, a real nice guy who takes care of himself, and you get zapped by a time bomb in your brain."

It was hard to stay worked up with Fernando's calm sympathy. "I bet a lot of your patients have it worse than me, huh?" At least the doctors claimed this stroke had been a fluke, a byproduct of a hidden defect in his brain. He was unlikely to have another, and although he was supposed to get regular checkups just in case, he wouldn't need to be on meds.

"They sure do," Fernando said. "Even the ones who walk out of here on their own steam like you're gonna do. A lot of them— You know, a real common effect of stroke is loss of speech. Imagine how it feels to have all those words bottled up inside you and not be able to get them out."

Kyle shuddered. "My voice is my livelihood."

"I know. Anyway, my point is that sure, you could have had it a lot worse. But that doesn't mean you don't have the right to grieve what you've lost. And you shouldn't feel guilty about being pissed off over it."

"Thanks." Kyle managed a shaky laugh, then scrubbed his face with his palms. "I'd hate to mix guilt with my fury."

"Can I give you some advice? We won't even add the charge to your bill."

"Hit me."

"This is something I've said to a lot of folks over the years, okay? It's tried-and-true wisdom. I should probably patent it."

Kyle smiled and motioned him to continue.

"Okay," said Fernando. "Here's the thing. Your life is never gonna be the same as it was before the stroke. There's just no getting around that. And some stuff is gonna be hard."

"If this is supposed to be a pep talk, it's a lousy one."

"Not a pep talk. I charge extra for those, plus the whole effect with my pom-poms would be lost on you."

Kyle's first real laugh in days surprised him. He knew from the way Fernando moved that he was a pretty big guy, although Kyle couldn't tell whether he was muscular or just heavy. Either way, Kyle could almost picture him in hospital scrubs, standing in the middle of the little room and prancing like a cheerleader. "Okay, sorry. It's advice you're giving me, not a pep talk."

"Damn right. And it's easy advice too. But let me tell you a little story first. I didn't grow up wanting to be a nurse. I don't think it ever occurred to me that I *could* be. I mean, all the nurses I saw on TV were women. Besides, nobody in my family went to college. We were lucky if we made it through high school. When I was little, I wanted to be a race car driver, except those were all white dudes. I guess I figured I'd end up like my dad and my uncles—in construction. I didn't mind that."

Fernando was silent then, perhaps thinking about his family. Kyle thought about *his* family, his childhood dreams. He'd wanted to be an actor. Well, no. He'd wanted to be a movie star. Maybe voice work wasn't as glamorous, but it wasn't so far off the mark.

"Anyway," Fernando continued, "I worked with my dad for a little while after I graduated. But then he messed up his back really bad and had to retire young. He was in a lot of pain, and man, that was hard to watch. He was a strong man, you know? Proud. Anyway, I watched him with all his doctors and nurses and I thought, wouldn't it be great if I could help him feel better too? So I joined the Army. Ended up serving in the Gulf War. And when I got out, Uncle Sam paid for me to go to school. Papa died a few years ago, but he got a chance to see me get that degree."

"I bet he was proud," Kyle said.

"Are you kidding? He'd stop complete strangers in the grocery store to tell them about me. But do you see the moral of my story?"

"Um, not exactly."

"It's not complicated. I figured I was gonna spend my life building houses, but Papa got hurt and here I am. Our lives take sideways turns sometimes. But just because things are different from what you expected, different from what you're used to, that doesn't mean they're worse. I *love* my job."

Kyle grinned at him. "You're good at it."

"Yep. Your life has changed, tiger. Doesn't mean you won't be happy. Just means it might be a different kind of happy than you planned on."

Fernando stood and patted Kyle's shoulder. "I have work to do. See if you can get some rest."

Suddenly exhausted, Kyle yawned, which made Fernando chuckle. "All right," Kyle said. "And thanks."

With another pat, Fernando left. Kyle lay down on the bed, but he didn't fall asleep. Instead he thought about happiness, and change, and never seeing what was around the next corner.

CHAPTER FOUR

STANDING ON the stoop of his greystone, Kyle awkwardly tried to balance his duffel in one hand and his cane in the other as he fingered his keys for the one to unlock the front door. Lily didn't offer to unlock it; he had to do it himself. He wasn't supposed to rely on sighted people for everyday tasks—but man, he was tired. He just wanted to be home.

As he opened the door, Kyle heard the familiar squeak of the hinge he and Matt never got around to oiling, and his throat tightened painfully. He stayed just outside the threshold and felt Lily brush by him. He was grateful that she didn't pressure him to come inside.

"Everything looks good," she called from inside the living room, her voice echoing slightly.

It smelled like home. Kyle stepped inside, set down his duffel bag, and closed the door. "Thank you for coming in and labeling everything."

"It was no big deal. Mom, Dad, and I stayed here while you were in the hospital. Matt sent the cleaning service a check from the joint account before he took his name off—and put me on, which was nice." Twice-monthly maid service had been one of their luxuries, since neither he nor Matt had been interested in tidying and their schedules were often hectic. "I'll call them tomorrow and find out how many more cleanings are left on that check." Shit. Another thing to arrange. Lily's shoes clacked on the wooden floor as she came closer. "I got a few basic groceries so we wouldn't starve to death tonight. We'll do a major shopping trip tomorrow."

"Lil, you don't have to—"

"Do too. And I don't mind. You can take me out to lunch. Nothing like tackling two big things on your first full day out of the joint." Lily laughed, and Kyle managed to chuckle. "Remember when we were in Germany?" Lily touched his arm. "When we found that sled saucer the other family left behind, and we climbed up the steep hill five minutes after we moved in?"

"Mom just about had a cow because we'd never gone sledding before and there we were, sliding down the hill at fifty miles an hour toward a hay barn."

"You were fearless at one time, Kye. And you can be again. Just think of this as an adventure. And I'll be here to help you out for a while."

Kyle could use her help. He might someday be able to buy groceries on his own, but that was far into the future, like jetpacks and flying cars. Besides, his sister loved to shop, even if they were buying only milk and produce. "You know you don't have to stay here."

"I do, Kye, for now. Then I'll move back to my place. This is just for a few weeks. Do you want help unpacking?"

He was still standing just inside the entryway as if he were a hesitant guest. "No, thanks. I think…. Don't take this the wrong way, Lil, but could you sort of… leave?"

Luckily Lily wasn't oversensitive, and she rarely threw fits. "Sure. You're due for some alone time. I'll be in the basement studio. Do you want me to make lunch?"

"No, I'll do it. I'll call you when it's ready."

"Looking forward to a gourmet lunch, then. Just call me if you need anything, okay?" She gave him a quick hug before going downstairs.

Moving cautiously, swinging his cane in an arc as he'd been taught, Kyle made his way across the living room. He had to think carefully about where the furniture was placed, and he hoped Matt hadn't moved things around too much before he left.

Matt.

With a noise suspiciously akin to a groan, Kyle collapsed into his usual spot at one end of the couch. Matt used to sit at the other end, and they'd balance a bowl of popcorn between them as they watched the TV over the fireplace.

"I wonder…," Kyle said out loud. He hoisted himself to his feet and, abandoning his cane, walked forward. He swore when he stubbed his foot into the coffee table leg, but at least he was wearing shoes. Besides, he used to trip over the damned thing even when he could see. He'd always assumed the piece of furniture had malevolent intent.

With his hand outstretched, he felt for the television. It was still there on the wall, mocking him. Matt obviously hadn't needed it, as his housing in South Dakota was completely furnished. It felt odd to have a television. It wasn't as if he could watch the thing, and if he wanted voices for company, the radio—which Matt had also left—would do just as well. He felt uneasy knowing that blank glass eye was staring at him, knowing he couldn't stare back. Well, he could stare back, but his look would be as blank as the screen.

Kyle's grandparents, knowing how much he loved the greystone, had left it to him in their will. It was in the Lakeview/Wrigleyville area, close to the activities in Boystown but far enough away for some peace and quiet during the big Pride events. Matt and Kyle had renovated the interior and furnished it with items from local shops and their world travels. He and Matt hadn't discussed the distribution of assets in much detail. They'd been a couple for so long that they'd acquired almost everything together. Hell, they even shared a few shirts and sweaters since they were the same size. Kyle had simply told Matt to take whatever he wanted, and Matt had sadly said okay.

All of a sudden, Kyle urgently needed to know what Matt had taken and what remained to him, but cataloging the house contents by touch would take forever. He turned too quickly and, disoriented, felt the floor tilt beneath his feet. He sank down onto his ass. "Don't let me fall off the world," he prayed to nobody in particular.

There he sat, inside a four-bedroom, 2100-square-foot house on a street that, conservatively guessing, contained a couple hundred people. His neighborhood was in a city of almost three million. Ten million souls called the Chicagoland metro area home. His sister was less than a mile away, or would be after a few weeks, and willing to come over at a moment's notice. Even Matt was just at the other end of the phone. So why did he feel so fucking alone?

No, he reminded himself sternly. *No more goddamn crying.*

He stood on wobbly legs, took a few deep breaths, and got himself resituated in the room. The stupid coffee table was directly in front of him, which meant that the entry door was to his left, the kitchen and hallway to his right, which led to the two staircases, one up to the bedrooms and bathroom and one downstairs to the workout room, the entertainment room, and the studio. And on the wall above the couch....

For several long moments, he remained motionless, unable to bring himself to explore whether Matt had taken the photo from over the couch. Matt had snapped the shot during their first trip to Japan. Kyle wasn't yet the voice of Ecos, but he had been working on an anime series. Matt was still freelancing in those days, hoping to sell some pretty pictures to magazines. But this wasn't a stereotypical shot of cherry blossoms, a temple, or Mount Fuji. Instead it was a street scene from Tokyo. Matt had captured a huge crowd crossing the street in the rain, multicolored umbrellas and neon light reflections providing splashes of color. Kyle had always loved that picture, and when they'd finished rehabbing the living room together, Matt had surprised him with a large framed print.

Finally able to move his feet, Kyle made his way to the couch and knelt on the cushions. He reached hesitantly to the wall—and found the picture still there. He collapsed onto the couch in relief. Although he couldn't see the photo, he was deeply comforted to know it remained.

"I need to unpack," he told himself. "And I need to start arranging my clothes." He had tagged the few articles of clothing he wore at the hospital, but now the entire closet awaited his newly gained skills. When he got better at learning braille, he would attach labels to the tags so he could identify the specific items. In the meantime, the people at the rehab center had told him that good organization was key. And not just with his clothes but also with the contents of the kitchen and bathroom, the cleaning supplies… everything. Even though the family had labeled more than half the house, they left some labeling for him. Getting used to the house and doing the labeling felt overwhelming and too much for today. First he needed to eat.

In the rehab center's kitchen, he'd spent a lot of time learning how to prepare food without poisoning himself, chopping off appendages, or burning the place down. He was pleased to discover that he faced few difficulties while fixing sandwiches, although he wondered what kind of artisan bread Lily had bought. It smelled weird. He sliced a few carrots and cucumbers into rounds to make healthy "chips." He was even happier when he managed to brew coffee.

He felt around the panel by the basement door for the studio call light. He pressed the button, notifying Lily lunch was ready. As he sat at the kitchen table and waited for Lily to join him, the mug clutched between his palms, he saw a wisp of movement over the top of his cup.

His breath caught, and as he watched, the vapor trail twisted in the darkness. Then, no matter how hard he squinted, it was gone.

LILY CHOSE a nice restaurant for lunch the next day, but Kyle was too busy concentrating—trying to eat without making a mess, looking for more movement—to appreciate the food. Even after the meal was over, his preoccupation continued. "But I *saw* it," he insisted for the hundredth time as they entered the grocery store and snagged a shopping cart. He had been trying to convince her since lunch yesterday, but she wasn't having it.

"You *thought* you saw," she corrected, steering the cart and Kyle down the canned goods aisle. "It was a trick of the mind. Like... like when you squeeze your eyes shut really hard and see sparkly lights."

"I don't see sparkly anything when I squeeze my lids. I don't see anything, because sparkles are not a trick of the mind—it's the ocular nerves being stimulated. And you can stimulate mine all you want, but the burnt-up part of my brain won't register it."

"Well, exactly. And if— You making your famous black bean soup?

"Yes, low-sodium black beans. And don't forget the fire-roasted corn," he muttered.

"Okay. Six cans of each?"

"Yes."

"The part of your brain that registers vision is too badly damaged, hon. The doctors said so. You didn't see anything yesterday."

He saw a blur of color shortly before he heard the metal cans thud into the cart. "There! I saw a blue-and-yellow flash!"

"Kyle, the black beans you buy are in a blue can, and the corn is in a yellow can. You're imagining it because you already know what they look like."

He wanted to growl in frustration. He didn't understand what had happened either, but he knew it was real. He wasn't hallucinating. "And I *did* see something. I was sitting there waiting for my coffee to cool, and I saw movement." He'd tried to explain this to her already but had trouble finding the words. He hadn't seen anything specific— not the mug or the refrigerator in front of him. Hell, he wasn't even sure if the kitchen lights had been on. But he'd sensed something right in front of him, a black shadow moving in the darkness. It was a little like knowing someone was watching you, even if you were turned the other way.

"This is a big adjustment for you," Lily said. "Things are going to be weird for a while. Maybe your other senses are compensating. Hey, do you think you'll end up with superhero hearing? That would be handy."

He sighed and kept a hand on the cart, following along as Lily guided them toward the produce. "Cross-modal plasticity," he said.

"What's that?"

"It's when your brain kind of rewires itself to make up for a sensory deficit. They told me about it in rehab. Some blind people end up with better hearing or touch or whatever. But it doesn't always happen, especially when someone loses sight later in life. Like, say, forty." He certainly wasn't counting on it. He'd always had good hearing in any case—he was excellent at picking up nuances of tone and inflection, which was one reason he made a good voice actor.

"Kyle—"

"Never mind. Just help me pick out some apples, okay?"

As they continued shopping, Kyle wondered if people were staring, feeling sorry for the blind guy who couldn't even grab a six-pack of beer by himself. But he didn't argue with Lily anymore. There was no point in it.

When the cart was full, Kyle paid with his phone. In rehab, he'd learned how to fold paper money so he could identify the denomination, but the phone app was easier: just tap and the phone announced the amount. He didn't even need to sign. Although if signing had been required, he was sure the scribble on the screen wouldn't be too far from his former signature, which was hardly more than a scrawl even when his vision was 20/20.

Kyle helped Lily load the groceries into the back of her car, then waited in the passenger seat while she wheeled the cart to a corral. He missed his own car, an Acura—nice but not fancy and only a few years old. He'd offered it to Matt, who already had a Jeep and didn't want two vehicles, so he'd sold it and deposited the money in Kyle's account. Kyle was doing okay financially—royalties on the voice of Ecos paid well—but he wasn't sure when or if he'd be able to return to work. A little extra cushion was good, especially with all the medical expenses insurance hadn't covered.

Lily grunted softly as she slid into the driver's seat.

"Everything all right?" Kyle asked as she started the engine.

"Yeah. Just tired."

Fuck. "I'm sorry, Lil. Babysitting me has pretty much taken over your life, and you have a job and—"

"Shut up." She didn't pull out of the parking space, and her voice was stern. "Don't you dare apologize for needing help, Kyle Green. You're my little brother, and nobody could stop me from helping you out. Besides, weren't you right at my side when I lost the baby? When Rich and I divorced? I seem to remember somebody letting me use him as a human Kleenex for weeks."

"But that was different. It was short-term. I'm never going to…. God, maybe I should just move in with Mom and Dad after all."

"Ha! I bet that would last about three seconds before you guys tried to strangle each other."

She was right. Kyle knew his parents loved him. When he had come out in his early teens, his mom and career-military dad had hugged him and said they were behind him all the way. Now in their early seventies, they were busy with their own lives and lived in a bustling retirement community in goddamn Arizona. His mom sold her handcrafted items through her website and on Etsy, and his dad was now a personal trainer—finding his niche in once again ordering people to do his bidding. Their little birds had flown the nest, and now there was no room, even for the blind baby bird.

Kyle had already considered his potential support network while he was in the hospital. His brothers had offered to help out, but there wasn't much they could do since they were both military. Paul was stationed in Texas, while Evan was… where the hell was he nowadays? Washington State, and doting on his first grandchild. That left poor Lily with Kyle as her burden.

"I like giving you a hand," Lily said softly. "God, I've been wanting to dress you for years. For a gay guy, you have a terrible sense of style."

He laughed. "I am not your personal Ken doll. I'll stick with my regular clothes."

"Not if I sneak into your closet and replace everything," she teased. "I'll swap out all those boring shirts for something with color and patterns, and you'll never know."

"You would take advantage of a blind man?" He put his hand over his heart, feigning outrage.

"I would if that blind man once hid issues of *Playgirl* under his bed and then told Mom they were mine."

"I was fourteen!"

"Old enough for criminal intent." Lily had been a paralegal until she found audio editing more her style. She laughed and then thunked the gears into reverse.

Although it was a short distance home, traffic slowed their way. Both Treasure Island and Whole Foods were within easy walking distance—well, easy when he had been sighted. He and Matt used to stroll the eight blocks to the grocery store and window-shop at the boutiques and small shops along the way. Now Kyle sat with his face turned toward the passenger window, wondering which familiar streets they were passing, the everyday sights he'd lost. Was the sky pale blue or covered in clouds? Did the furniture store still have a burned-out *ni* on its sign? Had the trees completely leafed out yet?

There must have been a green light and a momentary break in traffic, because Lily gunned the engine and the car shot forward. She had always been lead-footed. But as they accelerated, Kyle saw something again. Not a shape or a color or anything identifiable. He just had a firm sense that something was in front of his gaze. Or multiple somethings, more like. Buildings, other cars, pedestrians. His heart raced, but he didn't say anything to Lily.

LILY HELPED Kyle put the groceries away. He had purchased disposable braille food labels that, along with a strict organizational system, would help him identify canned goods, boxes, jars, and bags. As Lily handed him the cans and he put the labels on, he hoped he'd be able to keep track of everything.

"I never thought I'd end up with an alphabetized pantry," he said as he tucked away the last of the food.

"It's not a bad idea for anyone, actually. It always takes me forever to find things in my cupboards and drawers. Maybe I should try it too."

"Good luck with that." Kyle knew his sister lived amid perpetual piles of books and papers, and she had a tendency to lay things down wherever was handy. She would then get distracted and forget where they were.

"So, want to get dinner started while I go check on Mel's cat?" Lily asked.

"I'll start on the black bean soup. Dinner about six?"

"Sounds good. I've got other errands to run too."

He followed her out of the kitchen and to the back door, managing not to collide with anything along the way despite being without his cane. Yay for him.

"Later," she said, and she was gone.

SEVERAL DAYS passed, all feeling much the same. Kyle practiced his skills he learned in rehab, Lily stayed within earshot, Kyle cooked.

"Do you need me to help you today, Kyle? I can rearrange my schedule...."

"Lil, you have work to complete. Go downstairs to the studio and finish up your audio edits. My mobility instructor is stopping by, and we're going to walk over to the Bridge Center." The center was less than a mile away. Kyle was continuing his braille lessons there. The center also boasted a store that sold all kinds of gadgets intended to make life easier for the visually impaired. He might treat himself to a little shopping spree.

After a brief hesitation, Lily said, "Fine. Just call me if—"

"I know. I will. Now get to work."

He loved his sister very much, but he sagged with relief when she was gone. He savored the quiet of the house and his own sketchy independence as he finished getting ready for his outing.

Walking to the Bridge Center was slightly terrifying, even with the instructor at his side. City smells of exhaust and garbage and food, usually barely noticeable, were oppressive, and the sounds of traffic and pedestrians made him tense. He was relieved when he reached their destination unscathed. "You did well," the instructor assured him. She sounded young and perky. He pictured her as blonde, ponytailed, and dressed in bright colors. "A few more practice runs and you'll be ready to do it yourself. Then we'll master public transportation!"

Oh goody.

He concentrated hard during his braille lesson, desperate to read again. Yes, computers and smartphones and other technology could do a lot for him, but not everything. He still didn't know if he was ever going to be able to resume his career, which scared the shit out of him. *One thing at a time*, he reminded himself.

After the lesson ended, he bought a shopping bag full of stuff. Most of the things were for the kitchen, like a talking food scale and a plastic finger guard for when he sliced things. By far, his best find was a little device that would identify colors. Hah! Now Lily couldn't change all his shirts to orange plaid, or whatever her dastardly plan was.

The mobility trainer walked him home, chirping encouragement the whole way.

After the cacophony of the streets, his quiet house was a refuge. Kyle spent a long time sitting on the couch, listening to the hum of the refrigerator, the children in the backyard next door, the dog walker and her charges that passed by the house—all the comforting sounds of the house and the neighborhood—as he tried to calm himself. "It gets better," he said out loud. Fuck, it had to.

He was tiredly considering lunch options when his phone rang. He couldn't help but smile at the familiar sound of drums.

"Hey, Matt."

"Settled back in?" Matt's voice was deep, with just the tiniest hint of his father's French-Canadian accent slipping in every now and then, his mother's Lakota inflections adding some musicality to his tone.

"Getting there."

"Is… everything okay? Are you able—"

"I'm fine. Haven't killed myself or anyone else yet." Kyle hoped he sounded light and joking. He didn't want Matt to know how deep his despair could be. Breaking up had been the right thing—for both of them. But good medicine was often bitter. "How's the project going?"

"Amazing, man. Last night I got these shots just as the sun was setting, making the stone shine like gold, and…." And he was off, describing his work at length. His obvious joy made Kyle happy.

Eventually, though, Matt turned the direction of the conversation. "What about you? Are the lessons going well?"

"I guess. I walked to the Bridge Center and back with my instructor today. It was nice to get out a little." Which wasn't exactly a lie. Matt didn't need to know how the sounds of unseen traffic made Kyle want to jump out of his skin or how much Kyle yearned for the days when he could lift his feet and run. "And I think I've thwarted Lily's master plan to spice up my wardrobe."

Matt's throaty laughter filled the room. "She's still saying you're the worst-dressed gay guy?"

"I wasn't that bad, was I?"

"You and I know that Lily watched way too much of *Queer Eye for the Straight Guy*. And you're in show business. She expects way too fancy for what we are."

"Just plain guys."

They both chuckled. It felt warm and familiar, and it eased the melancholy that had plagued him for the past few days.

"I'm surprised she hasn't tricked out my cane yet, though that's sure to come."

"The cane's going to work for you?"

"It has to. I'm as allergic to dogs as I ever was. And you know I've never been a dog person anyway."

"That sucks."

This had been the best part of their relationship—the long talks about their lives, their opinions, their hopes and dreams. That didn't need to stop even though they weren't together anymore. Kyle could still act as a sounding board for Matt's sometimes unrealistic ideas, and Matt could still provide rock-solid advice, grounding Kyle when he felt lost.

These thoughts led Kyle to divulge something he hadn't planned to. "Something weird happened to me."

"Oh?"

"It was... I saw things, sort of."

"What do you mean?" was Matt's careful reply.

Kyle described what had happened over coffee, at the grocery store, and in Lily's car. He'd had a similar experience today, standing on a street corner and waiting to cross. A bus had rumbled by, and as it passed, Kyle could hear it, could feel the displaced air against his skin, and could *see* something. He hadn't mentioned it to his mobility instructor.

When the brief tale was done, Matt remained silent for a moment. "Would you mind if I tell someone about this?" he finally asked.

"Tell who?"

"A neurologist."

"Just… any random neurologist?"

"No."

Matt cleared his throat, and Kyle was struck with a realization. An odd mixture of emotions washed over him—jealousy, sadness, relief, happiness—making him a little dizzy. "How'd you meet him?"

"He's a friend of Dr. Walker's, from the university. His name's Gil. He came out to see the petroglyphs for a couple days, just being a tourist. And we… we hit it off, I guess. God, Kyle, I'm sorry."

"For what? Moving on with your life? Being happy?"

"But it hasn't been that long since we broke up, and—"

"Don't martyr yourself just because I'm blind!" That came out more sharply than Kyle had intended, so he made an effort to soften his voice. "Really. If he's good to you, then I'm really glad for you. You deserve that."

Matt sighed. "Thank you. And you—"

"Don't. I can't even cross the street by myself yet. I don't want to even think about the horrors of dating."

"Fair enough. But is it okay if I tell Gil what you saw?"

Kyle smiled at Matt's faith, at his belief that Kyle had truly sensed something. "Sure."

They chatted a few minutes longer, just about random bits and pieces. After the call ended and Kyle put down the phone, he felt calm. And possibly confident enough to craft a new recipe.

CHAPTER FIVE

A ROCKING chair. A fucking rocking chair was what the doctor ordered.

Things had been looking up since he spoke to Matt a few days earlier. Matt's new beau, Gil, was Dr. Gilbert McCauley, renowned neurologist and neurosurgeon, and he had connections. Really good connections, because the big-name neurologist Kyle couldn't get in to see all of a sudden had an opening. Sofia Balabanov and her ophthalmologist husband, Nathan Kane, had both worked on a few cases of something called Riddoch phenomenon with veterans returning from war and were familiar with what Kyle was going through. They ordered a few tests, including one where he could see a weird motion that looked like a blooming flower, and voilà! A rocking chair.

"Since you see movement and can see some colors, there's a good chance you may retrieve more sight," Dr. Balabanov said.

"A cure?" Kyle asked hopefully.

"It's not a cure, but your brain is learning a new way to get around the burned-out areas. The more you work it, the better you'll get."

"Neuroplasticity?"

"Precisely, Mr. Green. Your visual cortex is no longer functioning, but your eyes still are going strong. The brain is mapping a different route around the damaged areas. Many people have adapted to this condition and have lived good lives."

"If I use the rocking chair, will it get me to the point where I see faces again?" Maybe all would not be lost when it came to his career.

A heavy silence fell over the room.

"Mr. Green, the body is an amazing organism. The healing powers of the body constantly astound me."

"I hear a but coming…."

"Unless your brain creates new neural pathways to the specific facial recognition area, you will not be able to see faces."

Kyle sagged.

Her voice was warm. "However, one man was told he'd never ride his motorcycle again. He is able to do just that because he can see things in motion."

Really? Sweet, I can ride a motorcycle. Just not make any money. But then he had an idea. "Would that go for running too?"

"Maybe. Did they talk to you during therapy about a running guide? That would be your best bet if you want to try it."

Kyle left the appointment a bit more hopeful than he'd been in a long time.

LILY CLUCKED at him. "Kyle, you're going to rock a hole in the porch."

Kyle had tested several rocking chairs and ultimately decided that he needed both an indoor and an outdoor rocker. The faster he rocked, the more his brain worked on making the new pathways. Just like exercising muscles. Go brain cells!

"I'm sorry I doubted you about seeing things. The doctors were pretty sure you were going to be totally blind, so I didn't want to give you false hope."

Kyle kept rocking. "Lil, don't sweat it. I'll hold the grudge for a few more years and then forgive you."

"Ha! Well, just remember, you swore up and down you saw Miss Nishimori's Buddha statue cross the bridge. You've got a track record, baby bro."

"The Buddha statue did trundle across the bridge! You guys never believed me. I should have known I was born into a family of unbelievers."

Lily sighed. "Kye...."

"I can see a ball! It's a red ball moving toward our yard!"

Lily gasped. "Yes! It is!" She jumped up and hugged Kyle. "This is great news! You're seeing balls again!" Pause. "Wait, that didn't come out right."

They laughed for a few moments before growing more serious. "Okay," she said. "Tell me how this thing works. What's it called? Riddick?"

"Nope. That's a Vin Diesel movie. This is Rid*doch*, and it's a brain thing. My visual cortex got fried, but not the part of my brain that processes movements. So as long as something's moving—or if

I am—I have a chance of seeing it. Sort of." He didn't even try to describe the reality, which was weird streaks and flashes in a field of blackness.

"That's really great, hon."

He nodded. He wasn't sure if this pathetic bit of vision was a life changer. It was unlikely that he'd ever see faces, and he'd sure as hell never be allowed behind the wheel of a car again. Motorcycle, yes, car, no. Now that was an amusing sight to see in his mind's eye. It was still unclear whether he'd be able to resume his VO work. But blind beggars can't be choosers, right?

"Do you have to rock?" she asked. "I mean, are there other ways you can trigger this thing?"

"Yes, there are. Doc Balabanov said some patients shake their heads, but that felt weird. Probably annoys everyone else too. I'll stick with rocking for now, I guess." But even as he said it, a thought occurred to him.

"What?" Lily asked.

"*What* what?"

"You have that look on your face, like that time when you decided you could borrow Mom's car and she'd never know."

He tried to rearrange his expression into more innocent lines. "I don't know what you're talking about."

Lily huffed. "Right. Whatever you're scheming, I hope it's not going to result in four thousand bucks' worth of body repairs and six months of being grounded."

"We're too old to be grounded."

"Maybe." The other porch chair—not a rocker—creaked a bit as she settled into it. "But while we're talking about that particular youthful indiscretion—"

"*I'm* not talking about it."

"Well, I am. You stole Mom's car so you could go on a date, didn't you? With that Randy kid?"

He snorted. "Robby, and I didn't steal anything. It's not like she was using the car that night anyway, and I had every intention of returning it in the morning."

"Which you did—minus a quarter panel and a bumper."

He winced at the memory. Newly licensed, he'd been driving carefully but misjudged a parking space and hit a retaining wall. And then, instead of doing something about it, he'd driven the car home and left it in the driveway with vague hopes that his parents would assume someone had mysteriously crashed into the car overnight. Yeah, that went well.

"I was sixteen," Kyle said.

"Yep. And Robby was a cute little thing. But that brings me to my next topic, which is dating."

Kyle let out a long, noisy breath. "I just went blind and broke up with Matt. Dating is not a priority."

"Understood. But eventually it will be, right?"

"I didn't bug you to get back in the game after the divorce, Lil."

She was quiet for a moment before answering. "I kind of wish you had, though. 'Cause it's scary, right? So I kept putting it off and putting it off, and now…."

"You're not ancient. You could still—"

"I know. But now I'm set in my single ways, and even if I found a perfect guy, I don't know that I could fit him into my life."

Kyle wished he could see her face. He could judge a lot from tone, but she was good at hiding her emotions. Her eyes usually gave her away, though. That was why she never would have even considered stealing their mother's car. "You just need to find the right guy," he said.

"Maybe. But my point is that it doesn't get any easier. I don't want you getting so comfortable flying solo that you give up on finding a copilot."

He pointed at his eyes. "Not flying anywhere, Lily." *And not too much danger of getting comfortable either.*

"All right." She remained quiet for a while. His rocking chair squeaked, kids yelled, the garbage truck rumbled by in the alley. Then she sniffed. "But when you *do* decide you want to start seeing someone—"

"Not seeing anyone. Ever." He said it more harshly than he intended, but he was pissed off over what he missed, and sometimes that anger came boiling up to burn unsuspecting bystanders. He squeezed his useless eyes shut and grimaced. "Not like I'm gonna have potential suitors lining up for me anyway."

"Oh, hon. You don't think anyone can love you because you're blind?"

"I wasn't that great a catch to begin with. I'm way past my sell-by date as far as most gay men are concerned, and I'm boring."

"You are not!"

Kyle didn't know which part of his assertion she was arguing with. It didn't matter anyway, so he continued. "And even if I were young and hot and fascinating, nobody wants to take on a project."

She reached over to punch his shoulder.

"Ow. Blind man here."

"You're not a project! You're a great-looking guy—and have a great body too. Well, you're not a six-pack-ab Adonis, and you are a bit on the skinny side right now, but You. Are. Not. A. Project. I've seen plenty of those. You've done so much and learned lots of new things since you lost your sight. Soon you'll throw me, the old crutch, off—"

"Lily!"

"—while you go cruising Sidetrack or Hydrate."

"Lily!" Kyle's face flamed as hot as sriracha. By force of habit, he looked around to see if anyone was looking at them and then realized he couldn't see anything unless it was moving. Damn.

Lily ignored him and kept talking. "I'd like to go to Hydrate and look at the cute boys dancing in Speedos or boy shorts."

"Lily!"

"Oh, what are you getting so indignant about? You know you have a great excuse to feel up those boys now."

"Lily!" Lily was on a roll, and Kyle wouldn't get a word in edgewise until she finished.

"You'll be living independently soon enough, and you can bring them home without me cramping your style."

This had to stop.

"Lily, if you find a guy, I'll get one too and we can go on a double date."

"Is that a challenge?"

"Maybe."

Lily's phone rang inside the house. Thank God, now the subject could be dropped. After she left, Kyle had time to process what Lily had said.

He sighed, thinking of all the things he could never do on a date. He couldn't drive, obviously. Movies or any kind of performing arts? Well, Kyle could *hear* what was going on, but that wasn't the same.

Museums? Yeah, that'd be a laugh riot. Romantic little strolls with Kyle tap-tapping along with his cane, hoping he didn't trip and fall flat on his face. Boating excursions where he could not admire the city skyline. Little weekend jaunts to Wisconsin to not admire the scenic countryside.

Lily came back outside, evidently with a tray and some glasses. Fizzy water of some sort. He could hear the bubbles, and it faintly smelled of berries. She set the tray down on the table. "Your strawberry water, three o'clock."

"Thanks." Kyle got the glass on the first try and mumbled, "At least I tell time. I's got skillz."

"Did you say something?"

"Nothing," he said quietly.

Lily just sighed.

A WEEK after the uncomfortable little chat on the porch, Lily went out to check up on her apartment and then meet with a friend for lunch. She'd offered to drag Kyle along, but he declined. "I'm going to stay home and practice braille," he said.

"Okay. Call if you need anything. Want me to pick up something for dinner?"

"I'll make something." He was getting fairly accomplished at finding his way around the kitchen. Every now and then he came across an unlabeled can or box, but he'd recently downloaded a really nifty app. All he had to do was point his phone at something, and a sighted volunteer somewhere in the world would tell him what it was. He'd used it a couple of times, and it was pretty cool. Last time, some lady in Australia cheerfully helped him distinguish his laundry detergent from his liquid fabric softener.

After Lily left, Kyle really did work on his reading for a while. But as usual, he got frustrated quickly and pushed the book away. He sat at the kitchen table feeling restless and pissed off. It wasn't fucking *fair* that he'd lost his sight! And not even gradually, so he'd have some warning and have time to prepare himself. This hit him as suddenly and unexpectedly as getting struck by lightning, with similarly catastrophic results.

He growled and pounded his fist on the table. A coffee cup clinked at the impact, but he didn't feel any better. Then the phone rang.

"Call from... Michael Green. Call from... Michael Green," the phone announced as Kyle said, "Answer call."

"Hi, Dad."

"Hello, Kyle. How are things coming along?"

"Good. Good. They're good, Dad. Good."

Well shit, now the colonel is going to interrogate me.

"You usually say that when you're trying to cover something up. Come on, son, talk to me."

How could Kyle tell his dad he felt like a failure? That he used to be a fucking grown-up man and he just couldn't figure out how to be him again. He wanted to cry, damn it!

"I want a magic wand." That was family code for *I want a do-over*. But this was a more complex situation than hitting the croquet ball or having another chance at bat. This do-over was turning back time. It couldn't be done.

"When you were a little boy, even into your teens, you were my fearless child. You did the damnedest things, things that gave your mom and me gray hairs. Child safety locks didn't work with you. You were forever into something as a toddler. I didn't think you'd make it to the age of ten. As you got older, it only got worse. I thought we'd lose you before your next birthday," his father said fondly. "Remember the old barn in Germany? You created monkey bars made from ropes in the rafters, and you'd swing like there was no gravity, and there certainly wasn't a net."

Kyle chuckled a bit. "There was hay to soften the landing."

"Well, your mom and I didn't spot that right away, looking through only the top half of the barn door. We both nearly had a heart attack. And here you were, leading your older brothers and sister in a catch-me-if-you-can rope game."

"That was a lot of fun."

"And how about the zip line you rigged?"

"Which one?"

His father barked out a laugh. "That's right, there was more than one of those. In Italy. Florence."

"The one between the hotel and the fruit store?"

"Yes. The first thing I knew of it was when I saw you flash by the hotel window. No helmet, no protective gear, just zipping by at fifty miles an hour from seven floors above the street."

"I got Paul and Evan to zip down too."

"I remember that. And each time you zipped down, the shop owner would give you a piece of fruit." His dad, he could tell, was smiling. "I had some Rangers under my command that weren't as adventurous and brave as you."

"Was, Dad. I used to be adventurous and brave." *Not now. Don't cry now, damn it!*

His father's voice was steady and firm when he said, "You still are, Kyle."

"No, Dad, those days are long gone. My biggest adventure is going to the bathroom. If I feel lucky, I can piss standing up." Kyle sniffed and wiped his nose on his sleeve.

"Do you remember what you told me when I asked why you went down the zip line?"

Kyle sniffed again, struggling for control. "No," he rasped.

"You said, 'Vivi bene, ama molto, ridi spesso!' Though I think your motto was 'Be fearless and go for it!'"

Kyle couldn't help the sob that escaped. His father patiently waited until Kyle could pull himself together. "You are still the fearless, adventurous one. If you can just realize that this is another risky undertaking, you'll come out of it as you always do, with a few scrapes and a great story."

"Dad, I'm blind now."

"Well, that never stopped you when you leapt before looking. Just think of it that way—not-looking and leaping."

Kyle laughed. He remembered how he used to close his eyes before a big stunt. How he sometimes even used to go at a full run with his eyes squeezed shut. How he was Stupendous Man.

"Kyle, what can't you do? I know once you put your mind to it, there is no obstacle so high that you can't scale it."

"Is this a pep talk, Dad?"

"No, son, this is a reality check."

Typical Dad speak. And it occurred to Kyle that, yes, he had lost that sense of adventure, awe, and discovery. Maybe the stroke that burned out part of his brain affected his mood too. His dad was right; he needed to get off his ass and get doing what he needed to do. What he loved to do. He felt better, almost as if he'd purged himself of his pity party.

"Thanks, Dad."

"You're welcome, Kyle."

There was a pause.

"And Kyle?"

"Yeah, Dad?"

"Your mom and I need more gray hairs. And Lily does too. That girl needs to get some lift in her life."

Kyle laughed. "Okay, I'll do my best."

The talk buoyed Kyle's spirits. He could do anything. His dad had faith in him.

What did Kyle want to do? Run.

Then let's do it! What better way to start a new adventure than to run blind, as he had often done as a crazy-brave kid?

He made his way to his bedroom and changed into shorts and running shoes. But he couldn't make himself go down to the basement, to his workout room with the treadmill. The basement felt so confining, even if he couldn't see a damn thing. And besides, the treadmill was boring, definitely not adventurous or dangerous enough.

With a small determined nod and a smile, Kyle slipped his phone into an armband, found the house key, and headed outside. He locked the door behind him before tucking the key into the armband pocket. He hopped down the seven steps and felt like Rocky Balboa after the run through Philly. He jogged to the gate, opened it, closed it, turned left, and—without the celebratory victory arms above his head—started to run.

Over the past weeks, he'd been making his way to the Bridge Center by himself. He knew the route by heart and walked with a cane, but he'd noticed that if he walked really fast, he could see flashes of things. No details, no faces of other pedestrians, but images and colors—enough to keep himself on track and avoid collisions. He figured that if he ran, he'd see even better. No need for a cane, and definitely no need for one of those guides the people at the center kept talking about.

Foot traffic was light, which was fortunate. Kyle was beginning to see shapes of houses, trees, *color.* He was fascinated and distracted by his newfound skill, and he brushed by a few pedestrians. Some people grumbled as they ducked out of his way, but by keeping to the far right of the sidewalk, he avoided the worst of the problems. The faster he ran, the more he saw things take shape and the more colors brightened. A car drove by, and between his movement and the car's, he could see the car almost perfectly! He laughed out loud. Damn! Why hadn't he done this before? He felt great! For things that were not moving, he concentrated on sounds to keep his bearings: traffic as he approached cross streets and echoes alongside large structures.

He was doing pretty well, he thought. He wasn't anywhere near his former running speed, but at least part of that was because his hospitalization and recovery had left him out of shape. At least he was moving—fast—without a handy helper or the damned cane. For the first time since the fucking stroke, he truly believed that he'd be able to live independently. Happily, even.

And then he tripped.

He didn't know what he hit—something shin-high and plasticky. A kid's toy, maybe, like the Big Wheel he had as a kid or the tractor replica he gave his nephew for Christmas years ago. Whatever it was, the damned thing was enough to send Kyle sprawling, his head no doubt heading straight for the pavement. The fall seemed to take an eternity. He could see himself falling in super slo-mo, and he put out his hands to break the fall and hopefully not fuck up his head even worse.

And then strong arms caught him.

Kyle wasn't a small man, and for a moment it seemed as if his momentum would bring the other person down with him. But after some tangled legs and mutual grunting, they both managed to regain their balance. The other man kept his hands on Kyle's biceps. "Whoa!" the guy said. "Are you okay?"

"Yeah."

"You should watch where you're going. You'd have to be blind to miss that thing."

Kyle stood, panting, embarrassed, angry, and relieved. He thought his gaze might be directed at the other man, but he wasn't sure. He blinked a few times and then started to laugh.

"What's so funny?"

Kyle tried to say it, but it was like one of those jokes that was so funny you couldn't get the punch line out.

All he could say was "Blind!" before he broke into peals of laughter once again.

Kyle was sure his rescuer thought something had broken loose in Kyle's head. Fueled by embarrassment and absurdity, Kyle laughed even harder.

After several minutes, his laughter calmed into giggles, and with a heaving breath, Kyle thought the worst was behind him.

"Yes, I am blind."

"You must be to have missed that eye-bleeding pink contraption."

Kyle thought he looked in the direction of the obstacle but must have missed by a mile, because his savior tensed.

"Oh, fuck! You are vision impaired, aren't you? Man, I'm so sorry! I didn't mean anything by it." He had a pleasant tenor voice, and he still gripped Kyle's arms.

"Thanks for the save. I need to go." Kyle pretended he still had some dignity.

"I… yeah." The man let go of him, but Kyle could still hear him standing very close, his breathing slightly harsh. Either he'd been exercising too or Kyle's tumble had scared the crap out of him. "Sorry. I didn't mean to say something stupid."

Kyle sighed. "You didn't. I *should* watch where I'm going." He rubbed the sweat from his forehead. "This was an idiotic idea."

"So you, uh, don't normally run?"

"Not outdoors anymore, no. Thanks again for saving me. That was an NFL-quality catch." Was the guy staring at him as though he was a freak? Were other pedestrians rubbernecking as they walked by, wondering what the hell his problem was? God, as far as Kyle knew, the entire news crew from WGN was standing nearby, cameras pointed at the nimrod who couldn't even jog down the street without almost killing himself.

"It *was* a lucky catch," the man said. His voice was light, as if he were smiling. "And to think I always got picked last for the softball teams when I was in school."

"Well, you've redeemed yourself today. Thanks."

"Do you want— Shit. I don't want to say something asinine again. But do you want me to walk you home?"

Although Kyle bristled a little at the offer, he told himself to calm down. The guy was trying to be nice, and after watching Kyle's impromptu performance of street ballet, the man was justified in wondering whether Kyle could make it home in one piece. "I'll be okay, thanks. I'll, uh, walk. Slowly."

"Do you have a cane?"

Shit. Good going, Sherlock. Going to shake your head back and forth, looking like the eternal No Man?

"Ah, no. I don't have my cane with me."

"I can walk with you. I was almost done with my run anyway."

"I bet you didn't almost fall."

"Nooo. But if it makes you feel any better, my vision's 20/20 and I still ran into a light pole last month. I was trying to text and run. Inadvisable."

Kyle surprised himself by laughing. "Thanks for the pro tip."

"I'm at your service." There was a pause, and then the man snorted. "I just did this deep, theatrical bow because I thought I was being witty."

"Maybe you should stick to rescue operations instead of stand-up comedy," Kyle said with a grin.

"Probably. Um, did you know that you're bleeding?"

Kyle automatically touched the back of his head—the location of the stroke—even though that bleeding had been entirely inside his skull. But then he realized that his shin tickled. He bent down and discovered a sticky trickle on his skin. Of course, the wound immediately started to sting. "I must've scraped it on the… whatever I tripped on."

"It's a pink Disney Princess ride-on, and if you want to sue the little menace who left it there, I'll be happy to represent you. I bet we can get her entire allowance and half her stuffed animal collection."

"You're a lawyer?"

"More or less. Kind of. You're welcome to make the sign of the cross if you want, but it won't work on me because I'm Jewish. I'd suggest invocations against the Evil Eye instead. Oh. Shit." There was a muted thud, probably as the man thunked himself in the head. "I really am sorry."

"I told you to avoid the comedy," Kyle responded. He was grinning widely. He really wished he could see this man. There wasn't much Kyle could tell about him from his voice and their brief physical contact, apart from the fact that he was strong. He jogged, right? And he sounded neither especially young nor especially old, but that left a lot of territory in between.

"Really," the man said. "Let me walk you home. If I put my foot in my mouth again during the journey, you have my express permission to slap me upside the head."

"You'll even guide my hand to your head?"

"Naturally."

Kyle shrugged. Although he was still a bit humiliated by his collision, the man had been sweet about embarrassing himself in return. Besides, most of Kyle's adventurous spirit over solo travel had flagged a bit, and he wasn't up to walking home without his cane just yet. "Okay. If you really don't mind."

"Nope. Maybe it'll give me an excuse to explore more of the old neighborhood."

Kyle held out his hand. "Kyle Green."

The man's hand was warm, his grip firm but not obnoxiously so. "Nice to meet you, Kyle. Seth Caplan. Where to?"

Kyle rattled off his street number, feeling as if he were a kindergartener proud of knowing his own address.

"Impressive. You made it about twelve blocks from home before the obstacle portion of the course. May I?"

Kyle chuckled at the image of Stupendous Man splatted on the side of a tall building he'd missed as he leaped in a single bound. Seth took Kyle's hand and placed it on his arm near the elbow, as experienced guides do with the visually impaired. They started walking in the direction of Kyle's house, and then the adrenaline and the endorphins from laughing wore off and Kyle's leg began to hurt a little. He was probably going to bruise. "How gory do I look?" he asked.

"Minimal. I've done worse with a bad shaving job." They stopped at a crosswalk. "So, uh, I want to ask nosy questions, but you can tell me to shut my face if you want. Wouldn't be the first time I've heard it."

"Shouldn't I just lodge an objection?"

Seth gasped loudly. "You're not a lawyer too, are you?" He used the same tone of voice as if he were worried that Kyle was secretly Genghis Khan.

"No."

"Oh, thank God. I have spent way too many hours of my life with members of the bar."

"I guess that would be an occupational hazard."

The pedestrian signal chirped, indicating it was safe to cross, so Kyle stepped off the curb. He was always a little nervous about that initial step—what if someone ran the light or did a sudden right turn? But he felt a bit more confident with Seth at his side.

"So, uh, isn't it dangerous to run if you're vision im—"

"Blind. I like that word better. Fewer syllables. And yeah, I guess it is. The people at the Bridge Center have been telling me I should get a running guide."

"The Bridge Center?"

Distracted by the conversation, Kyle almost tripped again when he reached the opposite curb. This time he caught himself without Seth's help. "It's this place that does classes and things to help people adjust to blindness."

"Ah. But you decided not to take their advice?"

"Yeah," Kyle said with a sigh. How to explain to a stranger that he needed to regain his sense of fearlessness? "It just seemed... I don't know. Constraining. Or maybe it meant having to admit to myself that I have limitations now." He didn't know why he was pouring his heart out to a complete stranger, but it felt good to unburden himself slightly. It probably helped that he couldn't see Seth rolling his eyes or looking impatient or pitying.

"So the blindness is a new thing?" Seth asked carefully.

"Just over six months. A stroke. Just a random fucking by fate."

"Yeah, I know about those." Seth almost mumbled those words but then seemed to brighten. "You seem to be managing pretty well for a guy who's new to this."

"You just saved me from death by Disney Princesses."

Seth laughed. "A terrible fate indeed. But seriously, you didn't get run over by a truck. Or smash into a pole."

They'd reached another corner. Someone jostled Kyle while passing by, which reminded him of another good reason to carry a cane: it gave other people notice that you couldn't see them. And if they ignored the cane and invaded your space anyway, you could always take a swing at their legs and pretend it was an accident.

"I can see a little," Kyle explained. "Not much. Just... moving stuff or if I move fast enough. It's this weird neurological thing."

"Which would help when you're running."

"Somewhat. Not as much as I'd hoped, I guess." Then something occurred to him. "How'd you figure out so fast that I'm blind? Do my eyes look weird?" Maybe he should start wearing sunglasses.

"I did some volunteering with Sports Horizons. Have you heard of them?"

Kyle shook his head, realized Seth might not be looking at him, and said, "No, sorry."

"It was in San Jose. Maybe they have something similar here, I don't know. Sports Horizons does athletic activities with kids who have disabilities. Kind of like Special Olympics, only for physical disabilities instead of intellectual ones."

Well, that explained Seth's politically correct usage of *vision impaired*. "So you helped blind kids?"

"Sometimes. Man, you'd think I'd be more careful with what I say, right? Only, kids don't usually care all that much if you slip up. They either patiently correct you or they just laugh."

Somebody zoomed past on a bicycle, making Kyle flinch even though the bike was several feet away. Seeing sudden bursts of movement in the blackness was startling sometimes.

"So you don't just rescue random strangers," Kyle said. "You rescue children too."

Seth chuckled. "Those kids did not need rescuing. I volunteered because it was fun, that's all. And I like children and don't have any of my own."

For the next few blocks, Seth talked about his experiences with Sports Horizons. He told a couple of funny stories, like the time a little girl in a wheelchair was so busily distracted by flowers in the outfield that she didn't even see the softball coming until it landed neatly in her lap. He didn't say much about himself, though, and Kyle wondered why he'd moved to Chicago, why he claimed to be only "sort of" a lawyer, and whether he was truly as nice as he seemed.

"We're close to home," Kyle said as they turned the corner and approached his house. The familiar sounds of his block surrounded him, giving him a sense of home: the kids playing, the squeak of the baby stroller from three doors down, the classical music from Mr. Maxfield.

"I'm impressed. You know where you live. That's half the battle of getting home."

Kyle preened a bit. He recognized the familiar sounds on his street. Whoot for him! Stupendous Man might have superpowers after all.

"I live over on the next block." They stood awkwardly in front of his house for a moment or two. Then Seth cleared his throat. "Do you have someone at home to take a look at your shin?"

Was he fishing for an invitation inside? And if so, why? Not pity, Kyle hoped. "My sister. She's staying with me until I get my shit together." He didn't mention that she wasn't currently home. He could doctor his stupid shin himself.

"Okay." Seth sounded… doubtful? Disappointed? Relieved to be rid of the burden he'd just taken on? Kyle wasn't sure.

Kyle held out his hand. "Thanks again. I really appreciate it. Not just the good catch either. With your help, I managed to walk all the way home not feeling like an incompetent dork."

"It was a pleasure. I don't know a lot of people here, so thanks for putting up with my yakking." The handshake might have lingered a tad longer than usual.

"Well, I'd tell you I might see you around, but I won't."

Seth snorted. "If *I* made that joke, I'd be an insensitive asshole. But hey. Maybe you really ought to consider the running guide thing. In case I'm not there to catch you next time."

"I'll think about it. Thanks again." Kyle waved in what he thought was the right direction and then headed toward his front door.

Chapter Six

"Hey, Kyebye, how did the— What the hell did you do to yourself?"

Kyle was sitting in his favorite armchair, listening to an audiobook. He pressed the Pause button and removed the earbuds. "What do you mean?"

"Your leg!"

His shin was slightly sore, but he'd washed the wound after he got home, decided he probably wasn't going to bleed to death, and slapped a Band-Aid over the scraped part. Of course, since he was wearing shorts, it was probably easy for Lily to see any developing bruise. And pitch a fit over it.

"I banged my shin. It's no big deal."

"Banged it on what?"

He tried to think of a credible lie, but nothing came to mind, so he sighed. "A Disney Princess ride-on."

"A *what*?"

"One of those little plastic tricycle things. I'm betting this one was a hideous pink and purple, possibly with sparkly decals."

She stomped across the living room and, he imagined, loomed over him. He could feel her disapproving presence and could picture the exact scowl on her face. "Where was this?" she demanded.

"I don't know. A little over a mile from here. Some kid left it on the sidewalk and I tripped. It's no big deal."

"Why didn't you feel it with your cane?"

He sighed again, louder. "Because I didn't have the damned thing. I was running, okay? And doing perfectly fine until I ran into the trike. And even then, I walked home on my own steam. No amputation necessary." He decided not to tell her about Seth Caplan, whose involvement would only complicate matters.

"Kyle! You went running by yourself?"

Kyle tried to smother a laugh. "If I didn't know it was you standing there, I'd swear it was Mom. You sound exactly like her." He tilted his head and grinned smugly. "You said to be more adventurous, take more risks. I took your advice. Are you going to ground me now?"

"And if I didn't see the gray in your hair, I'd swear you were a stubborn teenager again. Seriously, Kyle. What were you thinking?"

His smile disappeared. "I was thinking I wanted to go for a goddamn run," he growled. "And I only have a *few* gray hairs."

She exhaled loudly as she flopped onto the couch. "I get that it's really hard not to be able to do everything you used to, but—"

"You *don't* get it. This isn't just, *Oh, slight inconvenience*. This is… everything. My job. Matt. Everything I've ever done or want to do. And it's forever."

Lily was quiet for a long time. "I'm sorry. You're right—I can't really understand what you're going through. I did give you a pep talk about being a brave little soldier, and you soldiered on. But do you remember what you said to me in the middle of my divorce?"

"That Rich is a fuckwad."

"Yeah, that," she said with a chuckle. "But you also advised me to accept that my life would be different without him. You told me to mourn what I'd lost—just like when I lost the baby—and then find joy in what was new."

Kyle nodded slowly. He'd thought it was good counsel at the time, but it was a lot easier to give advice than to take it. "I talked to Dad today."

"Really? Is that what prompted this run?"

"Kind of. He told me to take this as a new adventure. To be fearless and to be the intrepid explorer I've always been. Less pity party and more wonder, basically."

"Great advice, though I don't think running blind is what he meant." She laughed, and he heard the smile in her voice. "You used to do such stupidly dangerous things, Stupendous Man. I remember you loved *Calvin and Hobbes*. You channeled Stupendous Man so many times." Lily paused as if she remembered something. "Maybe Dad did mean for you to do this. Get on that horse, fall off, and get back on again. Though I don't think he meant for you to kill yourself."

"It's just a flesh wound."

She snorted. "Yeah, remember where that got the Black Knight."

"At least he could see."

He could almost feel her eye roll. "Get a guide, Kyle. Think of it as a sidekick, like Hobbes was to Calvin. It's not such an awful thing to have a running buddy, is it? And then you can go really fast and impress him with your machismo and athleticism."

He already knew he'd have to either give up jogging or find someone to run with, but that didn't mean he had to give in gracefully. "If I run faster than him, I don't see how he can do me any good."

"Well, he can look ahead and shout stuff at you. 'Princess trike at noon!' I might consider dropping Zumba and taking up running just to watch that. Or maybe I could just station myself somewhere along your route. Set up a comfy lawn chair, maybe bring a cooler…."

He wished he had a pillow to throw at her. He could probably hit her since she was close by and talking away. "Fine," he muttered. "I'll get a guide if you'll get off my back."

"Done," she said, slapping her palms on her thighs.

Kyle frowned and stuck his earbuds back in.

THREE DAYS after his ill-fated running experiment, Kyle was antsier than ever. He would have walked to the Bridge Center that day and begged for a guide, but it was Sunday and the center was closed. Lily had worked late the previous night, so when she finally entered the kitchen, her feet shuffled. He imagined she looked like a frowsy-haired zombie, which made him grin.

"It's too early for smiling," she complained. A cabinet door opened, a mug thudded softly onto the counter, and then liquid glugged quietly. "But I'll forgive you since you made coffee."

He asked Siri what time it was—nearly ten. "I've been up a couple of hours already," he informed Lily.

"Yay. You get the perky puppy award. I'll get you a medal."

"I'd prefer a trophy." He drained his cup, grimacing because the coffee was cold. "Did you leave me any?"

"No. But give me a sec to charge my battery and I'll brew more."

"Don't bother." Grabbing his empty mug, he walked around the peninsula into the kitchen, brushing Lily but not quite banging into her. After a bit of feeling around—Lily didn't always leave things exactly where they belonged—he found the coffee press. This routine had been one of the first things he'd learned in rehab. He rinsed the carafe, used a liquid height indicator to measure the right amount of water into the kettle, and carefully measured coffee grounds. As soon as the water boiled, he poured it into the press, added the grounds, and tapped a button on top to activate the timer.

Once his cup was newly refilled, he made his way back to the table. Lily sat there, clinking her spoon against the china mug. "Maybe I ought to switch to decaf," Kyle said.

"Blasphemy!"

"Yeah, except this is my third or fourth cup, and I feel like I'm going to jump out of my skin." He let out a sigh that was almost a moan. "I'm going nuts, Lil."

"Tomorrow you can go to the Bridge Center and—"

"Beg for a babysitter. I know. I will. But I don't just mean the running. I need to work!"

"Is money getting tight?" She sounded concerned.

"No, I'll be good for a while. I need a job for mental health reasons. I've been working since I was, what? Twelve?"

"You had a paper route."

He nodded at the memory. He'd used his earnings to buy comic books, mostly. That was before he knew about manga. "Even when we lived overseas, I always had a job. Some of them were crappy." Fast food. Campus cafeteria. Office boy for an asshole of a dentist. Delivery boy for a grocer. "But they kept me busy. And now I'm just sort of sitting around all day."

In his downtime he used to travel with Matt or just hang out and talk about their latest projects. Now that was gone too, and he had no trips to look forward to. He could barely get around his own neighborhood; venturing into the wider world was out of the question, at least for now.

Kyle turned his face toward Lily. "I know I can't do animation VO work, but do you think I could manage book narration? My braille's getting better, and I've always had a good memory for text. If I read the book a couple of times before we start recording and maybe practice a bit?" He knew he sounded almost pathetically hopeful, a dog begging for a bone, but he couldn't help it.

Lily didn't hesitate to answer. "It sounds like a great idea! We can practice in the studio downstairs. When do you want to start?"

He wanted to dance gleefully. Maybe it was the coffee. "How about when you're less like a zombie and more of a Lily?"

"How about you make me some of your yummy french toast while I take a shower, then we tackle blind-man narration?"

"Deal!"

KYLE WENT down to the studio while Lily took a call from the narrator on her current edit. It was like old home week. Kyle had stayed away from the studio as if it were off-limits, but now he felt like he could do this. The board he could operate blind. Well, he *was* blind now, so it was time to put that theory to work. He retrieved and hooked up the headset. Okay, obviously that muscle memory didn't get fried. Now to turn on the mic and start to read. Simple. It was like he never left. As his fingers felt the now-familiar passage he'd been reading over and over for the past several hours, he began the narration.

A light rap sounded on the door, and he stopped.

"Kyle! That was great. You're back in your own rhythm again."

"I just started. How can you tell?"

"Kyle, you've been down here forever. My call took longer than I thought. This newbie narrator was pissed at the edits I sent back to him. We argued. He's really bad."

"How bad?"

"Like having Paul read a bedtime story."

Paul, their older brother, was a horrible reader. No inflection, no emotion, no fun. His kids loved their father and put up with the bad reading just to hear his voice when he was home. But when Paul was deployed, his kids used to call Kyle at bedtime, and he would read them a story over the phone.

"Ugh. How did you become his editor?" Kyle asked.

"It was a favor to another one of my narrators. It's his cousin."

"Does his cousin know he sucks at reading?"

"I think he does, and he wanted me to break it to his cousin. I told the squirt—"

Kyle smiled and employed one of his anime character's voices. "You mean the young whippersnapper?"

Lily laughed. All the frustration drained from her voice. "Yes, that whippersnapper was told to get a speech coach or to enroll in some theater classes before contacting me again."

"Wow, Lily, you're on a roll!"

"And so were you. You've been down here for the last hour and a half."

An hour and a half—he hadn't realized it was that long. Probably because he couldn't see a clock or the timer. And he felt good because it had flowed naturally. His hands were flying over the braille. No stuttering.

"I've been watching you for the last fifteen minutes. You're poised and confident, and it was a great read. No stops and starts." Lily paused. "I think you're better than when you read with your eyes."

The compliment rang true. Lily wasn't a bitch by any means, but she didn't give false praise when it came to narration.

Kyle nodded. "Well, I could hear when I was turning the notebook pages."

Lily rewound the recording and listened for some time before switching it off. "I think that's your supernatural hearing, because I can't hear it in the first chapter at all. Maybe you're used to reading off a tablet and not turning pages when narrating. You'll be fine."

Maybe, just maybe, he could see the light at the end of the proverbial tunnel.

KYLE KNEW Lily was bouncing beside him on the couch because he could feel the cushions moving.

"I can do this by myself," he said, even as he knew resistance was futile.

"And how is that fun?"

"It's not fun. It's work."

She stopped bouncing. "And if you have that attitude, you might as well be making widgets. C'mon. You used to love this. You once told me that being a voice actor was your dream job."

"It was. But this is book narration."

"Is it really that different? I mean yeah, sure, cartoon characters are meant for people to watch. But a lot of book narrators do voices for the characters, so it's almost like listening to a radio play. And besides, you've done narrating before."

He swept a hand over the closed laptop and tried to think of words to explain. He wasn't sure he understood the problem himself. "It's not that different, not really. It's just... I used to do all sorts of stuff, but now I'm stuck in this little box. Like I used to have a five-course meal and now all that's left is the appetizer. And I can have lots of appetizers, so I'm not going to starve or anything, but... I miss the other courses."

"I get it," Lily said. "But you know what? The appetizer's just the start. So begin with that, and maybe the next courses will come along later. And okay, maybe you were used to Italian food and now you're getting Thai instead. But Thai's good too!"

He sighed. "Thank you for indulging me in my really lame metaphor." It was past seven in the evening and he hadn't had dinner yet.

"No problem. I'm hungry too."

He knew he was probably making a being-forced-to-take-medicine face as he opened his laptop and booted it up. He could have used his assistive software to help him with the next part, but if Lily insisted on being involved anyway, he might as well make use of her. He passed the computer over to her. "Here. Tell me what's open for audition."

The laptop keys click-clacked for a moment. "Okay," Lily said. "Let's narrow things down a little. What genres? Business? Language instruction?"

"Oh yeah, perfect. Make me figure out how to read Russian in braille. Let's stick with fiction, okay? I want... voices."

"Voices," she said in a bad imitation of, he thought, Donald Duck. Then she switched back to her usual voice. "Got it. Sci-fi and fantasy is cool, right?"

"Sure."

"Lots of voices there, but the names will all be, like, Zaxeron of Planet Sinixis or else Th'g'fae'nae of the High Elf Council."

Kyle snorted. "There were apostrophes in that elf name, weren't there?"

"You betcha. How about rooooomance?" She leaned sideways to bump her shoulder against his.

"Ugh. Lady Thistlewhite's bodice gets ripped by that rogue who's actually the Viscount of North Squashbottom? But he had amnesia and forgot."

"Gay romance, kiddo. *Lord* Thistlewhite's bodice gets ripped." She paused. "Do men have bodices?"

"Maybe Lord Thistlewhite enjoys cross-dressing."

"Someone should write that. I'd read it. Okay, romance, gay or otherwise it is. Let's see… accent. You can do a lot of them."

"Italian, French, Spanish, German, Japanese, Mandarin, Cantonese, Dutch, Queen's English, Cockney, Upper-crust British, South Korean, Gaelic, Scottish, Aussie, Kiwi—"

"What's the difference between those, really? Aussie and Kiwi. They both sound alike."

He shrugged. "Different as the Appalachian accent is to the Georgian accent."

"Fine, I'll put those down. Voice age… middle-aged."

"Hey!"

She cackled. "I'll leave vocal style blank. How about length? Is five to ten hours good?"

Kyle thought about that a moment. A lot of novels fell in that range, and he didn't want to tackle anything longer until he felt more comfortable with the process. "Sounds good."

"And… voilà. We have some contenders. Let's see…. Ooh! I know that author. She's good."

"You read gay romance?" Kyle asked, slightly abashed.

"Oh yeah. I'm all about Lord Thistlewhite. Okay, tell me what you think of this one."

The computer's annoying electronic voice began reading a passage in which a fireman lusted over a tattoo artist. The writing was good, and Kyle took an immediate liking to the tattoo artist character, but his face flushed when the scene turned steamy.

"What do you think?" Lily asked when the excerpt ended.

"I think I'm distinctly uncomfortable listening to that with my sister."

"Yeah, but could you handle reading it? And having your sister edit it for you?"

It was definitely a change of pace from Ecos. He did have a gay romance on the docket before the stroke. He originally thought it would be fun, with all the moaning and heavy breathing. And swearing. He never got to drop f-bombs when voicing Ecos. Or the Bible. "I'd like to audition for that one."

Lily made an undignified squee noise and clapped. "Yay! Thai food!"

CHAPTER SEVEN

KYLE HAD been so busy with the book narration project that he postponed his promise to seek a running guide. But as soon as his audition was submitted, he felt anxious and restless. The last thing he wanted to do was hang around waiting to see if he'd be offered a contract. He tried to use his exercise equipment in the basement, but even then, he could feel his laptop looming one floor above him, with maybe a new message lurking in the inbox. He was getting the word out slowly and carefully. People still sought him out for voice-over work, but he wasn't that confident yet.

He trudged upstairs and grabbed his cane. "Lily?" he called. "I'm going out."

He heard quick footsteps in the second-floor hallway, and when she answered, she must have been standing atop the stairs. "Want me to come with?"

"No babysitter necessary. I'm going to the Bridge Center."

"Okay. Back for dinner?"

He chuckled. "You're getting used to my cooking, aren't you?"

"Until the unlikely event that I obtain a houseboy, I'm going to enjoy having someone else make my meals."

"A houseboy. Why can't I get one of those instead of a running guide and this?" He waved the cane.

Lily's quick footsteps descended the top of the staircase and stopped just past the landing. *Hmm. She's wearing her Coco Chanel perfume. Something's up.*

"Who says you can't have all three? Um… and that sort of reminds me."

The tone of her voice sent shivers up his spine. "Yes?"

"I, uh…. Remember Tony?"

Kyle racked his brain. Ah yes, he remembered the guy. He'd shown up at Chicago's version of Comic-Con as a Klingon dressed in a Rebel fighter's flight suit. "Wasn't he that guy with the Star Wars/Star Trek crossover obsession?" Lily had dated him a few times but stopped after he began reciting Klingon love poems to her.

"Yup. He called last week and we were kinda catching up. He's really sweet."

Kyle could tell there was more. "Lily?"

"We met for coffee at Splash Dunk, and we hit it off. We're having lunch today."

Lily sounded more like a nervous teenager than the confident forty-three-year-old sister he knew. Kyle held open his arms. Lily ran down the last few stairs. He embraced her tightly. "That's great, Lil. Good for you." And he paused. "Let me know if he added Huttese to his vocabulary skills or if he's still only fluent in Klingon."

Air puffed against his neck when Lily laughed.

"Sure, I'll let you know."

Well, Kyle reflected as he left the house, at least now he had something to take his mind off that damned audition.

THE BRIDGE Center usually hummed with activity and always felt safe. Everything was set up for the benefit of those with limited or no vision—no princess trikes to trip on—and it was like a weird little alternate universe where functional eyes were an oddity instead of expected.

"Hello." Kyle immediately recognized the voice of the lobby receptionist, who was visually impaired.

"Hi, Mimi. It's Kyle Green."

"Kyle! I thought I recognized your foot tread. You haven't been around lately. How's it going?" She had a warm, round voice. He had no idea what she really looked like, but he knew she was tall and old enough to have grandchildren. He imagined her dark-skinned and bosomy with a ready smile. And she smelled spicy and floral, like ginger and gardenia.

"I'm managing. I was hoping I could talk to Dave about a running guide."

"Sure thing, honey. He's in his office. Go on in and I'll tell him you're on the way."

He thanked her, then walked to the elevator and pressed the button. He could have walked up the nearby stairs—it was only two floors—but he figured he needed a little more practice in working elevators. This one called out the floor number each time the doors opened, but that was unusual. In other buildings, he still worried about getting off on the wrong floor and wandering like an idiot.

He knocked lightly on Dave's door, which was ajar. "Come in, Kyle!" Dave called.

Dave's office must have had big windows, because on a sunny day like today, Kyle could feel the pools of warmth. The room held the faint odor of onions, perhaps the ghosts of lunches past. "Hey, Dave."

"I was just thinking about you yesterday. I ran across an article on Riddoch syndrome. Really interesting."

Kyle decided he didn't like the word *interesting*. "Yeah, I guess so."

"Do you find that you have enough vision left that it helps you?"

"A little bit, yeah. Not as much as I'd like. For instance, it turns out I can't run without risking breaking my neck."

"Hmmm, speaking from experience?"

Kyle blushed a bit. "I'm pleading the Fifth on that one."

"Did your vision get clearer when you were running?"

"Actually, it did. The faster I ran, the more things took shape. Though stationary objects at a certain level tripped me up." No use in outing the fact that he had been felled by a child's toy.

"A running guide would help in avoiding obstacles. Do you want to apply for one?"

"I guess so. I mean, yeah. I do."

"Great! Let's just get some information. We partner with the running clubs in the area. Want some coffee before we get started?"

"Sure, why not?"

Kyle sat in one of Dave's plush seats and waited as Dave fetched him a cup. He even remembered how Kyle liked it—black, no sugar. It wasn't as good as Kyle made in his french press, but Kyle knew he tended to be a bit of a caffeine snob.

The next part was easy. Dave asked a series of questions about when and where Kyle liked to run, how fast and how far and in what conditions. Kyle had never thought so carefully about his exercise habits. It was… just a good way to stay healthy and get rid of stress. One thing he'd always liked was that it didn't require tons of fancy equipment and you could do it almost anywhere—although he'd resorted to his treadmill during the worst winter days.

"This is perfect," Dave said after Kyle answered all his questions. "I'll send this to the local running groups we use. They have many levels of runners and all levels of experience as guides. We'll get you matched up with someone compatible. Shouldn't take more than a couple of days. Do you want the volunteer to contact you, or would you rather meet them here at the center?"

This sounded uncomfortably like a blind date. Well, at least they'd be screened, right? Kyle squirmed slightly. "You can have them call me."

"Okay. The guide or guides will call you. You can interview them over the phone, and you guys can meet up, confirm that everything works, and then you're good to go."

"What if they can't find a match?"

Dave chuckled. "Oh, they will. Your preferences aren't anything unusual, and the running groups have plenty of people who volunteer as guides."

That was slightly comforting, Kyle supposed. But it raised another question. "Why do people volunteer to do this, anyway?"

"Oh, everyone's got a different reason." Dave's chair creaked as he settled back into it with a quiet sigh. "Some people get a kick out of giving someone else a hand. Others have someone important to them who is sight impaired and they want to help the cause. Some enjoy running and like to spread around the love of pounding the pavement."

Those were all good reasons. In fact, now Kyle felt slightly guilty that he'd never signed up as a guide when he could see. Of course back then he'd never heard of running guides, and the need for them had never occurred to him. Now he knew better.

"Many of the people here at the Bridge need to get up and out. A lot of our clients have diabetes. A few people in particular were prediabetic and really out of shape when they decided to take up running with a guide's help. Now one runs marathons and another has gone on to do sprint-distance triathlons."

"No kidding?" Kyle was amazed someone could bike and swim blind, but he guessed with a guide, anything was possible.

"No kidding. She completed her first Olympic-distance triathlon in Chicago last August. She said if she can swim the lake, she can do anything. Now she travels to all the nonprofits for the visually impaired and encourages exercise. You never know what this first step will lead to."

Holy shit! Kyle didn't even swim in Lake Michigan when he was sighted!

From the creak in Dave's chair, Kyle could tell the director had leaned forward. "Studies show if you have an exercise buddy, you are more apt to keep up the routine. Plus it's a handy way to find someone who fits your exercise style. And from what I've read on Riddoch, you could gain more sight back."

Kyle and Dave chatted for a while longer. Kyle talked about his tentative foray back to work.

"Kyle, have you given any thought about joining a support group for the newly blind?"

"You said blind!"

Dave chuckled. "I did indeed. They meet once a week, and it's facilitated by some of the best social workers in the field—those who lost their sight and went on to get their master's in social work. All the people in the group have vision loss by disease, accident, or...."

"Freak of nature?"

Kyle could hear Dave's smile. "Or freak of nature. I've been color-blind all my life. Just as I don't know what it's like to see red or green, I cannot begin to know what it's like to suddenly not see at all. You've made some great progress. But depression can be a side effect for a lot of people faced with sudden vision loss, even more so for those that depended on their vision for their livelihood. The people in the group know that and have worked through or are currently working through those issues."

"My dad hinted about going to a group last time I talked to him. I guess it couldn't hurt to attend one session."

"That's the spirit!"

The conversation turned more casual after that. Kyle talked about his recent culinary accomplishments, and Dave described his teenage daughter's angst over deciding where to go to college. Dave was the kind of person who could relax anyone, so by the time Kyle set down his empty mug, he was feeling glad he'd finally listened to everyone's advice.

He thanked Dave, took the elevator downstairs, and exited into the kind of afternoon where children laughed, birds sang, and miracles seemed within reach.

HE FELT compelled to check his e-mail as soon as he got home. No response yet on the audition, but he hadn't been turned down flat, so he decided to think positively. Perhaps the publisher was so overwhelmed by the awesomeness of his narration that they hadn't yet gathered their wits—or appropriately enthusiastic words—to respond.

"You look happy," Lily said from the table when he entered the kitchen.

"I'm practicing optimism."

"Good for you."

Lily seemed to be happier too. Kyle guessed that she and Lieutenant Worf—er, Tony—had enjoyed a good lunch today.

"How was lunch with Tony?"

"Nice. We've got dinner plans on Saturday night."

"Good for you! Have a good time."

"Well, Tony and I were talking…. He has a good friend who's single. And gay."

Kyle stopped as he reached for a glass. "So why are you telling me this?"

"We thought…."

Oh my God, no! "You didn't. Tell me you didn't, Lily."

An ominous silence followed. *We have dinner plans. Shit!*

Then Lily cleared her throat. "The four of us are having dinner Saturday night."

"No! Dammit, Lily! I don't want—"

"You promised. You said if I found someone to date you'd double-date with us."

Kyle realized he was almost crushing the glass, and he forced himself to loosen his grip. "I said I'd find someone if you did. I didn't find Lieutenant Worf's BFF."

"You're not even looking."

He skipped the reminder that he *couldn't* look, thanks very much. "Lily—"

"It's one night. Maybe three hours. It won't kill you."

"Might give me a stroke," he muttered. Then he added, louder, "Does the BFF know I'm blind?"

"His name is Derek and yes, he does. Tony told me all about him, and he sounds interesting."

"*Interesting?* People who have their mother's taxidermic corpse stored in their basement, they're interesting."

"That's why we're going out for dinner. Reduced risk of corpses."

Once again Kyle accepted the uselessness of arguing with his sister. "One date, and you promise me no more blind dates. Christ. A blind man goes on a blind date. What do you call that?"

"Lucky. A double-blind double date." Then she laughed and walked away.

Kyle began assembling dinner ingredients. He'd decided he was in a pasta mood, so he took spinach ravioli from the fridge and put a pot on the stove. While the water heated, he set a couple of chicken breasts in a pan of hot olive oil and chopped veggies for a salad. Lily walked by him and opened a cupboard. A moment later, he heard her setting the table.

"Did you get a guide?" she asked as she clattered the silverware.

"Asked for one. Dave said it should take a few days for the request to make the rounds of the running clubs. I might have one or more people call me."

"Ooh! A variety? Way to go, little brother! A threesome maybe?"

He pointed the knife in what he thought was her general direction. "Running partner, Lily. Not *life* partner. I'm not in the market, remember?"

"That doesn't mean you can't make an impulse purchase."

No, you already took care of that, Kyle thought.

He growled and tossed the veggies into the salad bowl. "Here. Be useful and take this to the table."

She was humming as she carried the bowl. A moment later she opened the refrigerator. "What kind of dressing do you want?"

"Just oil and balsamic."

After flipping the chicken breasts, he squeezed a fresh lemon wedge over them and sprinkled some herbs on top. He took a moment to enjoy the aroma. Judging by the sound, the water was almost ready for the pasta. He thought about how easily he'd prepared this dinner—a simple one, sure, but with multiple components—despite losing his sight. If he could manage this well within months of going blind, maybe his dad was right: no need to cut back on adventure. Although if he was honest with himself, Kyle had become hesitant long before the stroke. Well, not hesitant, maybe. Staid. Settled. Dull.

"Why are you frowning?" Lily asked.

"Zip lines. When's the last time I did that?"

"Um… I don't know." She paused for a moment. "I guess there's nothing to stop you from doing it now. You wouldn't even need a guide."

"Good point."

Kyle carefully dumped the ravioli into the pot. "Siri, set timer for three minutes." Siri cheerfully confirmed.

"Why zip lines?" asked Lily, who could chomp onto a topic like a bulldog.

"It's time to rediscover my adventurous spirit." And then he added quickly, "I don't mean in romance!"

The timer on his phone signaled the pasta was done. He turned off the alarm, grabbed the pot, and carefully poured the contents into a colander he'd placed in the sink. After shaking the pasta to drain it, he poured it into a bowl and Lily fetched it. He removed the chicken from the pan onto a plate and carried it to the table.

"That's interesting," Lily said thoughtfully. Damn. That word again.

"What is?"

"Well, now that you can't see what someone looks like, you can't judge them based on how outwardly attractive they are. In theory, that could make you a less shallow person."

"I'm not shallow!" he squawked.

"No, not especially. But still. Now you have to go on what a person says and does. You'll never be lured in by someone like Rich."

He chewed a bite of chicken, considering. "I guess that's good," he finally admitted. "But I've also lost all the nuance of facial expressions and body language."

"But—"

Whatever Lily planned to say was interrupted by the ringing of Kyle's phone on the table beside him. He was going to ignore it, but Lily reached over and scooted the phone closer to him. "Go ahead. It's fine."

"Probably someone in India offering to fix my Microsoft Windows." But he picked up the call anyway. "Hello?"

"Uh, hi. Kyle Green?" The man sounded slightly nervous and also familiar, although Kyle couldn't place him.

"Yes."

"Dave from the Bridge Center said you're looking for a running guide. He thinks we might be good together."

"Dave told me he was giving my name to the running clubs in the area and it was going to take a few days." He was taken off guard and probably sounded a bit like an asshole—due to just being browbeaten into a blind date—but this was weird.

The guy laughed. "Uh, yeah, about that. Dave and I are in the same running club. I guess it was fresh in his mind, and he told me about you on our run. We live near each other."

"He told you where I live?" Kyle was immediately pissed off. His address should have been confidential until he chose to divulge it. What if the so-called volunteer was a con man trying to prey on blind people?

There was a long pause, then a noisy throat-clearing. "No, he just gave me your name and number. I, uh, already knew where you live." Another tight little chuckle. "God, you probably think I'm stalking you. I'm not."

"Who *are* you?"

"Seth Caplan. A few weeks ago I, um—"

"Caught me."

This time Seth sounded considerably more comfortable when he laughed. "That was me. You— Okay, let me repeat: not a stalker. But you mentioned you were going to ask for a guide at the Bridge Center, and I knew Dave worked at the Bridge Center. Then I started thinking it sounded pretty cool to be a running guide for an adult this time."

"You wanted a new charity project."

"Not charity. I don't know many people around here anymore, and I'd like a running partner that has a freer schedule than just evening or early morning runs. That stuff I did in San Jose with Sports Horizons was totally selfish too, because I like kids and it was a great chance to hang out with people who weren't lawyers."

Kyle regretted sniping at him. He needed to stop being so touchy. "Sorry."

"Forget it. I know I could be interpreted as a total creep here. Look, I didn't even know Dave had your request in hand and that I'd have a chance to meet up with you again, although to be honest, I was kind of hoping. You seemed like you'd be fun to run with."

Kyle felt the same way about Seth, who'd been funny and sweet and who'd done a great job rescuing him and getting him home without making Kyle feel like an idiot. If Kyle *had* to have a guide, Seth seemed as good a choice as anyone. But like a nervous bride, he wasn't ready to commit. "How about if we meet and talk it over. See if it'll work." He was about to invite Seth over, but then realized he could feel Lily's gaze boring into him. Nope—no audience necessary. "Are you free tomorrow sometime?"

"Sure. I'm sort of self-employed, so whatever works for you."

"Lunch?"

"Perfect. No better place to discuss exercising than over a meal."

They agreed on a Greek place a few blocks away before ending the call. Kyle put his phone down, picked up his knife and fork, and began cutting his cooling food.

Lily waited a whole thirty seconds before diving in. "Who was that?" she asked in a singsong tone.

"You heard the entire conversation."

"Just your part. Some of us don't have bat hearing."

Kyle ate a piece of ravioli, savoring the lemon herb sauce from the chicken before answering. "He might be my new running guide. We're meeting tomorrow."

"But you already know him?"

"He's the guy.... When I had my Disney Princess encounter?"

"Ah."

Kyle didn't know what that meant and didn't ask, instead attacking his chicken with vigor. He'd almost finished when he heard Lily open her mouth and prepare to speak.

"Don't," he warned. "He wants a running partner and that's all. I have no idea whether he's gay or straight, and I don't care. Neither should you. Can we.... Let's talk about whether I should try another audition, okay?"

"Okay." She launched into an extended monologue on royalty rates, which he gamely tried to track. Because that little thrill of excitement he felt over lunch with Seth? *That* was just plain dumb.

CHAPTER EIGHT

WHEN KYLE checked his e-mail the next morning, there was a message from ACX, the audiobook service. He hesitated several minutes before listening to it, first wading through the usual spam messages, phishing attempts, and advertisements from every business from which he'd ever bought something online. Even once he'd deleted all the junk, he sat at the table with the laptop in front of him and his coffee cup in hand.

Kyle didn't understand why he was so nervous. He was taking small steps to get back into the groove before posting on his website that he was open for limited business.

He'd been turned down for jobs before—it was part of the business. He'd long ago understood that a rejection wasn't necessarily a reflection of his lack of skill; it simply meant that someone else was a better fit. And he was also well aware that if this book didn't work out, there were plenty more to choose from. It wasn't a big deal.

Kind of like his upcoming lunch with Seth.

With that stomach-churning thought, he opened the e-mail.

"Hey, Lily!" he bellowed up the stairs a few minutes later.

"Yeah?" she shouted back.

"I got an offer!"

There was a pause, and when she spoke again, she was at the landing of the stairs. "An offer you can't refuse?"

"Well, I *could* refuse. I probably wouldn't end up with a horse head in my bed. But it looks like a good one, so I'm going to take it."

"That's great! Let me finish getting dressed, then I'll come down and you can tell me the details."

He walked back to the kitchen, wondering whether his sister had decided it'd be okay to chat with him while she was in the buff since he couldn't see her anyway. Ew. Better not to ask. He decided to make some breakfast while he waited.

After Lily joined him and read the offer, she agreed that he ought to take it. She clicked the buttons for him while he puttered around the kitchen, washing dishes and putting them away. "I downloaded the manuscript," she announced. "Want me to print it?"

"Yeah, thanks." He'd shelled out a hefty chunk of change for a braille embosser, along with a noise-dampening cabinet to put it in because that thing was loud.

"Done," she announced a few moments later. "When do you plan to start reading it?"

"Today. Maybe I'll be ready to record the first fifteen minutes in a week or so." His braille reading speed had improved, but he was still slower at reading than when he had been sighted. And he'd have to read through the text a few times before he was ready to narrate. But he didn't have much else going on now—just lunch with Seth and the dreaded blind date—so he could dive on in.

"Gotcha. Hey, Kyle?"

"Hmm?" He leaned against the counter and wondered what was coming next.

"You're doing pretty well here. Actually, you're doing great. I don't think you need me breathing down your neck all the time. How about if I move back home Sunday?"

"This Sunday? As in two-days-from-now Sunday?"

"Yes. I've been packing some stuff and taking it back to my place over the past few days."

A strange mixture of panic and relief washed over him. On the one hand, the idea of being alone terrified him. But… it also exhilarated him a bit, and besides, he did want a return of his privacy. He'd been aching for the chance to find out whether listening to porn did the trick as neatly as watching it. And Lily was probably eager to return to her regular life.

She must have taken his silence as hesitation. "I'll still be just fifteen minutes away, Kyebye, and it's not like you'll never see me. Just a phone call away if you get stuck. Plus I'm going to want excuses to come over and eat your cooking instead of just coming over and working."

"I'll be fine. Thanks for… being there for me. Jesus. I don't know how I'd have managed without you."

"You would have, somehow. But that's what family's for, right? Being the sand when your tires are spinning on ice?"

He nodded.

KYLE NEVER really got into the habit of collecting friends. He wasn't antisocial or anything. But when he was a kid, his family had picked up and moved too often to make lasting friendships practical, even when there wasn't a language barrier to deal with too. He'd mostly hung out with his siblings. Then he'd been busy with college and work, and when he settled with Matt, well, Matt had fulfilled most of his companionship needs. Since the stroke, Kyle had kept in touch with a few pals but hadn't felt the desire to get together with them. Aside from family and the people at the Bridge Center, he'd turned into a bit of a hermit.

All of which went a long way toward explaining why he was so nervous about meeting Seth for lunch. It was comforting to know that Kyle hadn't done anything in the twenty or so minutes they'd already spent together to scare Seth away, but a meal together—without the distraction of Kyle's princess injury—left open all sorts of opportunities for awkwardness. Beginning with Kyle's closet. He worried whether Lily had secretly followed through with her threat to replace his staid button-downs with colors and patterns. He had just finished organizing his closet too, but that wouldn't prevent Lily from switching things around. What if he thought he was putting on a shirt in plain forest green, when in fact it had leopard spots or bucking broncos or purple and orange stripes? He'd left his phone downstairs and couldn't use the volunteers-be-your-eyes app, so evidently his closet would be another trip into the unknown.

Yippee.

"Seth will forgive a blind man for an appalling outfit. And it's *not* a date."

Despite the attempt to embolden himself, his hands fumbled at the buttons.

Lily had gone out, so the house was silent as he slipped on his shoes and snapped his cane into form. Outside, he felt the warm sun on his face. It was that perfect time of year when the threat of winter was mostly gone but the heat and humidity hadn't settled in yet. He walked confidently down the sidewalk, his cane protecting him from lurking children's toys, the chirping traffic signals telling him when it was safe to cross the street.

He checked the time when he got to the Greek restaurant and learned that he was ten minutes early. He hovered uncertainly just inside the front door until a woman spoke up. "Can I help you?"

"I'm supposed to meet someone, but I'm—"

"Kyle!" Seth sounded as if he was hurrying over from the restaurant interior. He briefly touched Kyle's elbow. "I got us a table already."

Navigating through restaurants was tricky. Tables and chairs could be anywhere, not to mention servers with their arms full of food. And patrons didn't much appreciate having a cane whack against their legs. Kyle was grateful when Seth gracefully and expertly guided him through the dining room without making Kyle feel like a blind stegosaurus. Still, a small sigh of relief escaped him after he sat down.

"Would you like a menu?" asked a different woman.

"Not unless it's in braille."

"Oh, I'm sorry. The braille menu is in use right now. I can bring it over as soon as it's available."

"It's fine." Kyle turned to Seth. "Do you mind reading yours to me?"

"Sure. It's an epic menu, nearly as long as the *Iliad*."

Oh, so we're going for light and playful.

"You mean there is more to the menu than saganaki, dolmades, and hummus?" Kyle used one of his anime voices with a Greek accent. He didn't know what possessed him, but it felt good.

"Well there goes my excellent opportunity to impress you with my Greek pronunciation of avgolemono and spanakopita. Ooh! And tzatziki."

The awkwardness of not having a menu eased with the bit of levity. The waitress gasped. "Oh my God! You sounded just like the bad boy in *Werewolf PTA*!" She said it a bit too loudly, and the noise immediately around them abated a bit. "Can you say something else?"

Kyle ordered his drink in Terry James's voice. She was so excited she nearly forgot to get Seth's drink order. When Seth just ordered in his normal voice, she seemed disappointed.

"I horrified her, didn't I?" Kyle deadpanned.

"Slightly," Seth responded in kind. "I don't think she'll ever come back." They both chuckled. "Well, the only thing I can do is lawyer speak. Will that be okay enough for me to narrate the menu? If you fall asleep, I'll know I did my job."

Kyle laughed. "Let me be the judge of that before you audition through ACX." When Seth lapsed into puzzled silence, Kyle laughed again. "Sorry. It's what I do for a living, actually. Narrate books."

"Really?" Seth said, sounding slightly excited at the prospect.

"Yeah. Well, I used to be a voice-over actor, but I haven't figured out yet how to do that without sight. Narrating books is an easier fit for now."

"So you *are* the voice of bad boy Terry James in *Werewolf PTA*."

"Was. And yes, one and the same."

"That is *so* cool! Jeez, ex-lawyer sounds so lame compared to that. Plus you're totally going to judge my menu-reading skills."

Kyle leaned back in his chair and smiled. "I won't."

"What books have you narrated? Oh! I have the Audible app! I can look you up right now!"

"Um...." Kyle wasn't so sure he was ready to admit to the Bible and gay romance. "How about if we order first. I'm kind of hungry."

"Sure."

Seth didn't so much read the menu as discuss it with him, which was nice. They decided to share appetizers of saganaki, stuffed grape leaves, and hummus. Seth chose pastitsio as his main course, and after a moment's deliberation on the odds of impaling himself on the skewer, Kyle picked pork souvlaki. Then he remembered. "Do you mind if I eat pork?"

"I'm nonobservant. Hell, I'm as likely as the next guy to order bacon. So go ahead. But thanks for asking."

The waitress brought their iced teas and took their orders.

"She didn't sound so starstruck anymore," Kyle observed after she left.

"Nope. She's getting run ragged by the people two tables over. They have a toddler who's dropping everything onto the floor. Oh! She's slipped a bit on a dropped dolmades. Great recovery!"

Kyle smiled as he felt carefully for his drink. The waitress had left a straw on the table beside it, so he unwrapped the paper and stuck the straw into his glass. His nerves jangled as he felt Seth staring at him. "So, um, what are your running preferences?" Kyle finally asked.

"Flexible. Like I said on the phone, my schedule's flexible."

"No lawyer stuff?"

Seth snorted. "Ex-practicing lawyer, remember? I'm not even licensed in Illinois, actually."

"You sound… young to be retired." Yes, Kyle was blatantly fishing for information, but it was irritating not to have all those little bits of information a sighted person collected automatically upon meeting someone.

"Thirty-five," Seth said with a chuckle. "And not retired. Redirected. I was getting tired of the grind at the law firm and kind of considering doing something else anyway; then my mom started to fail at everyday tasks." His voice dropped a bit and lost much of its brightness. "I came back to Chicago to take care of her since, out of my siblings, I'm the most mobile. It was her wish before this started to be cared for in her home."

"What does she have?"

"Alzheimer's."

"I'm so sorry." Kyle tried not to think about losing his own parents to diseases of old age. Yes, they lived far away, but they were still his touchpoint in many ways. Maybe he was way too old for that, but he didn't care. His mom and dad were amazing.

"Thanks. I've found a fantastic set of caregivers. I'm glad I can spend this time with her, even though she's failing more each day. She's still a pretty cool lady."

"She must be pretty young for Alzheimer's."

"Well, I was the 'Surprise!' baby. My mom was forty-three when she had me. My sister is twenty years older and my brother is about eighteen years older than I am."

"And your father?" Kyle prompted, hoping he wasn't prying.

"Died when I was in high school. Guess that makes me an orphan now, or at least when my mom forgets who I am. Hmm. When do you get too old to call yourself an orphan?"

Never, Kyle thought. But he shrugged. "I don't know the official ruling on that one. Though you're not one just yet." He took a long sip of his iced tea.

"So anyway, here I am, back in the city of big shoulders. I haven't lived here since high school—man, half my life!—so I don't really know too many people around here anymore. And since I don't have an office to go to, I don't meet people at work either. Thus the stalking."

"I get it," Kyle said. He did, especially since he was socially isolated too. "Are you thinking about getting a job?"

"Oh, I work. I partnered up with a couple of buddies who ditched the big corporations, and I'm part owner of a start-up that produces adaptive technology. And I am *so* sorry—I imported that last sentence straight out of Silicon Valley. It sounds way less pretentious in San Jose."

Kyle chuckled. "What's adaptive technology?"

"Stuff to help people with disabilities. Apps mostly, and software solutions, that kind of thing. Like, we have this one app that basically adds closed-captions to phone calls or anything else you listen to on your phone. And we're working on a GPS system to help people with vision impairment get around."

Seth sounded so eager and enthusiastic that Kyle had to smile. "Does your system help with trike avoidance too?"

Seth's answering laugh was warm. "No, but I'm going to suggest it to the development guys. Maybe it could be like those curb feeler things they used to put on cars."

Kyle pictured himself walking around in leggings with thick wires sticking out. "You may need to work on that idea a bit."

"Just a bit," Seth agreed.

Before Kyle could ask another question, the waitress set some plates in front of them. "Here you go!" she trilled. "Enjoy! Nico will be by shortly with your saganaki."

Sensing Kyle's hesitation, Seth tapped each of the plates in turn. "Hummus and pita bread are at one o'clock. Dolmades at eleven o'clock. Feel free to poke with your fingers if you need to locate things. I won't be scandalized. I'll probably just be glad you can't see when I drip stuff on myself."

Kyle picked up his spoon and reached for the grape leaves. He really liked how Seth knew how to help him out in a way that felt natural and put Kyle at ease. That boded well for a running guide, right?

Only after he'd eaten a grape leaf and polished off a pita wedge dipped in hummus did Kyle resume his interrogation, only to be interrupted by the closeness of a man and the smell of Metaxa, the Greek liqueur.

"Opa!" the man exclaimed. Kyle flinched when the heat flared, not knowing if the flames were headed toward him. Once the flames were extinguished, the smell of fresh lemon and cheese permeated the air.

Although Kyle was adept in the kitchen and at his home table, he didn't want to burn himself on the hot dish.

"The plate is hot. Do you want me to serve you a piece of cheese?" Seth asked.

"Please."

"One piece of gooey cheesy goodness is on your plate."

"Opa!"

After a few bites of the saganaki, and what sounded like a cheese-induced orgasm from Seth, Kyle took the opportunity to continue the conversation. "So you don't do the development for your company?"

"Nah. Though I can tinker around with the coding, I'm more of an idea guy and an app tester. Back in California, my law firm's clients were mostly tech companies, so I know the business end. I also oversee the legal stuff and do some of the marketing too. Don't worry—I promise not to try to sell you anything!"

"It sounds—" Nope, not *interesting*. Kyle was boycotting that word. "Engaging."

Seth swallowed whatever was in his mouth. "It is. I mean, it's nice to know I'm indirectly helping people navigate their lives. But my partners are all back in San Jose—I telecommute—which means not much direct human interaction for me."

And that was a shame, Kyle thought, because Seth in person was charming and funny and nice to talk to.

"So how did you end up being a voice actor?" Seth asked.

Kyle described the somewhat wandering road that led to his career. As he was talking, their main courses arrived, but even as they were eating, the discussion continued. Seth seemed genuinely fascinated by what Kyle told him and downright gleeful when he learned that Kyle—as Ecos—was kind of a big deal in Japan. "I'm having lunch with someone famous!" Seth enthused.

"I'm not really—"

"I lived in California for eighteen years and never met a single celebrity, but here I am back in Illinois, and I'm having lunch with one."

Kyle could feel himself blushing. "I'm not a *celebrity*. I mean, do I look like Brad Pitt?"

"So you were going to tell me what books you've done," said Seth, apparently wishing to refocus.

"Um…." Kyle swallowed a bite of rice and washed it down with some watered-down iced tea. He really, really wished he could see Seth's reaction to this next part. "Well, many versions of the Bible, and now romance mostly. Gay romance."

Seth was silent, which made Kyle squirm a little. But when Seth finally spoke, it sounded as if he was leaning closer over the table. "Well, nothing like both ends of the spectrum. Gay romance? Seriously?"

"Yeah," Kyle said with a sigh. "There are some good books in the genre. They're fun to do."

He waited for the inevitable question. A lot of the men who narrated gay romances were straight—it wasn't as though they needed to be flying a rainbow flag to read the things, as long as they were comfortable with the idea. And Kyle had done VO work as a werewolf member of the intergalactic PTA, for Pete's sake, and he wasn't a shifter, a parent, or a space traveler.

But what came out of Seth's mouth was not a question about Kyle's sexual orientation. "I *love* reading gay romance!" Kyle suspected it had been loud enough to make people at the neighboring tables turn and stare.

Was he joking? "You do not," Kyle retorted.

"I totally do. When I was lawyering and would get bogged down with all the paperwork—all the *hereinafter*s and *wherof*s and *parties of the first parts*—I'd clear my head with one of those books. Like you said, they're fun. Some of them are really well written. And hot." His smile was audible as he said the last part. "Besides, nothing's better for a shriveled legal heart than the promise of true love and happily ever after."

Huh. So Seth batted for Kyle's team. Which was great, except blind men can't play baseball, can they? "I'm gay too," Kyle blurted. And then he blushed again.

Seth was quiet for a really long time. Kyle would have sold his soul to see Seth's face. "I, uh, I'm not looking for a date," Seth finally stammered.

Shit. This time Kyle's face flamed so hot it was a miracle he didn't spontaneously combust. Or melt like saganaki. "I wasn't trying to pick you up."

"Oh God." Seth reached across the table to cover Kyle's hand with his. "Oh God. That's not what I meant. I—" There was a dull thud, which Kyle suspected might be Seth's head on the tabletop. "I am such a fuckwit."

Kyle wondered if the waitress was anywhere within sight, and if so, whether he could wave her down. Maybe he should just fumble some bills out of his wallet, throw them on the table, and flee. But Seth was still holding Kyle's hand against the table, and Kyle was mortified into immobility.

"Kyle?" Seth said hesitantly.

"I'm just…. This was a mistake."

"No! Let's back up a little, okay? I did *not* mean to imply that you intended to pick me up. And I especially didn't mean to imply that I wouldn't want you, specifically, to pick me up. Because if things were different, you'd— Well, never mind. The point is, I've taken myself off the market for the foreseeable future. With my mom the way she is, among other things. And I just wanted you to know that despite the stalker-like thing, I'm not hitting on you."

Seth sounded sincere, and dammit, he was *still* covering Kyle's hand. A little of the flush receded. "I know you're not interested in dating me," he said quietly.

"But it's…." Seth sighed. "I almost said it's not you, it's me. Cliché much? Except it *is* me. 'Cause normally I'd be all over you, trying to convince you that you desperately want to date a socially awkward ex-lawyer. But I'm not normal."

It was sweet of Seth to pretend that Kyle was worth pursuing—so sweet that Kyle decided not to make a big thing of it. "Not really normal here either," he said, waving at his eyes. He could see the outline of his fingers as he moved his hand. "Anyway, I'm off the market too."

"I want to ask you why. But then I'd have to tell you my tale of woe, and I really don't want to go there. At least we've got it settled—we can be friends without benefits. And we can—" He stopped suddenly, then huffed loudly. "Unless I've scared you away."

"You haven't."

Seth squeezed Kyle's hand and finally let it go. "I should have warned you from the beginning—my mouth is a lot faster than my brain. Which is sort of an impediment to a lawyer and was why I wasn't a trial attorney."

Kyle smiled at him. "Voice actors get scripts. Safer that way."

"And it will give us both an incentive to run fast and hard so I don't have enough breath left to say anything stupid."

The waitress arrived and stood behind Kyle. "Mind if I clear your plates?" They told her to go ahead. "Can I get you anything else? Dessert? Coffee? Refills on your drinks?"

"Just the check, please," Kyle said.

After the waitress left, Seth cleared his throat. "We, um, haven't really talked about running. Did you decide not to—"

"No. Let's just go for a walk. It's really nice out."

Although Kyle was willing to pay for both of them, they ended up splitting the bill. Seth gently guided him out of the restaurant and onto the sidewalk. Seth let go of Kyle's elbow as soon as Kyle shook out his cane, and Kyle was chagrined to realize that he missed the touch. Seth's hand was long-fingered and soft, and his contact had been more a subtle suggestion than a firm steering.

It was early Friday afternoon on a fine spring day, and it sounded as if half the city was playing hooky from their jobs. They probably were, judging by the distant crowd noise from Wrigley Field. The scents of hot dogs, beer, and flowers carried lightly on the air. Kyle imagined women making the season's first use of their short skirts and sleeveless blouses and some of the men in shorts. It was a shame—he'd always been a leg man. He envisioned the promise of hotter days, when some guys would eagerly shed their shirts. That got him wondering what Seth looked like, which was not a productive direction for his thoughts. Besides, hadn't Lily told him that he was supposed to be all noble now, judging others solely on their inner selves?

"So," Seth began as they waited to cross a street, "we've already established that we both have pretty flexible schedules, which is great. When was the last time you ran?"

"Besides the Disney Princess run?"

Seth chuckled. "Yes, besides the obstacle course."

"I've been running at both the Bridge workout center and in my basement on the hamster run. I'm up to about six miles now, about seven-and-a-half-minute miles. But I hate the treadmill."

Seth chuckled. "Yes, the hamster run. I call it that too. Boring as hell, even if there's a TV to distract you from the fact that you're going nowhere fast."

"Amen!"

"You're familiar with the area, even though your sight is trashed. Where did you use to run before you lost your sight?"

"I ran in all weather and on all terrain with my former partner. We'd go up to either Belmont or Irving Park and cross over. Sometimes to Diversey and through the park. At times we ran up the Lakefront Trail to Jackson Park."

Seth let out a whistle. "Serious runner!"

"Well, we'd run to a place for breakfast in Hyde Park and take a Divvy Bike or cab back home. The most we ran was about fifteen miles."

The sun was warm as they walked down Broadway. Conversation flowed easily, as if they'd done it forever. Kyle had to stop that thinking. This was an exercise relationship, that was all.

"You know, even with sight, it's hard to get by all the cyclists, walkers, and tourists on the lakefront path," Seth said.

"I remember. Though really early in the morning or during the day on weekdays are good times. Forget weekends. The marathon groups, tourists, and various races use the path."

"Still, they might be good for training when we work up to it. How do you feel about running in a cemetery?"

"Graceland? They might chase us out. But I'm up for an adventure."

A comfortable silence. Yeasty smell with a tinge of cinnamon. Ann Sather was still pumping out those famous cinnamon rolls.

"How does the running guide thing work? Do you still lead me by the elbow?"

"No, but close. We run nearly side by side, connected by hand with a tether. As the guide, I run slightly ahead of you, but you set the pace. Since we're both about the same pace, that should be fairly easy."

"That's it? What about a Batmobile Big Wheel?"

"I'll let you know about any obstacles, change in terrain, curbs…."

"Potholes."

Seth laughed. "Yes, and potholes, of which there is no shortage around here. I'll say move right, pothole ahead, giving you enough warning so you can be prepared to move. Then you'll feel it on the tether too, before we get to them. Since you've not run with a guide before, it takes some practice. But I have no doubt you'll catch on quickly."

Seth told some funny stories about running, and Kyle reminisced about some trail runs out west. It turned out they were compatible on most points and flexible on the others. And Seth was just plain fun to talk to. Sometimes he commented on something they passed. He chatted a bit about the work his company was doing. And when the subject of books came up again, it turned out they enjoyed a lot of the same authors, both in gay romance and other genres.

Midway down a sidewalk, Kyle came to a sudden stop. "I have no idea where we are." He'd been so engrossed in the conversation that he'd lost track of which direction they were walking and how far.

"Yeah, that's where GPS comes in handy," Seth said.

"Or a guide."

"Does that mean we're going to run together?"

Kyle pretended to be nonchalant. "If you're up for it."

"Enthusiastically so."

"Good. I'll call Dave and let him know we connected." Kyle wondered if his wide grin made him look like a lunatic. "Um, can we start Monday?"

"Perfect. I can pick you up at your place at… is nine thirty okay?"

It sounded like a date. But that thought reminded Kyle that he had an actual date scheduled for the following evening—with Derek. He almost groaned.

"Something wrong?" Seth asked.

Kyle shook his head. "Not really. Just remembered I have to do something awful tomorrow."

Very quietly, Seth said, "Tomorrow I'm supposed to go through stuff in the attic. While my mom was a practical woman, there are boxes of my dad's things still up there. And then there are the clothes she no longer fits into. She's lost a lot of weight, and she didn't have much to begin with."

"I'm sorry." Kyle would have offered to help, but he wouldn't be much good at sorting things. Besides, sorting a deceased parent's and a diminished parent's belongings was an intimate act, and Kyle didn't know Seth well enough for that.

Seth patted Kyle's arm. "Thanks. It'll help that I can look forward to a good run on Monday."

They ended up walking to Kyle's house, not parting until they reached the front porch. "I'm glad we're doing this," Kyle said. "I'm glad you volunteered." That was the truth.

"God, me too. See you Monday!"

Kyle walked into his house, telling himself he did *not* feel like a teenage girl coming home from her first date.

CHAPTER NINE

"YOU ARE not wearing that!" Lily exclaimed.

Out of force of habit, Kyle looked down at himself. But since he was standing still, he saw nothing but blackness. "What? You didn't slip something awful into my closet, did you?" Because as far as he knew, he had put on a pale blue button-down and his favorite jeans, and his gadget confirmed it.

"No, but I should have. You look like a bank manager on his day off."

"I always dress like this," Kyle protested with a scowl.

"Yeah, that's fine for a trip to Osco. But this is a *date*."

Kyle crossed his arms. "One I didn't ask for and don't really want. Besides, weren't you the one who lectured me about not judging people by their looks? What I wear shouldn't matter to Derek."

She made an annoyed huff that meant Kyle had won this round. Probably they were both too old for sibling squabbles, but old habits died very hard. Smirking, Kyle found his light jacket and slipped it on. He'd dithered a bit about whether to take his cane. They were just going to a restaurant, where Lily could guide him. But he'd been enjoying the independence the cane gave him, so he grabbed it after all.

As Lily drove, Kyle looked out the window, enjoying the outlines of the buildings and people. It was a bit frustrating when the traffic was stop-and-go; unless something passed by quickly, his vision was a blank slate. But with the all the rocking he'd been doing, he'd improved his ability to see movement. Seeing and distinguishing something new was always a treat—kind of a visual surprise package.

"So how'd the running guide thing work out?" Lily asked, interrupting his reverie.

The car ride had been her first real interrogation opportunity. After meeting with Seth the day before, Kyle had avoided Lily's inquisition by burying himself deeply in the book he was supposed to narrate. Lily was always pretty good about not interrupting him while he was working, so she hadn't asked questions. He didn't want to seem petty, he just wanted to keep the happiness he felt after yesterday's lunch to himself. Okay, maybe he was being petty by punishing Lily for the blind date. Instead she had busied herself packing things up in preparation for moving back to her home. Judging by the sounds, she'd accumulated an impressive collection of stuff in Kyle's guest bedroom.

"Fine," Kyle answered.

"You sound like you're twelve and Mom just asked you how your day at school was."

She was kind of right. "He's a nice guy. We had a good lunch, and we're trying a test run on Monday."

"Does he volunteer to guide runners a lot? Because that would be a weird coincidence."

"He worked with kids and teens in the past. I'm his first adult."

Lily honked at someone for reasons Kyle couldn't discern. His sister was an aggressive driver, so not being able to see what she was doing was possibly a blessing. "Why does he want to volunteer for you? Not that you're not charming and everything, but...."

"He doesn't know many people around here and he wants someone to run with." Simple as that.

"Do they do background checks on their volunteers? What if he's a serial killer?"

Kyle shot her a glare even though she was watching the road. He hoped. "No, and he's not. I'm not defenseless, Lil."

"I know," she said with a sigh. "But you're still my little brother, you know?"

A few minutes later, she parked the car.

Kyle didn't know who'd chosen the restaurant; he hadn't asked. The menu was supposed to be New American cuisine, which was fine with him, but still he disliked the place as soon as they stepped inside. The noise level was terrible—loud conversations echoing off hard surfaces, clattering plates and cutlery, the wailing of a baby, some kind of sports on the TV in the bar, and the blare of eighties music over the sound system. The combined din hit him like a fist, nearly stopping him in his tracks. The smell was less than pleasant too. The kitchen had overcooked something. But he'd resolved to be a good sport tonight because he was grateful to Lily for all she'd done for him, so he didn't complain.

"Green," Lily shouted at someone, presumably the hostess. "We have reservations. The rest of our party's not here yet."

"Of course. Follow me, please."

He couldn't help but notice that Lily wasn't as good as Seth at leading him. Usually she wasn't bad, but nerves were probably playing into the regression of her skills. She clutched his arm instead of his elbow, and her grip was too tight. She wasn't very aware of where his body was either, because twice he banged into chairs. One of them was occupied, so Kyle mumbled an apology. He was glad when they reached their table and he could sit down.

Tony and Derek showed up fifteen minutes late, when Kyle was already halfway through his second beer. An advantage of being blind was that nobody was ever going to expect him to be a designated driver, and he suspected that a good dose of alcohol would make the evening go faster. While Tony was apologizing for bad traffic and lack of parking, Derek was intent on getting to know Kyle—very well.

"Do you want to feel my face?" Derek asked, sounding way too eager.

Kyle tried not to shudder. "Um, no thanks. I don't... really do that."

"Then how do you know what people look like?"

This was going to be a long evening.

Kyle took a long gulp of his beer and hoped a refill arrived soon. "I have supersensitive hearing, so sound waves bounce off faces and give me a visual image. You know, like bats."

"Really?" Derek sounded starstruck and wide-eyed.

"No, not really. I was kidding."

"Oh." Now Derek was disappointed. "But do you—"

Fortunately the waiter appeared just then to take their orders. Kyle had asked Lily to read him the menu while they waited for their dates, so he knew he wanted steak. As he waited for everyone else at the table to order, an idea occurred to him. Was there an app where you could point your phone at a menu and have the menu read out loud? That would be handy. He could ask Seth about it.

As soon as the waiter left, Tony involved Lily in a deep discussion about whether J.J. Abrams had improved or destroyed the Star Wars series. That left Kyle at Derek's mercy.

"Do you know Bob Rodriguez?" Derek asked. "He's blind too."

"Sorry, no."

"Oh. Well, he has a seeing-eye dog. Do you have a seeing-eye dog?"

"If I did, it would be here with me."

A *very* long evening.

Derek giggled, which was funny because he had a very deep voice. "Right. Of course. I think it would be cool to have a dog you could take into restaurants. Unless it was really slobbery or something. Like a Saint Bernard. Can restaurants kick out a seeing-eye dog if it slobbers a lot?"

"I'll have to check the handbook on that one."

"Ooh! There's a handbook?"

"Not really." Hoping to change the subject, Kyle asked, "What do you do for a living, Derek?"

"I'm an insurance underwriter."

Kyle couldn't think of a single intelligent thing to say about that. *Sounds interesting?* Not really. Finally he came up with "Have you been doing that for long?" There. That was safe and polite.

"About five years. Before that I was a claims specialist." Derek spent the next fifteen minutes describing the ins and outs of insurance employment in excruciating detail, which was Kyle's own fault for asking. The only thing that blessedly stopped the conversation was the arrival of their food.

Lily leaned close and discreetly let him know where the food was on his plate.

"Potato three, steak six, broccoli eleven."

"Do you want me to cut your steak for you?" Derek asked.

Kyle pasted on a smile. "Thanks, but I can manage." He felt Derek's gaze on him as he buttered a piece of bread.

"Wow! You're really good at that."

Christ. An interminably long evening.

No doubt sensing Kyle's annoyance, Lily tried to reboot the conversation by mentioning a vacation she was planning to San Francisco and asking Derek and Tony if they'd ever been there. Neither had, but that didn't stop Tony from going on about the different cons that happened in San Fran, and Derek from listing fatality statistics for pedestrians and calculating the chances of a major earthquake while she was there. But eventually that topic waned, and Derek again zeroed in on Kyle.

"How about you? What do you do?"

"I'm a neurosurgeon."

Lily kicked Kyle *hard*, making him yelp.

"Really?" Derek said. "Do you have computers and cameras and stuff to tell you where to cut, or do you go by sense of touch?"

The rest of the meal dragged on. Tony ordered dessert and insisted that everyone else do the same. Kyle polished off his fourth beer while eating chocolate lava cake and listening to Derek drone on about why the Cubs were better than the White Sox. Kyle liked baseball but wasn't a rabid fan, even though he was a Northsider. He hoped he nodded at the appropriate places. He wished for another beer.

At long last—at *very* long last—the ordeal ended. Derek suggested they could all go somewhere for a few drinks, and when Kyle replied that his doctors wouldn't let him stay out too late, Lily didn't kick him. Maybe she was tired of hearing Tony explain why the crew of the *USS Enterprise* needed a space ship when they could just teleport places.

Outside the restaurant, Kyle held out his hand to Derek, who pulled him in for an awkward hug and peck on the cheek. Derek felt sort of squishy. He most likely didn't run. Or lift. Or much of anything.

Silence reigned for most of the drive home. Finally Lily spoke up. "Sorry."

"If you *ever* do that to me again, I'm going to deafen myself too."

"Yeah." She sighed. "I was just trying to—"

"I know what you were trying to do. And I appreciate the thought, really. But I'm not pining away from loneliness. And I really, really don't want a matchmaker."

"All right." She didn't sound as resigned as he'd like. Or as contrite.

"So are you planning another date with Lieutenant Worf?"

She laughed. "He actually looks more like Captain Kirk—young, sexy Captain Kirk. And in case you're wondering, Derek bears a passing resemblance to Scotty."

Kyle pictured a man in a red polyester shirt sitting in front of a computer and huge stacks of paper. *We can't hold out much longer, Captain! The spreadsheet's gonna blow!* He snickered.

"I think Tony was a bit nervous. He wasn't like this on our other dates. He actually talked about topics that weren't star-related. I might pass on further dates with him," Lily said. "It seems he regressed just when he'd gotten more interesting."

"At least he didn't offer to cut up your food."

"God, Derek was pretty awful, wasn't he? And you know the worst part? I think he's really into you. He was making goo-goo eyes at you the entire time, and he gave me a thumbs-up right before we left."

"Ugh."

"He's a really *cute* Scotty, if that helps."

Kyle shook his head. "It wouldn't. Not even if I could see him."

"I am sorry, Kyebye. It's just... you're a really great guy, you know? You deserve to have someone special. Plus, well, I love Matt. You know that. But you guys never had that *spark*. Rich was a fuckwad, but for a while there, the thing we had was electric. Like, high-voltage. It was amazing. I want you to feel some of that."

Kyle frowned. Maybe he wanted that too, but he wasn't about to admit it. And he didn't *need* it. "The only sparks I'm going to feel with Derek are when I deliberately electrocute myself so I don't have to listen to him anymore."

She whacked his knee. "Come on—he wasn't *that* awful."

"But you know what he saw in me? A decent-looking, middle-aged freak show. He wasn't interested in anything about me except what I look like and that I'm blind. That's not the kind of man I want to date."

"I get that. But what kind of man *do* you want to date?"

"None, right now," Kyle answered, when he was really thinking *Seth.* "You should give Tony another try. Maybe he was trying too hard."

"We'll see."

SUNDAY WAS busy. Kyle helped carry boxes and bags of crap to Lily's car, assured her for the thousandth time that he'd be fine, and went for a solo walk with his cane and didn't trip over anything. Since he'd smelled those cinnamon rolls at Ann Sather on Friday, he decided to take a walk and grab one. Then, delighting in the first complete privacy he'd had since the stroke, he made sure the curtains were closed, took off his clothes in the middle of the living room, pulled up some porn on his laptop, and jacked off. The noisy, raunchy video he played helped get the job done, but it wasn't as effective as when he had visuals. And it wasn't *nearly* as effective as somebody else's hands on his body. "Getting too old for this anyway," he muttered to himself as he cleaned up afterward. Maybe he would become a monk.

He spent the rest of the day finishing the book he was going to narrate, which wasn't a chore since he enjoyed the story. It was well written, and the tale itself—about a fireman and a homeless tattoo artist—was angsty without being over the top. He already knew what voices he'd use for the main characters.

He had a light dinner, responded to Lily's texts by telling her he wasn't dead yet, and talked to his parents on the phone. They were probably checking up on him too, but they camouflaged it better than Lily did. He went to bed early, resolutely *not* getting excited over the next morning's run.

When he woke up just past six, long before the alarm went off, he was twitchy. He needed to do a reread of the book before he began recording, but there wasn't really time for him to settle in, and his attention wouldn't focus. A shower before running was stupid, and he didn't want to prepare and eat a heavy breakfast. Instead he listened to NPR as he assembled a chicken noodle thing in the slow cooker.

He started his prerun warm-up routine at nine o'clock. Finished it and checked his water belt for the third time.

"The time is 9:20." He told himself that he wasn't pacing as he waited for Seth—he was still warming up.

Seth rang the bell at nine thirty on the dot, and Kyle found himself grinning stupidly at the poor guy. "Do you want to come in first? Do you need anything before we go?"

"Nope. Drank and peed before I left my place. I'm ready."

Kyle locked the door and stored the key in his water belt pocket. "Where to?"

"I thought we'd start practicing on the Kelly Park path, where the only thing we need to worry about are moms and their strollers. Then we'll head back taking North Seminary, practice ditching some of those potholes and the garbage trucks, then back onto Kelly path, across Irving Park Road along the 'L' tracks to Montrose, then over to North Clark. If you're up for it, we can run into Graceland Cemetery. If we get kicked out, we'll do the Benevolent Cemetery next door, then back down Irving to Seminary, then home. I know it's not very far, but it will be practice on the different terrains. If we have time, we can do a second loop. Total time out would be forty-five minutes to an hour. How does that sound?"

"Sounds good. Oh, and I brought an old T-shirt, just like you told me to. What are we going to do with this?"

"This is our tether for today. We can try other items—rope, cloth—and they sell ready-made tethers too. We'll see how this goes first."

Kyle and Seth started to run, and the images started to form. Houses, the few people out, the mail truck.

"Crossing Seminary," Seth said. "Move right, curb up in five paces."

Kyle relaxed after a while, and the tether was just on the periphery of his awareness. He liked how Seth called out what Kyle needed to know, and it was timed just right. Seth kept up a running commentary on what was going on in the neighborhood, and it put Kyle at ease. Occasionally Kyle would mention something he could discern as they ran. Whoot! The more he ran, the more he could see. They successfully skirted potholes, strollers, and parked cars and navigated across major streets. Time flew by, and Kyle was disappointed when the run was over. They had gone just under six miles in forty-five minutes.

"Great run! We did a seven-thirty-minute mile. Not bad for the first time out," Seth said.

They both began to do a postrun stretch. Kyle was wondering if he should invite Seth inside when Seth broke his reverie.

"Run on Wednesday? Same time?"

"Sounds good."

"I have to go. I've got a conference call at eleven thirty with my California counterparts about a new app. See you on Wednesday!"

And Seth was off, leaving Kyle to make his way back into the house by himself. Still, his disappointment that the run had ended couldn't erase the joy he had while running and experiencing Seth's company. Kyle noticed that he still gripped the T-shirt tether. "I've got a book to narrate. After I throw these clothes in the laundry and take a shower," he announced, just to make sure the house and its contents knew his priorities for the day.

CHAPTER TEN

"YOU HAVE thirteen new messages. First message from Michael Plahm. Subject: voice-over needed for commercial."

After Kyle had completed his first poststroke narration, the word got out he was available. He was so flooded with requests that he needed to clear his e-mail inbox at least three times a day. He enlisted Lily as his booking agent to screen the requests. Most of the contacts didn't realize that he couldn't sync his voice with the lips of a character, so he was stuck with book reading and voice-overs that didn't require synchronization. That thinned the pack by half. But all of a sudden, he was in demand for gay romance novels and was booked solid for the next three months. He tried to send work to some of his fellow artists who'd taken over the workload when he was out of commission—Greg, Max, David, KC, Nick—but some authors said they would wait for him. He was going to get calluses on his fingertips from all the reading he was doing just to keep up.

And then there were the guest appearances. This was anime and comic con season. The first was going to be in North Carolina for Animazement over Memorial Day weekend. Then Anime Midwest in Chicago for Ecos in July, and the last one for him, YaoiCon in San Francisco in September. He used to enjoy cons, but now the thought of them terrified him. What would it be like to navigate them without normal vision?

He was swimming in work, but his first loves, anime voice-overs and movie dubbing, were out of the picture.

And then there was running with Seth, who was easy to talk to, and they got on well.

"You should invite him for dinner." Lily had brought over takeout Thai for their discussion of the latest bookings.

"Invite who?"

"Seth. I've yet to meet him face-to-face. I usually see his fine backside as he's running home."

"He has a fine ass?"

"Yes he does, baby brother. And since that was all I got to see of him, I googled him. He has a fine face to match that fine backside. Yum."

"Neither of us have time or inclination to date, Lily. We're both off the market."

Lily huffed. Kyle knew what was coming. "You can have him over for dinner without it being romantic. You've been running together for three weeks now. You're just being chickenshit."

"He works with people in California. He works late. That's why we run at the time we do. Plus he has his time with his mom."

"Uh-huh. All good excuses for avoiding a relationship. I know."

Kyle dug his chopsticks into the carry-out box with a bit more vigor than he should have and poked a hole in the bottom. The sauce from his pad thai dripped onto his lap. Of course it missed his napkin. Damn it!

He tossed the container on the table and reached for another napkin. "What did the box do to you?"

"Lily, just… just shut it. Okay?"

"Touchy touchy. Must be because you've not gotten laid for a long time."

Kyle gritted his teeth. Lily was happily dating a new guy. She and Tony had gone to a party and ended up leaving with different people. Evidently Lieutenant Worf found his Lieutenant Uhura. Or his Rogue One to his Rogue Two. Whatever it was, Lily was genuinely happy for him. Her new guy was a CPA who loved foreign films, just like she did. In her enraptured state, she was trying to stick Cupid's arrow where it didn't belong.

Lily put her hand on his. "Kyle, I'm just trying to help you."

He sighed. He knew that, but Eros's pointy tip was poking him in the most irritating places. And now that he'd found out that the man of his dreams was actually dreamy… well, it sucked. A man of his age shouldn't still be having wet dreams.

"I know, Lily. I'm just too busy right now."

KYLE WAS almost done grilling the fresh rockfish for dinner when the front doorbell rang. Lily was supposed to come over for dinner, and she must have forgotten her key. Again. He finished plating the fish and went to the door. "Did you forget your key again, Lily?"

"Um, I'm not Lily."

Seth.

"And I think you were expecting your sister for dinner instead of me."

She didn't!

Seth continued brightly, "She texted me the dinner invite yesterday. Evidently it's Japanese cooking, and I was instructed to bring a good sake."

Kyle was going to kill Lily. Then Kyle's brain kicked in. "Yes, it is a Japanese meal. Or at least my favorite Japanese dishes. Come on in."

Seth stepped into the small foyer. "Smells good in here. I usually eat what the caregivers make for my mom. It's a lot of Jewish comfort food. While kasha varnishkes and kreplach soup are good, a change of pace is nice."

"Come on into the dining room. You can pour the sake while I get the food on the table."

"Your place is nice."

"Thanks. Matt and I remodeled the place after I inherited it from my grandmother. It's been in the family for years and dates back to the early 1900s. I'll give you a tour after dinner."

Seth didn't ask who Matt was. Over the past weeks, Kyle had carefully avoided the entire subject of ex-boyfriends, which worked out well because Seth hadn't discussed his previous love life either.

"So what's on the menu tonight?" Seth asked.

"Grilled rockfish, rice, homemade pickled salad, okonomiyaki, and miso soup."

"Sounds delicious."

Kyle hoped he was successfully playing it cool, but his emotional state was anything but calm. Seth was here for dinner, setting Kyle's pulse racing as if he'd just sprinted a mile. And from the telltale sounds, Seth was strolling around a bit, checking out the downstairs living areas. Kyle was going to wring Lily's neck.

Seth's footsteps were whispery on the wood floor. He must have removed his shoes at some point. Kyle did not have a foot fetish, but for some reason the idea of Seth's bare feet made Kyle's face heat and fingers feel clumsy.

"That photo over the couch is amazing," Seth said. He clinked the sake cups softly against the counter.

"Thanks. Tokyo's one of my favorite cities."

"I've never been," Seth said, sounding wistful. "I've never been out of the US at all except for a cruise to Baja."

"You should go. I could give you tips. Or I could help you out with places in Europe. I've been around."

"I'd love that. But I think it's going to be a while before I travel anywhere. At least I hope it's going to be a while." He sighed.

"I'm sorry. I didn't mean to—"

"Of course you didn't. And for God's sake, don't tiptoe around the whole sick-mother thing with me, okay? You don't let me tiptoe around the blind thing."

Kyle turned his head to throw Seth a smile. "Deal."

"You know what would be better than you helping me plan a trip?"

"What?"

"You going with me."

Kyle raised his eyebrows. "You think having a blind guide is a good idea?"

"I think it's a fantastic idea! You still know where to stay and eat and how I can avoid acting like an ugly American, right? And you know the languages. Me? Restaurant Spanish and a couple of Hebrew prayers. Unless it's Hanukkah and you need your candles lit, that last part's not real helpful. And I can help you not trip on cobblestones or get run over by rickshaws."

"Tuk-tuks, and I can hear them coming." But Kyle allowed himself a brief moment of fantasizing, picturing himself strolling arm in arm with Seth along the Seine or through an alpine village. And hey, the blindness would make a great cover story if the locals objected to male-male contact. They could tell people that Seth was his guide rather than his boyfriend. Oh yeah—except Seth *wasn't* his boyfriend, was he?

Kyle paused in the middle of plating okonomiyaki. "Look, Seth. I love my sister and she's been a huge help since the stroke, but she sticks her nose where it doesn't belong. She always has. I had no secrets from her when I was a kid."

There was a slight pause before Seth responded. "Why the abrupt switch in conversational topics?"

"I want you to know that you don't have to be polite just because she called you. You can tell both of us to take a flying leap."

"I knew what she was up to. Lawyer, remember? We invented subterfuge." Seth padded closer but didn't touch him. "This is not me being polite," he said quietly.

"Then what *are* you being?" There was that stupidly pounding heart again, this time with the added bonus of dry mouth. He hurriedly finished sliding the food onto the dishes.

"Um...." Seth took the dishes from Kyle but didn't walk away. "I guess I'm being optimistic?" He said it just like that, with a question mark at the end.

"I don't—"

"This food smells amazing. Can we just eat it now and delve into deep motives later?"

That seemed like a reasonable enough request, although it left Kyle hanging. He joined Seth at the table and amused him by demonstrating his ability to make a toast in multiple languages. Then, while Seth made enthusiastic yummy noises—perhaps in deference to Kyle's inability to see his appreciation—they devoured their meals. It was natural that they'd discuss travel while they ate. Kyle talked about some of the places he'd visited, while Seth told funny tales about his cruise to Mexico, which had involved seasickness, overly aggressive souvenir salesmen, and a boyfriend who got so badly sunburned he wouldn't let Seth touch him.

After dinner Kyle made tea instead of coffee, and they took their warm cups into the living room. He smiled slightly as he watched the steam rise.

"That was a delicious meal," Seth said, then groaned as he settled into the couch cushions. "I can't cook. Mom never let me near the kitchen, and then I was too busy with school and work to learn how."

"But you haven't starved to death."

"I made ample use of the Bay Area's abundant restaurants, and nowadays Mom's caregivers do a lot of cooking."

"Cooking's not that hard. I could do it blindfolded."

Seth chuckled. "You could do a *lot* of things blindfolded. You're kind of amazing, actually."

"Because I'm not flopping around bemoaning my fate?" Kyle asked, bristling slightly.

"Because you've accomplished so much in such a short time. It had to have been such a huge life change, but you've been adjusting so beautifully."

Trying not to make a sour face, Kyle said, "Dave thinks I should attend a support group."

"Not a bad idea. I go to an Alzheimer's caregivers' group."

"Really?"

"Sure. Mom's doctor recommended it. It's just twice a month in person, although we can chat online too. It's a great way to pick up tips and advice and just… spend a little time with people who know what I'm going through."

Put like that, a support group made sense. Kyle certainly didn't judge Seth for making use of the resource, so why should Kyle hesitate to make use of one himself? Unless he was still not quite willing to admit that he was disabled—which was dumb and chickenshit. "Maybe I'll look into it."

"If you want. I figure it's not so different from the study group I had in law school. Well, law school involved more crying."

Kyle inhaled the sweet green scent of his gyokuro tea. "Whatever happened to the sunburned boyfriend?" he asked, feeling brave.

"After a week crammed together in that little cabin, we'd pretty much had enough of each other. He was history before I even shook all the sand out of my shoes."

Time to fish for more? Why not. "And since then?"

Seth laughed. "Man, you'd make a crappy lawyer. No subterfuge at all. Tell you what. You give me the dossier on this Matt guy you keep half mentioning and I'll spill my romantic tale of woe."

Despite his discomfort, Kyle grinned. "Quid pro quo, Clarice?"

"I hate fava beans."

A slightly awkward silence fell. Kyle sipped his tea and heard Seth sip his. The house creaked as it settled a bit more.

Finally Seth broke. "You don't have to talk about it. I was just—"

"It's fine. I mean, it's not like it was a Shakespearean tragedy or anything. Matt is—Matt *was* my boyfriend. We met in college, went separate ways, hooked up again and just sort of stuck. For a decade. He's the only person I've been serious about. He, uh, took that picture." He waved at the photo over the couch.

"A gifted photographer."

"He does it for a living."

"You're, um, using the present tense."

It took a moment for Kyle to parse Seth's meaning; then he groaned. "Jesus, sorry. He's alive and perfectly healthy. We just broke up is all." That sounded simple.

"When?" Was that an edge of anger in Seth's voice?

"About six months ago. Right after the stroke."

"That bastard!" Seth's teacup rattled against the coffee table, and he shot to his feet. "What kind of douchebag dumps someone when they're—"

"I dumped him, actually."

That must have taken the wind out of Seth's sails, because he thunked back onto the couch. "Why? Don't tell me you didn't want to be a burden or some kind of crap like that, because you're not a burden. Anyone with half a brain can see that."

"I *was* one at that time. Ask Lily. But no, that's not the reason. I guess I had a hospital-bed epiphany. I loved Matt—hell, I still do—and he loves me back. But we're not *in* love. It was time for us to go our separate ways." And that didn't sound at all clichéd. Well, why not add more platitudes? "We're still friends."

Seth made a little humphing snort. "If he's such a great friend, he could've stuck around to help you get settled."

Pleased to have Seth indignant on his behalf—even if the feeling was misplaced—Kyle shrugged. "He had a really exciting work opportunity, one he had waited for his whole life. He saw me to my dream career, so now was the time for him to have his. And I'm doing fine without him."

Seth gently took Kyle's teacup and refilled it from the pot, then poured more for himself. "Is Matt the reason why you don't want to date?"

"No. He's gone. Actually, he's dating someone else, and I'm genuinely happy for him." While Kyle was a little envious that Matt had been able to jump back into the pool so quickly, he wasn't jealous.

"Then?"

"I'm too old. And too... I don't know. I was never comfortable with that whole scene back when I was a kid with 20/20 vision. Now there are apps you're supposed to swipe, right? And stuff like that?"

Seth chuckled softly and moved closer on the couch. "Swiping happens, sure. But that's not the only way to meet someone. For instance, you could rescue a guy from a tragic trike collision, become his running partner, and learn that in addition to being sexy and talented—and a big deal in Japan—the guy is also really fun to talk to."

Kyle was too stunned to react to that immediately. He drank more tea while he tried to marshal his thoughts. Then he took a deep breath. "I thought you said you weren't interested in dating either."

"Yeah. I wasn't. Because there's Mom, and that's like an emotional black hole."

"Maybe you could use some extra emotional support, then."

"Probably I could use a lot. But that's not something most people are willing to take on for a new lover. 'Hey, nice to meet you. Do you mind if I cry on your shoulder for three nights straight?'"

"*Some* people might be willing," Kyle said.

"Not the kind of men I date. I'll be honest—I've been a swiper. Which was cool a few years ago, when I was too busy with work to even consider anything serious and too immature to want to settle down. I've had a very long record of one-night stands. Hans—the sunburn man?—he was one of the few who lasted more than a week. And that was mostly because we were stranded at sea."

"There's nothing wrong with being...." At a loss for words, Kyle stopped.

"A slut? Okay, I wasn't *that* bad. But Mom used to get so pissed off at me. 'You're wasting your potential on boys who aren't worth it!' She never thought anyone was up to her standards for me."

"You stopped because your mother disapproved?"

Seth laughed bitterly. "No. Nowadays, half the time she thinks I'm still in high school and starts lecturing me about my math grade, and the rest of the time she thinks I'm my brother. Either way, she has nothing to say about my dating habits. Which I guess is a relief."

"Seth—"

"It's like this. I don't want to be that swiper guy anymore, but I don't know how to be anyone else. And with Mom's illness in the picture, it seemed easier to just be a monk. A Jewish monk."

Kyle thought about how two very different paths could lead to the same place. Maybe not the place either traveler was expecting, but that didn't mean it was a bad place. One thing he'd learned as he'd trekked the globe was that while planning a trip was great, sometimes the surprise experiences were the best ones. He also thought there was something else to Seth's story, something he wasn't sharing. But Kyle didn't want to pry too deeply.

"Now you're having second thoughts about taking your vows?" Kyle asked.

"And third thoughts. You've...." He moved nearer, the couch cushion indenting under his weight, until Kyle could feel the warmth of his body. "I like you. If we stay friends, that's good. But I have to warn you, I've been thinking nonplatonically about you lately."

Kyle ducked his head to hide a blush. "Uh, me too."

"Seriously?" Seth closed the last inch or so between them, pressing himself against Kyle's shoulder and leg. "Care to specify the content?"

"Are you cross-examining me?"

"This is *direct* examination, Mr. Green." Seth's voice deepened into a purr. "Now, answer, please."

"Well. Lily might have said something about you having a fine backside. And I might have been wishing I could judge for myself. Nonvisually, of course."

Seth laughed delightedly. "She said that? Way to go, big sis!"

"Hey, I'm mad at her for the stunt she pulled tonight."

"Really?" Seth breathed warmly against Kyle's ear, and his voice dropped to a whisper. "'Cause I'm thinking I need to send her a bouquet of flowers."

Kyle turned his head so they were nose to nose. "She's allergic. Opt for chocolate instead."

And then, somehow, they were kissing.

Kyle hadn't kissed anyone in months, and it had probably been years since he'd kissed anyone with fervor. For the moment, it didn't matter that he was blind—he'd have closed his eyes anyway. All the better to savor the green tea flavor of Seth, the softness of his lips, the scratch of his late-evening stubble, and the springiness of his curly hair, in which Kyle's fingers soon became entwined. Seth laced his fingers behind Kyle's neck and emitted such sexy little gasps and moans that Kyle's head swam. God, and Seth smelled good too— soy sauce and woodsy soap—and his teeth were sharp against Kyle's questing tongue.

Kyle could have devoured him right then. Passion coursed through him like molten lava, obliterating regrets and misgivings, making him wonder when he'd last felt so alive. So powerful. Yet a cool island of reason remained, impervious to the fire, reminding him what Seth had said about his own history. Reminding him that he shouldn't take anything for granted.

With considerable difficulty, Kyle forced himself to release Seth and move his own head back several inches, bringing space and air between them.

"What's wrong?" Seth asked, voice roughened so deliciously that Kyle intended to copy it next time he narrated a sex scene.

"Nothing is wrong," Kyle assured him. "Opposite problem, really. That was a really good kiss."

"Top five for sure. But I'm guessing that with practice we can break into the top three."

"I think so too. But you know what I don't want to happen?"

Seth sighed and twisted his body slightly to snuggle up against him. It was the first time Kyle got a full sense of how Seth was built. Delicately boned, perhaps, his frame more compact than Kyle's rangier one, but with tight muscles that were a testament to his running habits. And he had nice biceps. "What don't you want?" Seth asked.

"To be a one-night stand. Then I'd lose a friend and a running guide."

"I told you. I'm over that. I don't want to give you up."

Despite the gravity of their conversation, Kyle smiled. "Then let's slow down. I don't think either of us has much experience in…." He tried to think of the word, grimacing a bit at the closest approximation he could find. "Courtship."

"Courtship?" Seth echoed, sounding amused. "Like, promenades in the park?"

"We've done that already. Well, running in the park. Same diff."

"Okay, then. Like I bring you corsages and you bake me apple pies and we try to hold hands when the chaperone's not looking?"

Unable to resist, Kyle snuffled at Seth's soft curls. "How about a couple of meals out together, sharing a cultural event that's not completely lost on the visually impaired, maybe a little clothed cuddling on the couch?"

Seth hummed thoughtfully. "How about some family meet and greets? Mom won't understand who you are and it's too late for you to see who she used to be, but still…."

"I'd like to meet your mother. And I'll also subject you to Lily."

"She's a dynamo on the phone. Can't wait to meet her in the flesh."

"Yeah, well, gird your loins. You've been forewarned." Kyle squeezed Seth lightly. "That woman is stubborn and devious."

"Excellent. I like her already."

"And you're okay with taking things slowly?"

Seth's nod felt firm against Kyle's shoulder. "Yeah. It'll be a new experience for us both. Besides, a little delayed gratification, a little sexual tension… those sound interesting."

That word again—*interesting*. But this time Kyle didn't hate it.

Seth insisted on doing the after-dinner washing up, taking care to ask exactly where everything went once it was clean and dry. Then they agreed on a time for a morning run, and Kyle walked him to the door. As they stood in the open doorway, cool night air wafting in with the scent of blooming trees, they kissed again. And this time Kyle couldn't help himself. He placed his hands on Seth's ass and gently squeezed, getting a lovely double handful of strong, denim-clad muscle.

"So?" Seth asked. "Was Lily lying?"

"Lily was telling God's honest truth." In fact, she might have underplayed things, although it was hard to be sure with all that damned fabric in the way.

"Do you want to know something stupid?"

"Of course."

"After your sister called, I spent fifteen minutes standing in my birthday suit, trying to decide what to wear."

Kyle snorted a laugh. "You could have just stayed in your birthday suit. I wouldn't have known the difference until just now."

"Your neighbors would have."

"I have the feeling they would have counted themselves very fortunate. Especially Mrs. Zdunowski across the street. She's been widowed for a long time. I'm sure she'd welcome a little eye candy."

"I'll keep that in mind for future excursions." Seth moved close to brush his lips against Kyle's cheek. "Thanks for dinner. And giving us a chance. See you in the morning, Kyle."

Then he was gone, leaving Kyle with the lingering taste of green tea and an urgent need for a cold shower.

CHAPTER ELEVEN

KYLE SAT on his porch the next morning, rocking, seeing flashes of the world in front of his eyes. It was one of those perfect spring days after winter's deep freeze had relented, before the sun started to come up distressingly early to fill Chicagoland with muggy heat. No thunderstorms yet, no tornado watches. Just the twitter of birds and the fresh scents of growing things—even here, deep in the city. He wondered if Mrs. Zdunowski had been out yet to clear away the yellowing daffodil leaves from her front yard and replace them with marigolds and geraniums. Maybe if he kept on rocking, he could catch a glimpse of bright oranges and reds.

And maybe if he kept thinking about Mrs. Zdunowski's garden, he wouldn't worry about Seth.

He'd thought about Seth all of the previous evening, his mind in such turmoil he couldn't read or listen to the TV. And when it came time for bed, he couldn't sleep either. In desperation, he'd jerked off to memories of the feel of Seth's lips, but even after he cleaned himself off and settled back down, sleep wouldn't come. God, he was as giddy and conflicted as a teenager with a first crush. What was *wrong* with him?

Well, the answer to that was obvious, at least. What was wrong was that he was a middle-aged blind man suddenly overcome with lust and longing for a man who wasn't any more certain about entering into a relationship than Kyle was. It was fucking terrifying, yet exhilarating at the same time. And he wasn't sure what scared him more: the possibility that Seth might back out, or the possibility that he might not.

"Morning."

Kyle startled so badly that he nearly fell out of the rocking chair. He'd been caught up in his own head and hadn't heard Seth open the gate or ascend the stairs. "Morning to you," Kyle said, grabbing desperately for his composure.

"Will any of your neighbors have a problem if I kiss you now?"

A stupid grin spread over Kyle's face. "Nope. Although Mrs. Zdunowski might pull up a lawn chair and watch."

Seth bent down to brush his lips teasingly just beneath Kyle's ear. "Would a kiss get better ratings from her than my bare ass?"

"Not having, um, assessed your bare ass, I couldn't tell you."

"Hmm. Well, I'm wearing compression running shorts. I'll position myself so she gets a good view." This time he kissed Kyle's cheekbone, then his lips, then just the tip of his nose. "Does this count as courting?"

"Possibly. But please stop."

Seth moved away at once. "Sorry, didn't mean—"

"It's not that. If you kept on, I wouldn't be in any condition to run. Comfortably, anyway."

With a laugh, Seth came closer. They almost collided when Kyle stood up, but Seth saved them both with a quick step backward. He lightly tapped a nylon strap against Kyle's hand.

Kyle grabbed the loop. Seth had bought the tether the previous week. It consisted of two comfortable loops with a short length of cord between them, and it kept Kyle attached closely to Seth while allowing some freedom of movement for both of them.

"You warmed up?" Seth asked.

"Yep." But a question occurred to him. "What color is the tether?"

Seth snickered. "Purple. Come on."

They had a particularly brisk run, but that wasn't the only reason Kyle's pulse rate soared. Mile after mile, he was increasingly aware that a *man* ran just at the other end of a few inches of nylon cord. A man who might be cheerfully calling obstacle warnings now, but twelve hours earlier had been pressed close, kissing him.

Despite Seth's warning, Kyle stumbled over a curb. Seth caught him. "Jesus, I'm sorry!" Seth exclaimed.

"For what? Me not paying attention?"

"Are you okay?"

Kyle breathed. "Only my dignity is damaged. Come on. I want breakfast."

They were less than a mile from home at that point, so soon afterward they were on Kyle's porch, taking in water and oxygen and stretching their cooling muscles. "Want to come in?" Kyle asked. "I make a mean french toast."

"I'd love to, but I have a Skype meeting to deal with."

"Sure."

But Seth didn't leave right away. "What are your plans for today?"

"Some narrating."

"More romance?"

"Yep." Kyle grinned. "High fantasy. We've got sexy elves and dragons—"

"Sexy dragons?"

"I wouldn't want to ruin it for you."

Seth's running shoe made a scraping sound when he shuffled his foot across the stoop. "How long do you spend narrating?"

"Not too long at once because my voice starts to go. I usually do an hour or two, take a break, then do another one or two sessions. Why?"

"So you're free around dinnertime?"

Damn. Just when Kyle's heart rate had returned to normal. "Sure. What did you have in mind?"

"Well, dinner. Out, I mean. But first…." He let out a noisy breath. "How about joining me and Mom for a walk?"

Meeting the parent. Fuck. And Kyle knew how important Seth's mother was to him. "I'd love to," he said, not entirely honestly.

Seth must not have discerned the ruse, because he sounded thrilled when he answered. "Great! I'll swing by at about five, if that's all right with you."

Kyle reached out, caught his arm, and pulled him closer. "Five is good."

This time when they tried to kiss, their noses bonked. Kyle couldn't tell whether his lack of sight was the cause or general inexperience. Either way, they chuckled as they fumbled, until finally they found a comfortable position to lock lips.

Mrs. Zdunowski must have been very pleased with the results.

"YOU ARE so, so dead."

Lily laughed, clearly unfazed by Kyle's threat. "How'd the Japanese dinner go last night, Kyebye?" She set something on the kitchen counter with a rustle and a muted thump.

"I spent it plotting your demise."

"You can't kill me. I stopped by Trader Joe's and bought you that masala simmer sauce you like, plus a bottle of balsamic. And sriracha potato chips!"

He cocked his head. "Sounds like somebody is hoping I'll make her dinner."

"I got chocolate-covered toffee chips for dessert," she crooned.

"I made a really good dinner *last* night. Which you slithered your way out of."

She collapsed into the kitchen chair opposite him with a *humph*. "I was doing you a favor. I figured you're pretty sick of my company anyway, and even if you and your buddy aren't getting up close and personal, you'd enjoy having a friend over." She paused a moment. "So, how *was* dinner?"

He didn't say anything, but he felt a blush on his traitorous face, and Lily responded with a triumphant squawk. "It *did* go well!" she crowed.

Dammit. "We just had dinner," he mumbled.

"Aaaand?"

"And nothing. We had a good conversation." He could feel her laser gaze boring into his skull, the same gaze his mother had used to extort confessions from him when he was a kid. Even if he couldn't see it, he wasn't immune. He hid his face behind his hands, but that didn't help. "We kissed."

"Ooh! And—"

"And that's it. Except we sort of decided to try...." God, it was going to sound even dumber when he said it to his sister.

She reached across the table to poke his bicep. "What? Try what?"

Kyle sighed. "Courtship."

Well, that shut her up for a moment or two. "What does that mean?" she finally asked.

"Nothing. We're going to go on dates and hang out a little and see... see how we fit. That's *all*, okay? Please do *not* start picking out your maid-of-honor dress."

Lily tapped a finger on the table. "But if you do get married, I *will* be your maid of honor. And I will wear a dress that makes me look fricking amazing, and the reception will be catered by the outfit that catered my friend Jennifer's wedding, because my God, the food was to die for, and you and Seth will honeymoon somewhere slightly exotic but also romantic, like Bora Bora."

He shouldn't have mentioned marriage, not even in jest. "Lily," he began.

"I know," she interrupted, her tone more serious. "I'm just teasing. Mostly. But I am seriously very happy that you and Seth are giving this a shot. Now, when do I get to meet him in person?"

Kyle groaned.

KYLE DECIDED ahead of time not to angst over what to wear. But still, he stood inside his closet, arm raised uncertainly. Then he imagined Seth showing up at his door naked—a clear image even if Kyle had little idea of what Seth looked like—and he grinned.

By the time Seth rang the doorbell, Kyle wore jeans, a thin green sweater, and a lightweight jacket. "Wow," Seth said as soon as Kyle opened the door. "You look great. That color is fantastic on you."

"Now *that's* an appropriate courting thing to say. Sorry I can't return the compliment."

"Well, you can picture me dressed however you want. Or undressed," he added slyly, clearly entertaining the same image as Kyle.

Kyle stepped outside and locked the door. Then he held out his palm. "Holding hands? More courtship. Unless PDA makes you uncomfortable." Sure, they'd kissed on the porch, but that wasn't the same as walking down the street.

"I haven't had a lot of opportunities to stroll hand in hand with someone. I'd really like to now."

So that was what they did, Kyle with his cane folded and tucked away, Seth keeping a running commentary on everything they passed. He was always talkative, but now he seemed a little manic. "Seth? Are you nervous about me meeting your mom? Because we don't have to do this today."

Seth squeezed his hand. "I'm kind of stressed, but I want to do this. It's just… I have never introduced her to a…. Shit. Are you my boyfriend yet? Or does that come after the courting stage?"

"I don't own a braille copy of Emily Post, but I feel confident in making an independent ruling." Kyle took a breath. "We're boyfriends now."

"Excellent. But I've never introduced Mom to a boyfriend. And she's a little unpredictable nowadays."

They stopped at a crosswalk, listening to the traffic zoom by. "Sometime soon," Kyle said, "I will introduce you to my sister."

"I talked to her on the phone."

"She sounds reasonable on the phone. But you will meet her in person, and she will tell mortifying stories about my childhood and generally act like I'm still a twelve-year-old kid she's stuck babysitting. She will ask you nosy personal questions and jump to ridiculous conclusions. And any uncomfortable moments we're about to experience with your mother will pale in comparison."

Seth was still laughing when they arrived at his house.

Kyle couldn't get much of a sense of the building itself, apart from its location on a quiet street and a short set of concrete stairs with a metal railing. He wondered whether Seth's home was old like his own or more modern, and whether it was faced in brick, wood, or stone. Was there a little garden in front, or bushes, or maybe just more concrete?

The entrance foyer felt slightly cramped and smelled of wood, lemon cleaning products, and of roasting meat. "Want a tour?" Seth asked.

"It'd be pretty much lost on me. Shit. I never showed you around my place last night."

"Next time. Hang on. I'll go get Mom."

Seth walked away, leaving Kyle near the door. He reached out and touched a wall, discovering that it was paneled in smooth wood, with an ornately carved chair rail. Expensive, he'd bet. Probably an older home, one with a certain dignity to it. Maybe the bathrooms had the original claw-foot tubs and octagonal-tile floors. Maybe the front of the house featured bay windows. Probably there was a daylight basement with a separate apartment—once for servants, now perhaps rented out. God, he'd love to see Seth's bedroom. Had he updated it since returning to Chicago, or did it still hold evidence of his teenage years? Later, Kyle decided, he would ask Seth whether posters of boy bands hung on his walls.

SETH'S FAMILIAR footsteps approached, along with another set that sounded slightly off-kilter, as if the person had a slight limp. "Kyle, this is my mom, Ruth Caplan. Mom, meet my friend Kyle Green. He's blind, Mom, okay? He can't see."

"Oh, that's a shame," responded a female voice. More youthful-sounding than Kyle expected. "It's nice to meet you."

"It's a pleasure, Mrs. Caplan."

She laughed. "Oh, don't call me that! My husband's mother is Mrs. Caplan. I'm Ruth."

Based on what Seth had told Kyle, if the mother-in-law were still alive, she'd be over a hundred. Kyle smiled at her. "I'm glad to meet you, Ruth."

"Now, tell me. Did you boys meet at school? My Seth's studying to be a lawyer, you know. His father and I are so proud of him."

Kyle remembered that Seth's father hadn't lived long enough to see his son graduate high school, let alone begin law school. It was kind of sweet that Ruth had it set in her mind that her husband was proud anyway.

Seth spoke next. "Kyle's my running partner, Mom. And a good friend."

"I'm glad to hear that. He seems much nicer than that Barry boy you're always hanging around with."

As Kyle raised his eyebrows quizzically, Seth sighed. "Mom, Barry was Aaron's friend, remember? I'm your younger son. Seth. But you're right—Barry was a jerk. He's a lobbyist now."

"Of course I know who you are, Seth. Are we all going somewhere?"

"For a walk."

"Oh, good. It's a lovely day."

They walked three abreast down the sidewalk, Seth in the middle with Kyle and Ruth on either arm. They must have been quite a sight as they strolled slowly, sometimes stopping entirely so Ruth could exclaim over something that had changed in the past forty years. Kyle found himself liking her. Her memories might be slipping badly, but she seemed like a cheerful sort. A lot like her son. Her comments were almost unfailingly kind and enthusiastic.

"Oh!" she said, stopping suddenly and nearly causing a three-pedestrian pileup. "What happened to Hoffman's Pharmacy? I fill all my prescriptions there. Mr. Hoffman is such a nice man, and his wife is sweet as can be."

"Hoffman retired," said Seth in a tone that suggested he'd said it many times before. "When I was a toddler."

"Oh, too bad. Is his daughter still around? She's very pretty. You could ask her out, maybe."

"I don't think so. Mom, Kyle is my boyfriend. We're dating now."

She paused a moment. "You're dating another boy?"

"Yep. I'm gay. Totally, completely gay."

Kyle waited anxiously for her response. Seth still gripped his arm, but not especially tensely. Maybe that was a good sign.

Finally Seth shifted slightly and Kyle heard Ruth kiss him. "As long as you're happy, sweetheart. That's all that matters to your father and me. We love you."

"Thanks, Mom." Seth's voice sounded a little watery, and after they resumed their walk, he whispered at Kyle. "I've come out to her now about a hundred times. And every damned time, she takes it like this. It's amazing."

What it was, Kyle thought, was both heartbreaking and heartwarming. His own eyes prickled with tears.

Ruth was the only one who seemed unaffected. She cooed at someone's dog, then started to reminisce about a dog she used to have—a terrier named Moishe who would follow her to school when she was a girl and come fetch her at the end of the day. She slipped into the present tense when speaking of him, but Seth didn't correct her. Why bother when she seemed perfectly happy?

They were stopped, waiting for a crossing signal, when Ruth asked a question. "Are you going to be a lawyer too, Arturo?"

"Mom, this is *Kyle*," Seth said, his voice tighter than Kyle had ever heard it.

"Yes, of course. Kyle. Are you also planning to go to law school?"

"Not me," Kyle answered. "I'm a voice actor."

"A voice actor? What does that entail?" She sounded genuinely fascinated.

Kyle gave her a quick rundown of VO work, but it was the book narration that really caught her interest. "Oh, that's lovely! I love books. Has Seth shown you our library?"

"Not yet," Kyle said, deciding there was no need to remind her he was blind.

"Well, make sure he does. My husband and I have been accumulating books for years. He jokes that soon we'll have to kick out the children to make more room for shelves. Please feel free to borrow any of them. Shared books are the best ones."

"Thank you, Ruth."

"What kinds of books do you narrate?"

When Kyle hesitated, Seth stepped in, a smile in his voice. "He does gay romances, Mom."

"Gay romances! I never heard of such a thing! Are they explicit?"

"Um, some of them," Kyle answered.

She giggled. "I may have to give them a try. I can't let Mama know, though. She gets upset if she thinks I'm reading anything remotely naughty. I hide the good ones in the bottom drawer of my dresser."

Kyle wondered if it was dizzying to move around in time as she did. It must be even more frightening to lose memories than it was to lose vision. He should consider himself fortunate—his life had changed, but his fundamental sense of who he was remained intact.

"What's your favorite book, Ruth?" he asked.

"Oh, that's a hard one. Let me see. I almost always teach the classics because the curriculum demands it, and because young people need to have an understanding of our literary roots. Even if it's like pulling teeth to get them to read those things! But to be honest, when I relax, I like a good mystery. Or maybe a horror novel."

Kyle was going to ask her another question, but then she made a slightly distressed noise. "It's getting late! Aaron, we need to get home. I don't have tomorrow's lesson prepared yet."

"Sure, Mom," Seth said. "We're just a couple blocks away."

"No, that can't be right. I don't recognize any of these shops."

"I promise. We'll be home in ten minutes."

"We'd better. You know how I feel about facing a classroom unprepared. It would be like you failing to look at a patient's chart or Seth showing up in court without having read the briefs."

Kyle startled slightly when a skateboarder whizzed by, but Seth kept him out of harm. It was quite a talent to carry on a conversation with his confused mother while keeping his blind boyfriend from getting into collisions. Boyfriend. Kyle couldn't help a goofy smile at that thought.

Ruth continued to chatter about her plans for the next day's class, while Seth took it all in stride, even when she kept calling him Aaron. Few people in Kyle's experience had the skill and care for those losing their memories. He remembered that Matt's French-Canadian grandmother, Gran, had Alzheimer's. The Lakota family had taken her in when the memory care facility failed to take care of her properly. A few of Matt's cousins were nurses and took turns giving Gran care at home. It was heartbreaking to see her decline over the years. When they went to visit her, Kyle noticed that Matt and his family just took things in stride as Gran's memory failed. They answered to whatever name she called them and treated her with loving-kindness. Gran had not remembered Kyle's name, as he was new to her memory. He was a variety of men in the Labrecque family, but mostly Peter, Matt's childhood best friend.

"It's such a lovely evening," Ruth said when they stopped to wait for another light. "Although I'm sure you're used to good weather, Arturo, seeing as you're from California. I'm so glad Seth finally persuaded you to pay a visit to the Midwest."

"Mom—" Seth began.

But Ruth ignored him. "Now, I know you boys are busy, but please promise me you'll make sure Seth takes care of himself. Sometimes he works so hard he forgets to eat, and I'm sure when he *does* eat it's mostly pizza and hamburgers. Arturo, will you make him eat some vegetables once in a while? He'll listen to you better than he does me."

Seth's grip on Kyle was almost painful, but Kyle kept his tone light. "Of course, Ruth. I'll force broccoli into him daily."

"Not broccoli," she said firmly. "It gives him terrible gas."

Kyle bit his lip hard to keep from laughing.

When they arrived back at the house, a woman with a pleasantly warm voice greeted them and then bustled Ruth away, leaving Seth and Kyle in the foyer. Seth let out a long, deep sigh. "Are you still up for dinner?"

"I'm starved. Where are we going?"

"Someplace with booze."

The place with booze was just a short walk away, and Kyle liked it at once. Probably because the noise level was barely above a hush and the sound system played something soft and instrumental. It might actually be possible to have a conversation here. It smelled nice too, like candle wax, flowers, and olive oil. A woman with a slight eastern European accent led them to a table and, without fuss, handed Kyle a braille menu. She promised their waiter would be right with them, then left.

"Fancy," Kyle said, taking note of the cloth tablecloth and napkin and the wineglass already in place. "Am I underdressed?"

"You're fine. This place is courtship-worthy, but not schmancy."

The waiter poured water, took their drink order—Kyle had wine, but Seth asked for whiskey—and rattled off the specials. "This was an interesting choice," Kyle said after the waiter left. "Are you a fan of Istrian food?"

Seth barked a laugh. "Actually, I've never had it before. To be honest, I was trying to impress you."

Kyle made a saluting motion with his water glass. "Well, you've succeeded. I didn't even know there was an Istrian place in Chicago. Bravo!" But with a pang, he remembered the couple of weeks in Istria several years before, when Matt had landed a photo assignment for a magazine. They had driven around the Croatian peninsula as Matt shot picturesque fields and charming little hill towns. Between shoots they lounged in cafés, enjoying the local wines and interesting food. They'd driven down the Croatian coast and back up again, catching a ferry to Italy. It had been a wonderful trip.

Of course Kyle could return. But he'd never again see the rolling greens of vineyards and forests, the warm earth tones of the stone houses, the impossibly clear blue of the Adriatic. He wouldn't catch sight of a school of silvery sardines darting in their aquatic ballet, drink in the view from atop ancient city walls, or marvel at a flock of bats circling over an orange tree in a courtyard.

As punishment for wallowing in self-pity while he was having a nice dinner with a wonderful man, his brain loosened his tongue. "Who's Arturo?"

"I don't want to talk about it."

Kyle backed off immediately. "Okay. No problem. I think I'm going to order the squid ink risotto, but maybe—"

"I'm sorry. I didn't mean to be rude."

"You weren't. It's not a comfortable subject for you, and that's fine. We'll talk about something else. How 'bout them Cubs?" He winked, then wondered whether that looked weird. Probably not. His eyes were still perfectly normal; it was his brain that was zapped.

Giving Kyle's hand a quick squeeze, Seth snorted. "How about my mother? Now that you've met her, are you ready to run for the hills?"

"We're in Illinois. There are no hills. Anyway, I like her."

"Really?"

"Yeah, I—"

The waiter politely interrupted, setting their drinks on the table before taking their orders. Kyle decided on the risotto after all, along with wild asparagus. Seth ordered a seafood stew. "No broccoli?" Kyle teased after the waiter left them.

"Oh, God. You know, that part wasn't even the Alzheimer's. Mom has always had an amazing ability to embarrass me."

"That's what family's for. Besides, she's just about bursting with pride over you."

"Eh." The ice cubes in Seth's whiskey clinked when he took a drink. "She's proud of her son the lawyer. I don't think she really gets the whole app development thing."

"It must be so hard to see her...."

"Deteriorate? Yeah. God, she was so sharp. She raised three kids and taught high school English and nobody ever got away with *anything* under her eagle eye. She was one of those moms who could help you whip up a science fair project on a moment's notice while also giving you a lecture on responsibility, cooking a brisket, and grading a huge stack of essays. Supermom. And she was funny too. But she could be really scary if she thought someone wasn't doing right. She was active in the ACLU, the ADL, all the liberal letter organizations."

Kyle shook his head slowly. "It must be so hard on you. Are your sibs helping out?" There was Aaron the doctor and Judith the university professor, but Seth rarely mentioned them.

"Not much. Since they're almost two decades older than me, they were more like an aunt and uncle when I was growing up, and I was basically an only child. I think they kind of resent me because by the time I came along, Mom and Dad were middle-aged and steady and wanting to spend a lot of time with their kid. Aaron and Judith got them in the super-hectic youthful years."

Kyle could understand that. The age spread between him and his siblings wasn't nearly as wide, but he knew they had experienced a different childhood than he had. For one thing, as military strict as his father was, he'd loosened up a little by the time Kyle hit the obnoxious years.

"I'm sorry they're not backing you up," Kyle said.

"Thanks. They have spouses, grandkids, less flexible jobs. And they moved away. Judith's in Seattle and Aaron lives in Minneapolis. They can't uproot, and nobody wanted to move Mom. I'm just lucky Mom had plenty of money set aside and has a good pension, so good care's not a problem. And I'm happy to get this time with her, even if she's not wholly who she used to be."

"She adores you. And *not* because she thinks you're still a lawyer."

Seth sniffled. "Verklempt. But yeah. The way she takes it every time I come out to her. God. Some people can't come out to their people even once without getting rejected, but I can do it over and over and she rolls with it."

Their food arrived soon afterward and the conversation turned lighter. Seth gleefully informed Kyle that the risotto was turning Kyle's tongue black and then snuck a few bites so his own would match. Kyle had a second glass of wine and described the offer he'd just received to do VO work for a car commercial. "It'll be my first real VO job since the stroke, but we think it'll work out because I don't have to sync my voice to visuals."

"So you get to be one of those 'and now, something so spectacular you'll crap your pants' guys?" He used a deep, dramatic announcer's voice.

"Nah, that guy's more for movie commercials. For a luxury car, we're going for sexy and commanding. Like this: 'Drive this overpriced hunk of plastic and metal and nobody will suspect you have a very small penis.'"

Seth laughed so hard he nearly choked and had to wave down the waiter for more water.

They skipped dessert and then strolled slowly down the sidewalk in the direction of Kyle's house. "I should be the one seeing you home," Kyle said. "I'm better off walking in the dark than you are."

"Next time."

"You've spent a lot of time on your feet today."

"I don't mind." Seth bumped gently into him. "I've had good company."

When they reached Kyle's house, Kyle smiled at him. "Want to sit on the porch for a bit?"

"*That* sounds like a perfectly courtshippy thing to do."

Kyle took the rocker, while Seth scooted the Adirondack chair a little closer before sitting down. They sat quietly and listened to the city's night noises, the creaking of the rocking chair, the canned laughter of a TV show wafting through an open window. And then Seth reached for Kyle's hand and held on tight.

"Let me tell you about Arturo."

CHAPTER TWELVE

KYLE GENTLY squeezed Seth's hand as Seth took a deep breath and seemed to gather his thoughts.

"I got a full-ride soccer scholarship to Caltech and majored in computer science. I loved Chicago, but I wanted to go somewhere I could spread my wings, so to speak. And I wanted warmer weather and more sunny days." Seth laughed softly. "The school had a freshman mixer where we were paired up for skill-based games. I got paired with a gorgeous guy who had the darkest blue eyes I'd ever seen. He had this deep, rich voice and a dazzling smile. Arturo Muñoz had to repeat his name twice before I realized he was talking to me."

Seth was quiet for a long time, no doubt lost in the memories. Kyle held his hand and waited. He loved the sound of the creaking chair, like a favorite song playing softly in the background. Despite the movement, he couldn't see anything in the darkness, but that was fine. He was home; he knew what everything looked like.

With a tiny chuckle, Seth continued his story. "Once I got enough saliva back into my mouth, I introduced myself and then remembered we were supposed to be playing a guessing game. We each had the name of a famous person pinned to our back and had to guess who we were based on the clues our partner gave us. I was Marie Curie and he was Buckminster Fuller, and we traded snarky clues, cracking each other up. We were supposed to change partners, but we were having too good a time together. We discovered we were in the same dorm—on the same floor, even—so when the mixer ended, we sat outside the dorm and talked about everything. We clicked, you know?"

Kyle nodded. "It's happened to me a couple of times."

"Well, I told Arturo I was gay, and he said he was not. I realized that this love at first sight was going to be one-sided, and I had to decide if being friends was what I wanted. In the end, I thought not having him at all would be harder than remaining friends. I didn't tell him how I felt about him. I probably should have just walked away."

"Do you wish you had?" Kyle asked.

It took a few moments for Seth to answer. "No. No, I don't. The next year we moved off campus and roomed together for the rest of our stay at Caltech. After we graduated, a big law firm recruited us to act as consultants for all their cyber stuff—Internet, coding, privacy. Arturo's uncle was one of the partners. Part of the deal was that they would send us to Stanford Law School. It was an offer we couldn't refuse. Arturo and I remained roommates, and once we had our legal training, we were full-time heads of the firm's cyber division."

"It sounds like interesting work," Kyle said.

"It was. It was a *lot* of work, though. As new associates, we were expected to put in a zillion billable hours. Maybe that's why the thing with Arturo worked as long as it did. I lusted after him, but I didn't have time to dwell on it. Too busy with memos and briefs."

Seth let go of Kyle's hand and stood. Kyle heard the quiet drag of Seth's foot on the cement porch as he paced.

"All this time," Seth said, "Arturo had a string of girlfriends. I had a few boyfriends, but mostly to keep my mind off Arturo. I even dated guys that were the total opposite of Arturo, just so he wouldn't guess I had it bad for him.

"A few years later, we made junior partner, which meant more money, less grunt work, *and* the acquisition of minions. We went out to celebrate with the people at the firm, got totally toasted, and sang in the cab on the way home. As we stumbled up the stairs to the apartment, we were laughing our asses off and saying, 'I love you man,' 'No, I love *you*, man.' You know, just being silly. Mostly."

When Seth continued, his voice was soft and faraway. "I remember, clear as day, falling against him as we closed the door. Arturo caught me, we looked into each other's eyes, and I kissed him. He asked me what I was doing, and I told him I was celebrating. He laughed it off—until I unzipped his pants and pulled out his cock. He was hard, Kyle. I'd have stopped if he wasn't." Seth sighed. "At least, that's what I keep telling myself.

"Anyway, I dropped to my knees, but just as I started to blow him, he pushed me away. He was pissed. Told me to fuck off 'cause he didn't swing that way. He stormed into his room and slammed the door. I went to bed thinking I'd tell him in the morning that I had been drunk and stupid. I never got the chance. Arturo left before I got up, and a few hours later he was killed in a car accident on I-880 by, of all things, a drunk driver."

Seth's voice broke. "I fucked up big-time. If I hadn't kissed him and tried to blow him, he'd still be alive today. I found out at the funeral that his girlfriend was pregnant. I was so fucking stupid! I gave into my crush, lost a great friendship, and ruined so many lives. Guilt ate me up. I worked a lot of hours and lost a lot of weight. I slept at the office because I couldn't face going back to the apartment. Whenever I was there, that night kept playing back over and over. I could see him standing in the living room with his pants unzipped, this… this *fury* in his eyes."

Seth crossed the porch and sat beside Kyle again. He didn't take Kyle's hand, though. "About six months later, I got word my mom was beginning to fail, memory-wise. And out of the blue, an old high-school friend needed someone full-time to head up the legal department of his growing specialty-app firm. Biggest incentive, I could work from home. I quit the California law firm and found myself back in sweet home Chicago."

When Seth remained silent for a long time, Kyle searched for an appropriate response. "So, guilt-driven celibacy?"

There was no humor in Seth's laugh. "Pretty much."

They were quiet awhile longer. "How many people have you told about this?"

"Only you."

Kyle remembered a quote from *Macbeth*. *Give sorrow words; the grief that does not speak whispers the o'erfraught heart and bids it break.* "Thank you for trusting me enough to tell me."

Seth stirred from his chair. "Thank you for listening. I hope you won't think too badly of me now that you know the story." He sounded worn and sad, a shadow of his usual ebullient self.

Kyle reached out and, with a lucky grab, connected with Seth's hand. "I don't think badly of you at all. And one day, you won't think badly about yourself."

Seth stood, then kissed Kyle on the forehead. "Sounds like advice from one who's been there. I'm going to take off. I had a great time at dinner."

"I did too. Run tomorrow?"

Kyle could hear Seth's hesitation.

"Sure."

As KYLE was getting dressed the next morning, his phone rang.

"Hey, Kyle." Maybe it was just the phone connection, but Seth sounded a little off. Strained. "I'm feeling a little under the weather today. Do you mind if I cancel our run?"

"Of course not. Anything I can get you?"

"Nah, thanks. I think I just need to lie low for a day."

"Sure." Kyle shifted from one foot to the other. "Tomorrow?"

"Um, give me two days, okay? I'll be fine by then."

After they ended the call, Kyle felt uneasy. The phone conversation had been... weird. It had felt more like rescheduling a doctor's appointment than a chat with his boyfriend. Or maybe Kyle was just reading it wrong. He couldn't expect Seth to be a ball of cheery energy if he felt like crap.

Kyle removed his running clothes and put on jeans and a tee instead. Then he made his way downstairs for breakfast. He had plenty of work to keep him busy.

He didn't hear from Seth the rest of that day. Kyle thought about calling or texting to see how he was, but if Seth was sick, he probably didn't want to be disturbed. When Kyle had a virus, all he wanted to do was wallow in bed with a glass of ginger ale nearby and feel sorry for himself. It had been a point of dissension with Matt, who had a tendency to hover at the bedside, offering soup and Kleenex and NyQuil until Kyle was ready to scream.

The following morning he went grocery shopping with Lily, carefully steering the conversation to Lily's new CPA flame. "He's divorced," she informed him while picking out canned beans. "Amicably, he says. His ex lives in Romeoville with their kids."

"Kids?" Kyle idly pushed the cart back and forth a bit.

"Girl, ten, and boy, thirteen. Gary and his wife have an arrangement. Weekdays, she's in Romeoville and he's in the city. Which makes sense because he works downtown and she's a kindergarten teacher in Naperville. Then on weekends, he stays out in the 'burbs and she's in the city apartment."

"That's... interesting."

"Yeah." Lily held the cart still so she could put some cans in it. "But I guess it works. The kids don't get uprooted, the grown-ups don't have to commute too far. Gary thinks the ex is kind of living it up on weekends, but he doesn't blame her."

"I don't know if I'd have that much patience."

"You seem to be dealing pretty well with Matt and his new guy. Um, what's his name?"

Kyle shrugged. "Gil. I'm fine with that. Happy for him. But I don't know—maybe I wouldn't be if I actually saw them together. Or in my case, heard them together."

Lily took control of the cart, pushing it slowly down the aisle. "Watch out, Kye. Display of cake decorations sticking out on your right."

Thanks to the warning, he deftly avoided a collision. "Why are there cake decorations in the canned goods aisle?"

"Because shoppers will feel so virtuous over buying peas and green beans that they'll decide to reward themselves with a treat. Dropping the topic of Matt, how are things with Mr. Goodbuns?"

"Really?" he exclaimed, glaring in her general direction. "He has a name."

"Seth. How are things going with Seth?"

He ignored the slight anxiety. "Fine."

"That's it? Fine? No juicy details?"

"Nope." And he stomped ahead of her, hoping no additional displays blocked his path.

WHEN KYLE'S phone rang that evening, he grabbed it right away.

"Hi," Seth said.

"How are you feeling?"

"Okay. But Mom...." Seth stopped and cleared his throat. "Mom fell this afternoon."

"Shit! Is she okay?" Now there was a stupid question.

"They admitted her to Saint Joe's. Fractured tailbone. We're waiting to find out about treatment and prognosis, and in the meantime she's kind of freaking out because she keeps forgetting why she's in the hospital."

"Dammit, Seth, I'm so sorry. How can I help?"

Seth paused before responding. "Everything's under control. I need to stay with her, though, at least for now. So our running date tomorrow...."

"Postponed. I understand."

Another silence fell, this one slightly awkward. Kyle wanted to ask whether everything was all right between them, but with Seth's mother in the hospital, it seemed like the wrong time to bring it up. "Hey," he finally said. "Take care of yourself."

"Thanks," Seth said.

This time after the call ended, Kyle's unease blossomed into full-fledged worry. Seth's reasons for canceling were completely justified, but he'd sounded so distant. Maybe Kyle hadn't been sympathetic enough. He'd never had to face a family crisis—hell, he'd *been* the crisis—and he couldn't fully understand how Seth felt. Probably Seth had exhausted all his emotional energy between his illness and his mother's fall. And the last thing he needed was some blind guy tagging along and getting in the way.

Over the next few days, Kyle and Seth exchanged nothing but a few texts. When Seth wasn't at the hospital, he was busy with a potential lawsuit at work. His messages were… well, not quite curt but definitely to the point. When Kyle tried to push a bit, hoping for a real conversation, Seth responded with one- or two-word replies. So Kyle pulled back, wondering whether he'd said or done something to offend Seth, or if Seth was having second thoughts about tying himself down with a disabled man when he had so many other issues in his life. *Maybe he just needs some space to deal with his mother and work*, Kyle told himself—but he wasn't convinced.

On the scheduled run days, he ran on the treadmill in the basement with the window open, tether in hand, and pretended he and Seth were still together.

CHAPTER THIRTEEN

LILY ARRIVED at Kyle's house just as he was putting on his shoes. "Hey, Kye, I've not seen Seth's fine ass running away lately. Did you guys change your schedule?"

Kyle answered with a noncommittal grunt, which she ignored. "So where are you headed off to now? The Bridge Center?"

He didn't have permission to share Seth's story, so he went with "His mom is in the hospital and work is crazy for him right now. I was going to take a walk over to Saint Joe's and pay his mom a visit."

"Are you looking for company on your adventure?"

Kyle thought about it. If Kyle was lucky, Seth would be there, and it would be harder for him to get rid of Kyle if Lily was there.

She must have thought she needed to sweeten the deal. "On the way back we can stop at the new Asian place, Rhys and Noodles."

"Yum! I've passed by that place a few times, and I've been meaning to try it. It has a lot of five-star reviews on Yelp! They even have a kimchi bar. And you can get bibimbap to go."

"Let's swing by my place so I can get my walking shoes."

"And let's take the route past the florist. I want to pick something up."

ON THE way to the hospital, Kyle told Lily about Ruth's dementia, gave her a rundown of the names in Seth's family, and instructed her to run with whatever Ruth called them. Remembering back, Kyle said, "Matt's gran loved visitors, and she would attach a name, any name, to them. Over time, I was a number of people from the Labrecque family, including her husband."

Kyle hated hospital smells; they reminded him too much of his own ordeal. But he ignored that as much as possible, walking beside Lily to Ruth's room. One of Ruth's caregivers recognized Kyle and invited them in. Seth wasn't there, which was both a disappointment and a slight relief.

Ruth seemed delighted to see them. "Kyle! I'm glad you brought Judith with you! How nice. Did you meet in the hall?"

He was surprised Ruth remembered him. "Yes we did, Ruth. I hope you like flowers."

"My favorites! Gardenias and irises!"

"Hello, Mother," Lily said warmly.

They visited for a little while. Whenever Ruth expected them to know something that they didn't, Kyle or Lily prompted her to tell the story. Ruth seemed to enjoy such an appreciative audience.

About a half hour into the visit, the door to the hallway opened and closed. "Uh, hello," Seth said, sounding puzzled. Kyle's stomach knotted.

"Oh Seth!" Ruth called out happily. "Kyle and Judith met in the hall. We've been regaling him with some of the stories of when you were small."

"Kyle?"

"Yes, of course. Your new young man. Stop hovering and come in, Seth. You know, Kyle can't see anything, but he can do different voices. He does a very good Jack Kennedy and Bugs Bunny. He could be on *Johnny Carson*, he's so talented."

Lily got up and, judging by Seth's slight grunt, gave him an enthusiastic hug. "It's so good to see you again, little brother! And this time from the front!"

Seth laughed and hugged her back. "You must be Lily," he whispered, just loudly enough for Kyle to hear.

"One and the same." She giggled.

Kyle didn't get up, and Seth didn't say anything to him. But when Seth scooted a chair closer to the bed so he could sit down, he placed the chair next to Kyle.

They all chatted for a while, but Kyle was weirdly uncomfortable with Seth so close. Besides, Ruth was beginning to sound a little tired. "We should go now," Kyle said, standing.

"Of course. Judith, bring the children next time, please."

"Um...." Lily hesitated, then apparently decided on the middle road. "They're in school now. We'll come on the weekend."

That seemed to satisfy Ruth. In a sunny voice, she asked, "Kyle, have you met Arturo, Seth's best friend? I'll bet you two would get along well."

Seth inhaled sharply, but Kyle didn't miss a beat. "No, Ruth, I haven't. Arturo is out in California, but I've heard all about him."

"I always thought that Seth liked him more than a friend. But the way he talks about you, I'm glad he's finally found someone who can make him happy in the love department. He's a good boy."

"Mom!" Seth protested, sounding mortified and very young.

"Out of the mouths of babes and women over seventy," Lily laughed.

"It's just nice to see you finally coming to your senses, dear." Ruth sounded as if she were smiling as she said it.

After a heavy sigh, Seth dropped his voice. "Kyle, can I see you in the hall?"

Kyle nodded, got up, and made his way to the hallway. Seth followed close at his heels, but Lily remained with Ruth.

"What are you doing here?"

Kyle kept his voice neutral. "Visiting your mom."

"I got that, but why?"

"I thought your mom could use some company. Hospitals suck." While those statements were true, they weren't the whole truth. "And I hoped I'd run into you."

Kyle could hear Seth blow out a breath. "Thanks for visiting with Mom. I'm sorry I've been avoiding you."

"I know you've been really busy. But it's more than that, isn't it?" Kyle braced for the reply, hoping he didn't look too needy.

"I just don't want to see disappointment on your face. I don't want you thinking I'm a charity case."

"Whoa there, buddy! Let me be the judge of my own feelings. Why the hell would I think that about you?"

"Because of what I did to Arturo."

"You didn't—" Kyle stopped himself and placed his hand on Seth's arm. "The way I see it, we both looked for love—quoting the great country-western song—in all the wrong places. You with your straight friend, and me with a guy who was a best friend and, essentially, a brother."

"Not the same thing. You didn't kill Matt."

Kyle gathered his thoughts. "Look, Seth, I think we're both guilty of a lot of things. Poor judgment is one of them. I prevented Matt from finding the love of his life, you loved your friend in a different way than he wanted. You didn't kill Arturo; the drunk driver did. Who knows what would have happened if Arturo didn't leave that morning? What if you got up early and delayed him from going out? Would you still be friends, or would you have lost the friendship completely? You can play that game forever. When I was in the hospital, I kept wondering what would've happened if I'd had more regular checkups. Maybe the doctors would have discovered I wasn't right in the head—in time to save my sight."

"Could that have happened?" Seth asked quietly.

"I don't know. The docs say it's very unlikely, but that didn't keep me from thinking about it. Seth, the what-ifs and the guessing take you out of life. Time is too short to allow regrets to consume us." His throat felt raw with the intensity of his emotions.

Kyle grabbed Seth into what he intended to be a hug, but errant fumbles created something akin to pawing rather than an embrace.

"Kyle, stop!" Seth was half laughing, half sobbing as he wrapped his arms around Kyle. "I'll stop running away from you."

"Good. Now we both have a common goal."

Seth sniffed. "I guess I make a shitty guide if I don't even let you know where I am."

"You don't have to stay tethered to me." Kyle forced the next words out. "Maybe being tied to a blind guy is more—"

"Stop. I'm not tied to a blind guy—I'm falling for *you*. Which scares the crap out of me, if you want to know the truth. And no, not because you can't see. That's a pretty minor issue compared to some of my baggage."

"Then why are you scared?"

"I've never done this before. What if I fuck it up? Jesus, I already almost did."

Kyle thought for a minute. Then he remembered the discussion he'd had with his father about rekindling his sense of adventure. "Zip lines," he said.

"Huh?"

"Have you ever ridden one?"

Seth chuckled. "I don't think they let lawyers anywhere near those things."

"Then you've been missing out. Here's the deal. You *might* fall and break your neck. You *might* crash into a tree. So you do your damnedest not to fall or crash, and in any case, it's a hell of a ride. If you sit on the ground worrying about what could happen, you're not going to have any fun."

"You're a zip line, huh?"

"I encourage you to substitute the analogy of your choice if you don't like mine."

"Zip line is good." Seth rested his head on Kyle's shoulder.

The weight of the world didn't disappear from Kyle's back, but it sure did feel a lot lighter.

They stood there awhile before ending the embrace. "Let me say good-bye to your mom," Kyle said. "Who knows who I'll be when I go back in there."

"I can't believe she remembered who you were."

"I've heard Alzheimer's can be unpredictable, though less so as it advances. I don't care who she calls me. I'll be whoever her mind needs at the time. And if she calls me Arturo from now on, it's okay with me. I know that she's interested in your welfare and can identify people who loved you and who you loved back. Now let's get back in there before she tells Lily some embarrassing things about your childhood."

"Oh God, yes. Thanks."

"Yeah, I want to hear those stories firsthand."

Seth laughed as they walked back into the room.

"Oh, Seth and Kyle! I'm glad you've come to visit. Judith needs to rest after traveling so far to see me. She tells me that Kyle will take her back to the house while you visit with me."

"See you again soon, Mother." Lily leaned over and gave Ruth a kiss, and Kyle followed.

Seth sat in the chair next to his mother's bed, and Kyle heard them talking as he and Lily left.

"Kyle is such a good man. Did you see the flowers he brought for me? He's a keeper."

Seth laughed. "Yes he is, Mom. Yes he is."

LILY WAS uncharacteristically quiet during the walk home, but Kyle could hear the gears turning in her head. Finally she spoke up. "I like her. She's a pistol, even with Alzheimer's. And she adores you."

"She hardly knows me."

"But she thinks you're good for Seth. In fact, she thinks you'll make a much better son-in-law than Judith's husband, who isn't smart enough for Judith and has awful taste in music, clothes, and home décor."

"Poor guy," Kyle said with a laugh.

"Maybe that's why he and Judith live on the West Coast—to avoid Ruth."

"Well, I like her. But the in-law thing—that's a lot premature." A bus roared by, its multicolored side briefly visible as it passed.

Lily made a thoughtful humming noise. "I'm glad I finally got a chance to meet Seth. He seems like a really good guy."

"He is."

"So you want to explain the secret hallway conference? The one you both returned from with red-rimmed eyes?"

Shit. "We had a little crisis. I think we're past it now."

"What kind of crisis? He's not having issues over your sight, is he?" She sounded angry, ready to lead a righteous charge on Kyle's behalf.

"Nope. It was a baggage crisis, and the baggage had nothing to do with me. But we're good."

She gave his bicep a quick squeeze. "How serious are you two?"

"We're still trying to figure that out." Kyle could have told her that Seth made him feel giddy and weak-kneed in a way nobody else ever had. With Matt, love had been a slow burn, a cup of hot chocolate on a cold winter day. Seth, though—that was more like chili peppers and firecrackers. But Kyle kept that information to himself.

Chapter Fourteen

"I CAN'T believe I'm helping somebody else pack," Seth said as Kyle handed him several pairs of socks. "I am the world's worst packer. I always bring fifty pounds of crap I don't need and forget at least two critical things I *do* need."

"That's why you're the assistant packer and I'm in charge." Kyle knew what he wanted to take, and he was pretty sure he was grabbing the right things and placing them in the correct packing cube. Seth's job was mostly quality control, making sure Kyle really was packing what he thought he was. Besides, Kyle was enjoying Seth's company. Although Seth was no longer avoiding him, his work and his responsibilities to his mother had meant they couldn't spend much time together. And now Kyle was leaving town for several days.

Kyle opened a dresser drawer, counted out four pairs of boxer briefs, and gave them to Seth.

"This is not how I've been dreaming about your underwear," Seth complained.

"You've been dreaming about my underwear?"

"Oh yeah." Seth's voice went husky. "Among other things." He caught Kyle's hand and tugged him close.

"You know, an advantage of dating a blind guy is you don't have to waste money on sexy clothing," Kyle pointed out.

Seth thought for a moment. "Yeah, the finer points of Andrew Christian might be lost on you. Except you can *feel* sexy stuff, right? Leather? Silk? Lace?"

A warm thrill traveled down Kyle's spine. "Lace?"

"Sure. Don't get me wrong—cross-dressing has never been my thing. But then I never slept with a blind guy before. I'm thinking that now maybe I ought to make an effort to *feel* really interesting." He chuckled evilly.

"I have a plane to catch," Kyle replied in a slightly strangled voice.

"I know. But when you get back…. Don't you think it's time to take our courtship to the next stage?"

Kyle smiled. "Pledging troth?"

Seth brushed his soft lips against Kyle's cheek. "You already have all my troth, babe. I was thinking more like third base. Or a home run, even."

"Now it's a baseball metaphor?" Kyle said, shivering slightly at Seth's touch. "I gotta warn you, I can't see the ball, so I can't catch."

"I'd be perfectly happy for you to pitch instead. And you don't have to *see* any balls, just—I think I'm done with the innuendo. Kyle, I want to make love to you."

"Plane?" Although catching his flight suddenly seemed a lot less important.

"I know. When you get back. We'll have a private welcome-home party. And in the meantime, happy underwear dreams."

They eventually finished packing, with a few gratuitous gropes and kisses thrown in for good measure. Then Kyle checked to make sure he'd turned off the stove while Seth checked that all the lights were off. Kyle followed Seth out the front door and locked it behind them.

"I wish I could go with you," Seth said as he pulled the car away from the curb.

"Me too. It would be fun." They'd talked about this a lot over the past couple of weeks. Kyle had been booked as a guest at Animazement a year earlier, well before the stroke. He could have bowed out—the organizers would have understood—but that would have felt like defeat. Besides, fans hoped to see him, and if Kyle wanted to resume his anime voice-over work eventually, he needed to keep in the public eye.

But flying to Raleigh and navigating a busy con all on his own scared the crap out of him. Lily was chairing the committee in charge of an editors' conference in Chicago. Seth was tied to the city with his job too. The executives of his company were coming to town in advance of the big E2 conference at McCormick Place. As the chief legal counsel of the company, he was tapped to give a presentation on the necessity of good legal advice when starting up a new business. Plus he had his mother to worry about.

Kyle was a grown-up. He could handle it.

He'd deliberately booked a flight from Midway rather than O'Hare, hoping he'd find the smaller airport a little easier to handle. And he didn't have to navigate it by himself, because Seth parked his car and joined

Kyle at the check-in counters. The lady there gave Seth a pass so he could accompany Kyle to the gate.

"Like I'm a little kid," Kyle groused as his insecurities surfaced.

"No, like you're a man who needs some help. Besides, this way we get a little extra time together." Seth squeezed his hand as they made their way down the escalator to the security checkpoint.

They sat next to each other at the gate. Airports always bustled with activity, and Kyle saw little streaks of movement when people hurried by. Seth kept up a running commentary, making up little stories about who other passengers were and where they were traveling. "There's a lady at the next gate," he said. "She's in her late sixties, maybe five feet tall on her tiptoes. Gray perm. Beige polyester pants, lavender sweatshirt with a drawing of cats, enormous purse. Her name is Shirley, and she's on her way to Las Vegas, where she will fulfill her lifelong dream to dance in a topless chorus line. She told her husband she's going to a scrapbooking convention, but he saw her stuffing feathers and spandex into that purse, and now he's sitting at home in Schaumburg, feeling suspicious."

"Who's sitting near her?" Kyle asked through his laughter.

"Tall kid in his early twenties. Longish hair slicked back from his forehead into a man bun."

Kyle chortled at the man bun comment.

"A bristly mustache, a beard to make a lumberjack proud. He has a plaid shirt, a red bow tie, and sleeve tats. And a messenger bag that's supposed to look like a boombox."

"Where's he going?"

"His name is Eugene, and he is also pursuing his dream, which is to open an artisanal gin distillery in Oregon. Sadly, he's about to discover that he has a terrible allergy to juniper berries. But it'll all work out. He'll end up working at a doggie day care instead, and he'll find that he has a talent for soothing puppies with separation anxiety."

Kyle laughed so hard he snorted.

When it was time to board, Kyle got to be one of those special snowflakes who hit the Jetway first, owing to his need for assistance finding his seat. Seth gave him a passionate kiss before leaving him in the care of the gate agent, a perky short girl with a slight Spanish accent. As she guided Kyle into the plane, she cooed over how adorable he and Seth were together.

Being first one on the plane, he'd chosen the bulkhead aisle seat for the extra leg room and so his seatmates could get to and from their seats easily. A lead-footed, heavy-breathing man plopped down in the middle seat; he was wide enough that his thigh impinged on Kyle's space. Before Kyle could get his earbuds in place, the guy started talking and never left a long enough pause for Kyle to politely withdraw. Not only that, but after he realized Kyle was blind, the man spoke slowly and in a near shout, as if Kyle were also deaf and not very bright.

Once everyone was seated, the young woman sitting across the aisle offered to lay hands on Kyle and pray for a cure. That time he did stick in the earbuds, ignoring her insistence that it was the Devil making him skeptical and that he'd never be happy until he found Jesus.

"I'll look for him in North Carolina," Kyle snapped. Then he turned the volume way up, hoping both the rude and the clueless could overhear the steamy passage in the romance novel he'd recently finished narrating.

At the Raleigh airport, an airline employee met Kyle at the gate and shepherded him to the baggage claim to help get his luggage. As they were walking from the gate, he caught snippets of several conversations. He wondered what stories Seth would have told about the people, such as the man yelling angrily in Italian into his cell phone. Kyle picked up the gist of that conversation—the guy was royally pissed off at his brother over some kind of investment mistake.

Just as the airline employee pulled Kyle's small roller case off the conveyor, a volunteer from the con approached. His name was Jun, although he had a Southern accent rather than Japanese. He was a huge fan, chattering nonstop about his favorite episodes of *Ecos*—which were pretty much all of them—and driving so fast and erratically that Kyle was grateful that he couldn't see much of the journey.

At the hotel, Jun hovered while Kyle checked in. Then he accompanied Kyle to his eighth-floor room and very broadly hinted that he wouldn't mind being invited inside. Kyle put him off gently but firmly. "I need to call my boyfriend and get some work done. But why don't we chat later? I'd love to hear your thoughts on the season-three arc. I've never been sure how I felt about the way Ecos dealt with that orphaned flying cat."

Clearly disappointed but also mollified, Jun informed him that one of the organizers would be back in two hours to take him to the guest appreciation dinner in the hotel restaurant. Jun bid him good night and let him know the next day he or someone else would show up in the morning to take Kyle to the convention center. As soon as the door closed, Kyle locked it, dragged his suitcase against a wall, and collapsed backward onto the bed. He was exhausted, but worse than that, he felt lost. He wanted to curl up under the bleach-scented sheets until it was time to fly home.

But then his phone played the ringtone he'd chosen for Seth— Jackson Browne's "Lawyers in Love"—and Kyle immediately felt a little better.

"How's it going?" Seth asked. Music was playing in the background. Perry Como, Kyle thought. Ruth had apparently been very fond of him when she was younger, and now when she was feeling especially confused, those old songs seemed to soothe her.

"Made it to the hotel," Kyle said. "Where I ignored being hit on by some kid named Jun and am now enjoying the king-sized bed with the four zillion pillows."

"Hit on, huh?"

"Yep."

"I neglected to take into account the presence of groupies. I'm getting on the next flight to Raleigh."

Kyle grinned. "Don't bother. I'm very good with the new superweapon in my arsenal—the Cane of Pain. I will whack all those who get too close. Besides, I get to try it out at the pre-con dinner. I'll excuse myself after the main course, wield my CoP against any that get in my way, and thereby return to my room and crash. And maybe dream about underwear."

"I don't have a superweapon at my disposal, but it sounds like a plan. Meet you in your dreams?"

"Done."

WHEN KYLE had attended previous cons, he'd gone to a lot of panels. They were fun, and he always learned something new. This time, however, after enduring last night's dinner, he decided to stick to the events he was required to attend: a panel discussion with two other voice actors and, the following day, an autograph session. He was a little disappointed that he wouldn't be able to browse Artists' Alley or admire all the cosplay.

In the past, depending on the country and the con, he had been mobbed or admired from afar. Matt had always been able to get them out of potential pickles by pointing his camera and having people pose or by guiding Kyle through the back service halls. Now Kyle didn't have any safety net except for the con promoters. They assured him they had people who would get him from place to place without him being overwhelmed.

His volunteer handler for the day was supposed to meet him in the hotel lobby. The ride down in the elevator was a bit crowded. A young woman complimented his Matt Murdock cosplay. Kyle had to think for a minute, and then he remembered he was wearing a suit vest and the glasses Seth gave him before he left. The girls were giggling and whispering that he was *soooo kawaii!* Not knowing where he was supposed to meet his guide for the day, Kyle skulked against a square pillar in the lobby, alongside a large potted plant.

He smelled coffee from the nearby Starbucks and longed for an Americano. He was about to go off in search of breakfast when someone stepped close and grabbed his arm. "Kyle Green?" asked a man, sounding slightly out of breath.

"Yes." Kyle wished he could extricate himself, but the guy had grasped him firmly.

"Excellent! I'm Toby Fisher. One of the volunteers? I'm in charge of you this morning."

Great, Kyle thought sourly. "Do you think we can find something to eat before heading over to the con?"

"Oh yeah, totally."

Toby didn't ask where Kyle wanted to eat. Instead, he gripped Kyle's arm as if he were being arrested and towed him outside and down the sidewalk. The situation made it impossible for Kyle to use his cane, and Toby didn't know to warn him about curbs. As a result, Kyle tripped several times, and each time Toby tsked sadly. It was a relief to enter a nearby restaurant and sit down.

The waitress seemed slightly flustered when Kyle asked for a braille menu, but she found one and brought it to him. He discovered then that this was a vegetarian diner. Lovely. Scrambled tofu.

"How come you don't have a guide dog?" Toby asked.

"I have a cane."

"Oh. Dogs are way better than canes. My cousin Deedee? Her grandmother—not the one who's also my gran; the *other* grandmother—is blind, and she has this awesome golden retriever. He's like Lassie or something. And he lets her do almost everything normal people do. Except drive, of course."

"I'm allergic."

That made Toby pause, but only for a moment. "You could take antihistamines. Dude, you totally need to get a dog. I can ask Deedee where her grandma got hers, see if maybe they can hook you up."

Kyle was spared having to answer when the waitress appeared. "What does he want to order?" she asked, clearly aiming the question at Toby.

"*He* is able to order for himself," Kyle said, trying for pleasant. "And I want the tempeh Benedict, home fries, and please *God* tell me you have booze."

"We have kombucha," she said hesitantly. "The regular and the higher alcohol version."

Kyle sighed mournfully. "Fine. I'll take the higher alcohol version."

"Are you allowed to drink?" Toby asked.

"It's not like anyone's going to expect me to be a designated driver."

"Yeah, but you're blind."

"Visually impaired," Kyle snapped, just because Toby was pissing him off. "And that is no impediment to enjoying all of the same vices sighted people indulge in." Feeling the tension, he added with a laugh, "Well, I guess I'd make a crappy Peeping Tom."

The waitress giggled.

The food actually wasn't bad, although it wasn't bacon. He had two green kombuchas, which gave him a pleasant buzz. He seriously considered a third as Toby continued to expound on what blind people should do. Kyle tried not to be an asshole, he really did, but the effort was almost superhuman.

On the way back, Kyle managed to avoid Toby's grabby hands and insisted on using the cane instead. That didn't stop Toby from yelling loud, confusing, and often contradictory instructions to him as they walked. By the time they reached the convention center, Kyle was ready to throw one or both of them in front of a bus.

Then they entered the building, the roar of the crowds surrounded him, and he decided he'd had far too little alcohol.

People didn't intend to be rude. But there were a lot of attendees, most of them highly distracted, and they tended to bash into him. Or they stopped in the middle of the path, blocking the way. Their mingled perfumes and body odors and the sickly sweetness of candy made him slightly dizzy. Toby, as distracted as everyone else, was a useless, shitty guide. He didn't clear the way for Kyle through the crowds, and the cane was difficult to use properly in such close quarters. Kyle felt as though he was stuck inside a video arcade game.

He crashed hard into a pillowy woman who had stopped in front of him. She whirled around furiously. "Watch it! What are you, blind?"

Kyle lifted the cane.

"Oh," she said after a moment. "Sorry."

Judging by the acoustics, the room for the panel discussion was large. Probably one of those spaces where they'd folded back a few walls, combining several small rooms into one. Kyle had arrived early, but conversations already buzzed loudly. It sounded as if they'd have a good crowd. Toby took him to the front of the room and parked him at the table for the three-person panel. "I gotta go deal with this thing. I'll be back for you later!" He zoomed away, leaving Kyle unsure whether anyone else was near.

His heart pounded. He'd never minded public speaking—he was an actor, after all. But now he had no idea how many people were there and whether they were gazing at him with pity or disgust. His dark glasses provided far too little to hide behind.

Kyle jumped a little when somebody plopped into the seat next to him. "Hey," said a familiar voice. "It's good to see you again."

"Hi, Reggie," Kyle said, a bit of his anxiety fading away. "Sorry I missed you at dinner last night."

"You were in and out of there like a shot."

Kyle winced. "I needed my room. Travel takes a lot out of me." That hadn't always been true, but it sure was now. Then he smiled at Reggie. "I heard you landed a new gig. Congratulations."

"Thanks. It's a good role in a great show. I just hope it catches on. I'd love to be as popular as Ecos."

They talked quietly for a few minutes, never once mentioning blindness, and Kyle briefly felt ordinary again. Then the other panelist joined them—a woman named Belle, whom he'd met at another con a few years back when she was just starting out—and the moderator picked up the mic and addressed the crowd. Kyle and his colleagues took turns speaking about their work, joking a bit with one another as they went, and that was good. Comfortable.

Then the moderator started taking questions.

"Mr. Green?" said someone in the audience. "I love what you do."

He smiled. "Thanks. That's why I do it."

"I read the manga, and in the next arc Ecos is silent, right?"

"Yeah, that's true. His voice gets stolen by the poisonous ice giant."

"Okay, yeah, but that kind of sucks. We like to *hear* Ecos, Kyle. When's that going to happen again?"

His mouth felt dry, and he had to clear his throat. "I don't know. I'm just as much in the dark"—the audience snickered—"as the rest of you." He reached for and knocked over the bottle of water in front of him, but it was capped and nothing spilled. He unscrewed the lid and took a big swig.

"But, like, you are coming back, right?"

The million-dollar question, the one he'd avoided asking himself. "I've been keeping really busy with a lot of other voice work," he hedged. "Book narration, mostly. A couple of commercials. You might recognize me in some car ads."

"But I love Ecos." A round of applause signaled the audience's agreement.

Kyle took a deep breath. "Me too. He's a great character, and when Kurokuma-sensei decides to give Ecos his voice back, I'll be ready." Kyle then repeated one of Ecos's famous lines, and the crowd applauded. And then, because he couldn't face this issue anymore, he turned to his right and asked in his Ecos voice, "Hey, Belle. Why don't you tell everyone what happened when you tried to record that underwater scene?"

Belle took the mic, everyone laughed at her story, and the remainder of the panel went smoothly. But while Kyle was shaking people's hands and posing for photos, while Toby ineptly led him back to the hotel, while Kyle sat in the chair in his room, all he could think about was his future. He was going to spend the rest of his life being Kyle Green, the guy who used to voice Ecos.

THE VOLUNTEER babysitter for Kyle's autograph session was a man named Eric. Kyle had the impression that Eric was a big man—his voice rumbled and he exuded a definite presence, even though the only time he touched Kyle was to shake his hand. Mercifully, Eric had no advice on living with limited vision. In fact, he didn't say much at all, choosing instead to silently clear a path for Kyle and then lurk behind the signing table. Kyle didn't mind. It was like having a bodyguard.

A lot of people wanted Kyle to sign things for them. He had a thick stack of papers bearing images of Ecos, and a lot of the fans were thrilled with those. With Lily's help, he'd worked out ahead of time where best to scrawl his signature on them, so all he had to do was measure the distance with his fingers. But people brought other things as well: different pictures, plastic Ecos figurines, T-shirts, posters, DVD cases, tote bags, hats. A few of the fans wanted Kyle to autograph their arm or chest, which he always thought was a little weird but went along with anyway. Whatever needed signing, he just asked the person to place the Sharpie tip in the right spot so he could do the rest.

Almost all of the fans wanted him to say something in Ecos's voice in both English and Japanese. Many of them wanted to photograph Kyle, either by himself or—more often—posed next to them. Eric snapped most of those shots. The fans asked questions about the show's storylines and gushed about their favorite parts. They gave him their opinions on which other characters he should voice. There were a few that wanted *Werewolf PTA*'s bad boy Terry James's voice or Screll from *Seahorses in Love* and *Seahorses in Love to the Rescue*, a very old series and one of the first animes he voiced only in Japanese.

Kyle was used to all of that. As long as he took a moment now and then to sip some water and shake out his aching hand, he was fine. But a lot of people made comments along the lines of "Wow, you're doing so great for a blind guy!" And every time Kyle heard that, something inside him twisted a little tighter, until his heart felt like a compressed spring. It became increasingly difficult to smile at his fans and make nice, and a nasty voice in his head insisted he was no longer Kyle Green, voice of Ecos, but instead Kyle Green, that pathetic blind guy.

He almost sobbed with relief when the autograph session ended.

ERIC WAS leading him back through the crowds when a familiar voice called out, "Hey! Kyle!"

"Hang on," Kyle said to Eric, then waited for a slightly breathless Belle to catch up.

"Man, you *booked* out of that room!" she exclaimed. "But if you're desperate to pee, you're out of luck. Huge bathroom lines, even for men. I blame the costumes—they increase undressing time exponentially."

Kyle relaxed a bit, enough to grant her a small smile. "My bladder can wait. I just need some peace and quiet."

"I getcha. Such a zoo. Not that I don't feel incredibly lucky to have rabid fans, blah blah blah, but *jeez* this is a lot for my poor little introverted soul."

"You're an introvert?"

"Yep. But I can pass as extro." She moved slightly closer and dropped her voice. "Can I ask you a huge favor?"

"Sure."

"You know that film Yasu and I have been wanting to make?"

"The one about the peach boy?" Belle and her husband, Yasu, had been talking for a few years about doing an animated version of the Japanese folktale.

"That's the one. We have a Kickstarter campaign to fund it. And to drum up interest in the campaign, Yasu filmed this silly little documentary about the story. I act out all the parts. We're going to show the doc later today. We have some giveaways and stuff—it'll be fun. And... I was hoping you'd come, maybe give us a plug. Pretty please?"

All he wanted to do was curl up in his room, but he couldn't refuse her request. "I'd be happy to," he lied.

Belle gave his arm a quick squeeze. "I owe you so, so big. How about if I meet you at your hotel room in a couple of hours and take you to the screening?"

"I'm upstairs in the Marriott, room 825."

"Perfect. We're staying here too. See you then." She squeezed him again and hurried away.

When Kyle returned to his hotel room, he undressed and lay down in bed, hoping a nap would help him feel better. But he couldn't sleep—his head was too filled with storm clouds—so he brooded instead. Then he ordered and ate a sandwich from room service, checked his e-mail, and brooded some more. He didn't paste on a smile until Belle knocked on his door, and then he wasn't at all sure he looked sincere.

Belle gave him a hug anyway. "Thanks again for doing this, Kyle. Did I tell you I owe you big? If you ever need someone to pimp any of your projects, I'm your gal."

"How do you feel about gay romance?"

She laughed. "I've listened to a couple of your books. Whew!" He felt a movement of air and realized she was fanning herself. "Good stuff!"

She didn't grab him as they left the hotel, and she chatted lightly as they walked, telling him about the Kickstarter campaign and the documentary. "We're going to hand out cards with a QR code so folks can donate while they're sitting here today. We've got all sorts of goodies for people who support us, like I can record their voice-mail message in the octopus queen's voice or Yasu can do a sketch of them as an anime character." She gave a little chuckle. "You'd make an adorable anime character, by the way. I'm going to tell Yasu to draw you."

He grinned at her, but he was picturing himself with enormous sightless eyes.

Belle, bless her introverted soul, took Kyle to the screening room through the service hallways. He was grateful to avoid the crowds. As they entered the room, it sounded as if it was filled to capacity. Belle had saved Kyle a seat up front, and Yasu greeted him with enthusiastic gratitude in English and Japanese, then handed him a metal box of Japanese sweets. "Belle says these are your favorites," Yasu said.

"Ah. She planned ahead. Well, thank you. I'll enjoy them."

He listened to Belle and Yasu give a short spiel about their project, both of them sounding so passionate that the crowd clapped and cheered. Then, at Belle's prompting, Kyle stood and gave an impromptu little speech about how wonderful their peach boy film was going to be. He even said a few words in Ecos's voice, pretending that Ecos was best buds with the peach boy. As he sat down again, the room erupted into wild applause. Then Belle and Yasu started the movie.

Kyle hadn't paid attention to TV since the stroke. He'd rarely watched the boob tube even when he could see, so there didn't seem much point picking up the habit now. Still, he'd wondered if he might be able to see what was on the screen since the images were moving. He hadn't been brave enough to find out.

It was a strange experience. At first Kyle saw nothing but the usual darkness, a black more complete than the darkest room. He and Matt had once visited a cave in California, and during part of the tour, the guide doused the lights, plunging them into absolute darkness. That was what Kyle experienced all the time now—unless there was movement. And as he stared attentively toward the screen, he saw streaks and blurs. In the documentary, Belle bobbed around, pretending to be a peach floating down the river, and he saw her shoulders move up and down. A few minutes later, she was a talking monkey—and Kyle saw her body as she hopped from foot to foot and moved her arms like she was scratching her sides. Then she was a demon chief, growling hilariously, and he saw her arms wave. He grew excited—he could see the movie! He leaned far forward, as if doing so would clear the picture.

But he couldn't see her face.

No matter how much Belle capered and danced on the screen, no matter how animated her expressions must have been, no matter how hard he squinted, the most Kyle could make out was a vague pale oblong with ears and hair but no facial features, no facial expressions. His heart sank as rapidly as it had risen. He couldn't see her mouth at all.

If he couldn't see a mouth onscreen, he'd never be able to sync his voice properly. And his most fervent ambition was to return to voice acting for animation. To be Ecos again, and all the other characters he'd grown to love. He was their voice, and they were part of him. And now he knew he'd never be them again.

Somehow he made it through the remainder of Belle and Yasu's event. He clapped when the documentary ended and listened politely while his friends gave away prizes to the cheering audience. He stood and bowed when Belle thanked him. But as soon as some members of the audience began to crowd around him, he mumbled an excuse about another engagement, hastily wished Belle and Yasu luck, and made his way to the exit. Belle called after him, offering to take him back to the hotel, but he refused. He could find his own way.

He probably would have been fine if he'd been calmer. But his head was in such turmoil that he quickly became disoriented, and the roaring noise of the busy con set him further off his bearings. He ended up sagging against a wall with his cane in one hand, Japanese treats clutched in the other, and tears prickling his eyes.

"Excuse me? Mr. Green? I'm a huge fan." The person addressing him sounded like a young woman, slightly breathless and hesitant.

He took a few calming lungfuls of air. "Thanks. And it's just Kyle. What's your name?"

She giggled, and he imagined she was blushing as well. "Stephanie. Or just Steph."

"Steph, could you help me out?"

"Of course!"

"If you could show me the way to the main hotel lobby, I'd really appreciate it." From there, he thought he could find the elevators on his own.

"Wow, Mr. Gr—I mean, Kyle. Of course. This is so cool! I missed your appearances 'cause I had to work, and I was so bummed I wouldn't get to see you."

She was chatty and sweet, which made him feel ancient and slow. But she effectively guided him to the stairway that led out of the convention hall and to the hotel, which was considerably farther away than he'd guessed. He posed for her selfie of the two of them, signed her program, and recorded his voice as Ecos on her voice mail. She was thrilled. Then he thanked her and walked to the bank of elevators.

He made it all the way back to his room before he began to cry.

CHAPTER FIFTEEN

"ARE YOU angry at me?" Seth asked as he drove them from the airport to Kyle's house.

"Why would I be angry?"

"I have no idea. But you didn't really want to talk last night, and now you're still awfully quiet."

Kyle closed his eyes and leaned back into the headrest. "Sorry. It was a rough couple of days. I don't mean to take it out on you."

"You can vent, though." Seth rested his hand on Kyle's leg. "No point having a boyfriend if you're not going to vent to him."

Kyle's answering sigh sounded pathetic, even to him. "Thanks. I don't have the energy for it right now. Let's just go home."

"That has a nice ring to it," Seth said with a smile in his voice. "Do you think you can hold on to the UST just a little bit longer?"

"UST?"

"Unresolved sexual tension. God, so unresolved. So tense. But you're not in the right frame of mind for a resolution."

"We could—"

"Let's make our first time good, okay?"

Kyle chuckled softly and hummed a few bars from "Like a Virgin."

"Fine. But I would like some company if you have time. We can just hang out."

Seth crept his hand slightly upward toward Kyle's thigh. "Sounds good. Mom's set with her caregivers, and the guys from work went to Wisconsin on a fishing trip, so I'm in no hurry. We're supposed to get a storm this evening. I wouldn't mind just sitting with you and listening to the rain hit the windows. Maybe we'll get some thunder. Good thunderstorms were one thing I really missed when I lived in California."

Cuddling on the couch sounded wonderful. They could pull a soft blanket over their laps, eat popcorn and drink some decent pinot grigio, and talk about something besides how pitiful Kyle felt. Yeah, that was a good plan.

"So you can see moving pictures?" Seth was popping the corn on the stove, adding a savory spice combination that made Kyle's mouth water.

"Yeah. I was stoked when I saw the movement, the body features. I think I leaned so far forward on my chair to see more, I nearly toppled onto the floor. I could see everything, the buttons on the blouse, the waves in the water. Everything except the face. I can see the ears, but nothing between the ears. It's just a blank space." Kyle hung his head, rubbed his face hard, and grabbed his hair. "Arrgh! It's frustrating!"

Seth poured the last of the popcorn into the big bowl and carried it to the couch. After setting the bowl down, he pulled Kyle into his arms and hugged him hard. "Did I hear you brought back Japanese sweets? That would complete our movie food menu."

Kyle laughed, knowing that Seth was trying to distract him. "Yes, though I'm not sure I want to share my stash."

"Are you a Pocky hoarder?"

"Hardly. More like a dark-chocolate-Kit-Kats-and-green-tea-wafers hoarder."

"Oh ho! The good stuff!"

Kyle smiled. "Yeah, the good stuff. It's in my carry-on. I was *not* going to entrust it to my checked luggage."

Once they'd settled on the couch, food and drink within reach, Seth selected an old black-and-white movie on a local station, and they relaxed. Twenty minutes later, a weather-warning ticker ran across the bottom of the screen.

Kyle, who'd been slumped against Seth, shot up straight. "I can see the ticker! Shit! Severe thunderstorms and a tornado warning." It was the first time in his life he'd been happy about nasty weather. "I can read the ticker!"

As if on cue, lightning flashed, followed almost immediately by a crack of thunder so close it made them jump. The rain that pummeled the street, windows, and roof was deafening. A nearly simultaneous thunderclap and flash of light across Kyle's vision urged him to stand. "Let's take this to the basement just in case that rare city tornado drops in. I don't want to end up in Oz."

Seth stood and gathered the foodstuffs and the booze.

"I have a survival kit in the hall closet that has a flashlight and a hand-cranked weather radio," Kyle said. "It's in a red bag on the top shelf. Would you get it, just in case?"

"I never pegged you as a city survivalist."

Kyle bumped Seth's shoulder. "One of my soooper seeecret identities."

They made their way to the basement with popcorn, Japanese treats, wine, and survival kit in hand. Kyle practically bounced down the steps in his excitement. But he paused when a thought struck him. "Will your mom be okay?"

"She'll be fine. The caregivers are great, and they can get her into the basement if they need to. They'll call if they have any problems."

"Okay. Good."

"This is amazing," Seth said as they placed the edibles on an ottoman that served as a table.

"That's right, you never got the whole house tour. We were distracted before the tour began." Kyle winked in Seth's direction. "There's no time like the present. Let the lower-level tour commence."

"Most people call it a basement."

"Not with the money, time, and effort that were poured into this area. It's the lower level."

Seth grunted, and Kyle continued. "This is the entertainment room with surround sound. Couch is comfy and pulls out into a queen-size bed for guests who didn't get rooms upstairs."

"Ooh, a pullout bed in the basement. How convenient." Seth placed his hands on Kyle's hips from behind and pulled him into an embrace. Seth leaned in and breathed into Kyle's ear. "We can make out in the basement like teenagers."

Kyle stumbled just a bit but didn't push away from Seth immediately. Instead he reveled in the closeness. Then he grabbed one of Seth's arms and continued forward before he got too hard to walk comfortably. "Now, Mr. Distraction, please allow me to complete our expedition. I don't want any complaints that you didn't get the full tour."

"Does the full tour include the pullout couch?"

Kyle's blood pressure spiked and just about took his head off. "It's the last stop, but we have four stops before that point. So come on."

"Come on what?" Seth said with a giggle.

Really? It's going to be like that? Kyle pulled Seth onward. "Bathroom."

"Nice. Full. Bathtub." Seth made every word sound like sexy innuendo. "And here is my office and studio."

Seth was silent as he looked about. "It looks like a recording booth and two sound board booths."

"Basically. One of the sound board booths is for Lily when she needs to edit what her clients send to her."

"I thought she could do that anywhere."

"She can, in a pinch. But she prefers the setup here. The soundproofing is much better than just the headset she has. We also have a backup generator in case the power goes out and an automatic backup and queue for when the power comes back on."

"Wow." Seth moved slightly away, perhaps to inspect things more closely. "And the recording booth is your space?"

"Yes. It's got baffling in each wall and six layers of drywall. All the seams, the door, and the air return are sealed, which makes it as silent as a tomb in there. So much so that your ears ring in the silence. You can't even hear the vibration of the rain in there."

By the way Seth moved past Kyle and by the pace of his breathing as he moved through the space, Kyle was sure he was impressed.

"Sweet setup—you can stand or sit while recording."

"Yeah, it's a pretty ideal space with all the customizations, and I really enjoy working down here. Okay, enough drooling over my workspace. On to the next stop of the lower-level tour." Kyle made a grab and managed to catch Seth's hand.

It didn't take long to visit the storage and utility area, the workout room, and the walk out from the basement into the backyard. "I can't believe that all the doors blend into the walls so invisibly down here," Seth said.

"Matt and I saw it in a house we toured while abroad, and that gave us the idea to do the same here."

"Have we now reached the final leg of the tour?"

"Eager, are we?" Kyle rubbed up against Seth, who smelled deliciously like popcorn and spices.

Just then, Seth hummed. "The power's out."

"I think we can generate a bit of a glow by rubbing together." Kyle almost laughed as the words left his mouth.

"I can't see anything. It's black as night in here."

Kyle wasn't at all concerned. Not only was this his turf, he had been through this area sighted and blind. "Don't worry; I've got you." This was a situation where he could be the guide instead of the guided. He got to be useful instead of feeling useless. They made their way back to the entertainment room, where Kyle had Seth sit in a chair and work on getting the flashlight and the radio going while he turned the couch into a bed. Seth was having little luck with the flashlight.

"You just need to shake it for thirty seconds," Kyle said. "It'll provide light for twenty minutes."

"Shake it how? Like I'm jacking off?"

Kyle barked out a laugh. "Yes, just like jacking off."

Kyle heard a rush of air past his ear, then a thump against the far wall.

"Oops."

"You've got a strong arm there, Caplan. Use that arm a lot?"

Seth laughed. "Yes. Don't even know my own strength."

"You must need a powerful pull."

"Oh yes. I've got a powerful push and pull."

Kyle could practically hear Seth's eyebrows waggle up and down. And knowing Seth, he had a leer going as well.

Kyle approached the chair. "Don't worry, I got you. We don't need no stinkin' flashlights." Kyle leaned down and kissed Seth. "Let's get comfortable," he whispered in Seth's ear and then pulled him up. But when Seth rose from the chair, his foot caught on the leg, and he elbowed Kyle in the solar plexus.

"Shit!" Kyle wheezed.

"Sorry! Are you okay?"

The blow had taken Kyle's breath away. He bent over and gasped, trying desperately to get some air. Once he could speak again, he joked, "So much for romance and seduction. That's going to leave a mark."

"God, I'm sorry."

"No big deal. It's what happens when the blind lead the blind, I guess."

They both chuckled until Seth, not knowing where Kyle was, turned and elbowed Kyle in the temple.

"Shit! Sorry, Kyle!"

Kyle put his hands out in front of him and grabbed Seth. "Stop moving around! You're going to kill me if you move again without my help."

"Okay, I hear you. You obviously have the advantage in this environment. Are you okay?"

"A bit battered and bruised, but I'll be fine. Let me put my arm around your waist, and I'll guide you over to the pullout. It's ten steps away, slightly to the right from where we are."

Seth squeezed Kyle's waist. "Hey, you're a good guide! I bet I could run after dark with you."

"Only if you're in my house."

"I'd be up for a game of blindfolded 'chase me, chase me.'"

"More like Marco Polo!"

The absurdity of it all triggered a bout of giggles.

Seth cautiously stepped across the room with Kyle, who pushed him down onto the mattress. "For a pullout, it's nice and comfy," Seth noted. The springs squeaked slightly as he moved.

"Stay right there. I'll be back." Kyle stood back up.

"Where are you going?"

"Just over here. Hold on."

Kyle cranked up the weather radio, and it hissed to life. Glowing letters briefly flashed in Kyle's sight before they were lost to the dark. He handed the device to Seth. "You'll need to put in the zip code so we can get an accurate account of what's going on out there."

The radio kicked in and said a tornado had been sighted just north of them, moving out over the lake. Flash flooding was possible, with severe thunderstorms continuing until two in the morning.

The NOAA feed repeated over and over again. Seth turned down the volume, and the bed creaked as he placed the radio on the ottoman.

"It holds a charge for about fifteen minutes before it has to be cranked again," Kyle said.

"Come here, Kyle. There's just enough light from the display so I can avoid whacking you."

"You sure? I think there's a part of me that is still undamaged."

Seth reached up and brushed Kyle's cheek. "Come join me."

Kyle bent down and kissed Seth slowly, exploring through touch, trying to convey his need through the connection. He wanted Seth so badly that his skin ached.

Seth pulled Kyle down, and somehow they both lost balance. Kyle collapsed on top of Seth, bumping their heads in the process.

Kyle groaned. "We're going to have sex, even if it kills us."

"The *Trib* headline: 'Two Men Knocked Unconscious during Raging, Sexually Charged Storm. See back page for photos.'"

"Are you happy to see me?" Kyle rubbed Seth's groin.

"Yes, but that's the bottle of lube. Let me get that out of my pocket; it's getting painful in there."

"You brought lube?"

Seth licked Kyle's neck, making them both shudder. "Yeah. I know we originally agreed on only cuddles for tonight, but I wanted to be prepared, just in case."

"Boy Scout." Kyle went in for another kiss just as Seth pulled the bottle out of his pocket, and Kyle got a fist into his abdomen.

"Oof!"

"Kyle, are you okay?"

It wasn't as stunning as the solar plexus blow and not as sharp as the temple blow, so he was calling it a win. "I'm fine. I want to move on to second base. So far we're as bad as the Cubs."

"I think we're trying too hard. Let's just relax."

They scooted up the bed without injury. Seth wrapped his arm around Kyle, and Kyle placed his head on Seth's chest. The sound of the rain pounding against the upstairs windows drifted down the staircase.

"It seems that the more I want something," Kyle said, "the farther out of my reach it gets."

"Is this a pity party? 'Cause I'm still hopeful we will get tab A into slot B at some point within the next twenty-four hours. Maybe even in the next hour or so, if we don't keep flailing about like fish on a dock."

Kyle laughed against Seth's chest before growing more serious. He very much wanted to get to the tabs insertion, but it was suddenly more important that he unburden his heart. "When I was at the conference, the fans were so angry that Ecos is silent. They demanded to know when Ecos would speak again. I had no answer for them. It's up to the mangaka, and they are waiting on me. What if I'm the downfall of their anime? I'll probably have to give it up to another VOA. I think I'll skip the rest of the cons this year. They're painful reminders of who I once was."

It was easy to speak in the dark because that was all Kyle had now. Darkness.

Seth was quiet for a moment before answering. "I think you're not giving yourself enough credit. You've adapted well to what is, for right now. You'll evolve. It hasn't even been a year yet, and you're back in the studio. It's not the same as being the VOA for Ecos, but who knows what the future holds? It could be even better than before, in ways you can't imagine right now. You can already see much more outside when we run. In fact, we've been running side by side lately. And you've been able to see movies and the weather ticker across the screen. Those are all improvements, Kyle." Seth gave him a gentle shake.

"Yes, they are," Kyle admitted.

"Don't worry. We'll figure things out as we get to them."

"Yeah, you're right. Thanks for talking this out. I've been feeling a bit low since the con." Kyle started to unbutton Seth's shirt. "Now maybe you can help me with something else. If we don't coldcock each other."

Seth pressed his groin against Kyle's. "Nothing cold about my cock right now."

"Oh, that's terrible!" Kyle laughed, pushing back into him. An enormous peal of thunder shook the house, and Kyle groaned as the storm's electricity seemed to course through his body. His hands shook as he fumbled at the last buttons of Seth's shirt. "Warm," he said when he finally stroked Seth's chest.

"Told you." Seth's voice was unusually hoarse. "I, uh, hope you're not averse to a little body hair. I don't manscape."

It was more than a little, but Kyle was definitely not averse. To prove it, he touched his lips to Seth's sternum.

"God," Seth said, clutching at him. "I feel like I'm eighteen and it's my first time." Another thunderclap sounded, and Seth laughed. "And I'm going to go off just like that too."

"I think tonight's going to be more a sprint than a marathon for both of us."

"Smooth analogy, Kyle Green," said Seth, tugging at Kyle's shirt. "Can you get this damned thing off?"

Although it would have been sexy to let Seth undress him, Kyle decided that additional bodily harm was more likely than not. Instead he'd save sexy disrobing for when Seth could see him. Tamping down pointless anger over the fact that he'd never get to see Seth, Kyle pulled off his shirt. After additional groping and scrabbling, they were both completely, gloriously naked.

"Holy *shit* you feel good," Seth panted, squeezing handfuls of Kyle's ass. "Why the hell was I dreaming about underwear when I could have been dreaming about this instead?"

"Reality's better," Kyle responded breathlessly. He was trying to slow things down, but his heart beat to the rhythm of the pounding storm, and he couldn't stop his hands from roving over Seth's compactly muscled body. Their cocks rubbed together, hot and hard and slightly slick.

Seth's next words came out slightly strangled. "K-Kyle? We'd better—"

"Yeah."

It turned out that Kyle's blindness was no impediment to lubing and stretching Seth. If anything, the lack of sight was a benefit, allowing Kyle to focus more carefully on the tight heat around his fingers and the deliciously ragged sound of Seth's breathing. They both moaned when Kyle pulled slightly away, but it was only long enough for him to find and unwrap the condom that Seth had the foresight to bring. Kyle batted away Seth's reaching hand and rolled on the condom.

"Hurry up!" Seth urged.

"We've waited this long—"

"And I have no more waiting left in me."

To be honest, neither did Kyle. With his teeth gritted, he entered Seth as slowly and carefully as he was able. They uttered twin whimpers of relief once he was fully seated. "G-good," Seth said, pulling Kyle's hips to urge him more deeply inside. "Really good."

Kyle answered him with a long kiss and slow rocking of his hips.

Above them, the storm raged. The house creaked and shuddered against the wind and rain, windows rattled, thunder roared. For all they knew, a tornado was bearing down on them, ready to carry them over the rainbow. Kyle didn't care. Didn't care that he was a little sore in the stomach and head from Seth's accidental blows. Didn't care that he couldn't see and would no longer be able to pursue his dream job. Didn't care that so many things he'd once taken for granted were now lost to him. All that mattered in this moment was Seth beneath him, clutching him hard enough to bruise, calling out Kyle's name.

If not for the stroke, Kyle might have continued in his comfortable life. But then he might never have met Seth and experienced the intense passion he felt now—the bone-deep urge to join with Seth, the electrifying tingle of his nerves, the pure heat radiating from his heart. The love. Jesus Christ, he'd fallen well and truly in love.

Now was as good a time as any to say so. He stopped moving, bringing an anguished cry from Seth. "Kyle! Please!"

But Kyle placed his mouth at the shell of Seth's ear and barely voiced his whisper. "I love you, Seth Caplan."

Seth's breath hitched. "I love you too, Kyle Green."

The orgasms that followed soon afterward weren't exactly anticlimactic—their bodies trembled with the force of them—but they paled in comparison to the warm happiness that bathed Kyle as they cuddled afterward. The storm hadn't subsided at all, yet Kyle felt calmer and more at peace than he could remember.

Seth spooned him from behind, lazily tracing shapes on Kyle's sticky belly. "That was so worth waiting for," Seth said.

"It was."

"Which isn't to say we should wait that long again."

Kyle laughed. "Can you give me a couple hours at least? I have a few years on you, remember. The old guy needs recovery time."

"I suppose I can wait a couple hours." Seth kissed Kyle's nape and squiggled a bit, settling more fully into the mattress. "I mean, we have all night, don't we?"

"We have all… everything. If you want," Kyle added hastily, suddenly insecure. Maybe he was reading more into their relationship than he ought to be.

But Seth sighed happily. "Everything. Have we reached the everything point in our courtship? The forever part?"

"That makes it sound like a fairy tale."

"It is. Once upon a time there was a poor lonely lawyer…."

"Who got stumbled into by a poor lonely blind man."

"And they lived happily ever after," Seth said firmly. "Some of the details might be a little more complicated than fiction, though. Cinderella had an evil stepmother but didn't have to worry about a mother with dementia."

Kyle stroked the back of Seth's hand. "It's fine. I know your mom can't take a lot of change and upheaval. We'll take things as they come."

"As they come," Seth agreed, giving a credible Beavis and Butt-Head snigger.

They lay silently for a long time, petting each other languidly, listening to the storm blow itself out.

"Power's back on, isn't it?" Kyle said eventually.

"How can you tell?"

"I can hear the fridge running."

Seth held him a little more tightly. "Can we stay down here anyway? I'm not ready to face the real world yet."

"Me either."

They slipped into a doze, with the hope of future happiness bright around them.

Chapter Sixteen

"HEY, KYLE." Matt's voice was warm and soothing, even over the phone lines.

"Hey, Matt. How goes the petroglyph documentation?"

"Great! That's why I'm calling you."

Kyle settled more comfortably into his armchair. Nearly a week had passed since the storm. Seth had been over nearly every evening, and contentment had settled on Kyle like a friendly cat in his lap. "Unless those drawings hop off the rocks and move rapidly, I'm not going to be much use."

"Well, we are making a documentary short, and I was wondering if you'd be interested in doing the narration. I know it's not the book you said you would narrate, but still."

Kyle was so stunned he couldn't reply at first. "Uh, sure! I'd love to! When do you need it?"

"We're trying to get the script finished. The crew is piecing together the film, so you should have the final script and film copy by the end of the week."

"Wow. Why the rush?"

"Yeah, well, they thought they could pass it around and get it Oscar-eligible before September 1. It'll help us get more funding for this project. If this year doesn't work, we can go to September 1 of next year."

Kyle smiled at the obvious enthusiasm in Matt's voice. He could easily picture the sparkle in his eyes. "I thought you were funded through a five-year grant."

"We are, but we need to start the new grant-writing far before the funds run out. It's a constant cycle, man."

"I get it." Kyle had seen Matt go through that in the past. "Sure, I'll do it. How long can I have it before you need it back?"

"It's about thirty minutes, so a week?"

"Sounds good."

"What's your fee?"

Kyle clicked his tongue in annoyance. "I'll do it for free."

"Kye, you don't have to."

"No, really, I'll do it gratis. Reinvest the money into the project."

After a brief pause, Matt said, "Okay. As long as you promise to show up for the Oscar ceremony."

"Kinda optimistic there, aren't we?" Kyle asked with a laugh.

"Power of positive thinking. C'mon. You look really sharp in a tux. And I want you to meet Gil." Matt cleared his throat. "Um, if you do go, will you bring a date too?"

Smiling at the folly of planning imaginary attendance at the Academy Awards, Kyle said, "I think so."

"Really?"

"My running partner. Seth Caplan. He's... we're...." He fumbled for the words before settling on simple ones. "It's true love."

"Jeez, Kye. I'm so glad to hear that. I hope he's good enough for you."

"Well, he's a lawyer, but I'm willing to overlook that," Kyle joked.

"Bring him when we go collect our Oscar. I have a story or two I want to tell him about you."

"Sure. As long as I get to dish to Gil."

Matt laughed loudly. "Done."

WHILE KYLE collected plates and Seth set the table, Lily sat and waited, secure in her role as food provider. She had, after all, been the one to contribute the boxes full of delicacies from their favorite Chinese place. "So what do we have?" asked Kyle after taking his seat. He'd put in an especially long day finishing a book in which one protagonist spent two hundred pages not telling the other guy he was the biological father of the tennis prodigy the other guy had been coaching. Consequently, Kyle's throat was a little sore and he was sick to death of rackets and nets.

"Kung pao chicken's directly in front of you at six o'clock," Lily said. "Move clockwise for rice, mongolian beef, hunan shrimp, and szechuan vegetables. Pot stickers are in the middle."

"Sounds like someone was in the mood for spicy," said Kyle as he reached for the carton of chicken.

"As if you two aren't spicy enough already," she said. Twice in the past few weeks she'd walked in on them while they were making out. At least they were clothed each time. Now she made a point of ringing the doorbell when she showed up at Kyle's house.

Seth plopped down next to Kyle. "Spicy food's good for you when it's hot out. It increases blood circulation and sweating. Cools you off."

"I do have air conditioning," Kyle pointed out.

"Sure, but I figure we need all the help we can get after today's run." An early heat wave had settled on Chicago, and even though they'd set out at 5:00 a.m., they'd been miserably overheated by the time they returned to Kyle's house. Of course, that hadn't much deterred them from a tumble in Kyle's bed. But then it would take a bigger force of nature than high temps to accomplish that feat. They'd been doing a whole lot of tumbling.

Kyle silently cursed himself, wishing he'd put off this line of thought until after taking a few bites of food. Then he could have attributed his flush to capsaicin.

For a while all three were busy with food, but then Lily tapped her plate with a chopstick. "Hey, you guys want to come to Grant Park tomorrow afternoon? The orchestra and chorus are rehearsing for this weekend's festival performance, and Gary and I thought it would be fun to go. Lunch alfresco and free music, right?"

"I can't—" Kyle and Seth began in unison, making her laugh.

"You guys are adorable. What are the excuses?"

Kyle spoke first. "I have to go downtown and record that SUV commercial."

"That's our Kyle," Seth said, giving Kyle's shoulder a quick squeeze. "The voice of overcompensating vehicles."

"That's me. And then I have a support-group meeting." He'd been attending twice a month, and although at first he'd been skeptical, now he had to admit they were worth his time. If nothing else, he got a lot of great tips on living with limited vision. Plus everyone shared their stories, and it was heartening to hear about other people occasionally blundering their way into difficult spots. It reminded him that mistakes were human.

"Well," Lily said, "you can join us, Seth, even if boring brother is boring."

"Thanks, but I'm boring too. I have this thing at work."

Seth had been spending a lot of time at work over the past couple weeks. Some new project, he said, and he seemed really excited about it but refused to divulge any details. "If it works, you'll hear about it eventually," he'd said. "And if it flops, no use getting hopes up." Which drove Kyle crazy, naturally, but he was trying to be an adult about it. Things were otherwise pretty damn wonderful with Seth despite their complicated lives, and Kyle didn't want to let this one thing upset their balance.

"Fuddy-duddies," Lily said with a sigh. "Pass the shrimp, please, Kyle."

He handed it over, but not before snagging a little extra for his plate. "Gotta pay the mortgage somehow," he said.

"I've seen your schedule, Kyebye. You're booked. No problem keeping up with the bills."

That was true enough. His inability to do anime VO work still hurt, but the pain was eased by his popularity for audiobooks and advertisements. Matt's documentary had turned out well too. "Yeah, I'm keeping busy."

"That reminds me! We need to go over the schedule for Anime Midwest. Daniel and Aero are going to need time with you, plus there are the panels and—"

"I'm not going."

He could almost hear her gape. "What?"

"Not going." His dinner sat heavy in his stomach, the good flavors gone bitter in his mouth. He'd been avoiding this conversation for some time—avoiding even *thinking* about it. Now the con was only two weeks away.

"But it's right here in Chicago," Lily protested.

He shoved his plate away. "I know where it is."

"C'mon, Kyebye! You've got fans clamoring to see you, and—"

"Clamoring to see the voice of Ecos, you mean. I'm not him. Not anymore." Because anime faces were the same as flesh-and-blood ones: black holes. Blank canvases. He couldn't see the mouths to get the words synced properly, couldn't see the expressions to get the emotions right. Anime and movie dubbing, the two things he most loved to do, were now lost to him forever. He needed to face the fact that he could no longer be Ecos, in any language. Or be Daniel Craig, for that matter.

Appearing at cons and signing autographs for people who loved Ecos, doing all the familiar voices—these were just ways of keeping a dead dream shambling around like a zombie. He needed to lay that corpse to rest and move on.

"Have you told the organizers you won't be going?" Seth asked softly. Not accusingly at all, and Kyle could have kissed him for it. Would probably convey his thanks later, after Lily was gone.

"Not yet. I've been too chickenshit. And I haven't had the balls to tell Daniel and Aero-Sensei either."

"Okay," Seth said thoughtfully.

Lily made an aggrieved sound. "It's *not* okay! This con is right here in our front yard, so you don't even need to fly anywhere. Aero's coming all the way from frigging Japan, and—"

"Lily!" Seth sounded firm and confident. "I know you love Kyle and want the best for him, but you really need to lay off on this. Bullying isn't going to help."

For a moment Kyle was chagrined to need defending. But then he remembered that Seth defended people for a living, and so he took the role naturally. Besides, a partner's role was to help buffer you when relatives were troublesome, right? Just like Kyle willingly played along when Ruth confused him with Arturo or Seth's brother or—once, but memorably—a rabbi. And after a lifetime of being the baby of the family, the one who everyone else felt entitled to give advice to and boss around, it was nice to have backup.

"I'm not bullying," Lily said in a tiny voice.

"I know you don't mean to, Lil," Seth replied. "But let Kyle make his own decisions. He's a big boy. I don't think he's making this choice lightly."

After a long pause, Lily said, "You're right. I'm sorry, Kyebye. You're amazing. I shouldn't expect you to be superhuman."

Kyle made a lucky grab for Seth's hand and held tight while smiling at Lily. "Thank you for worrying about me. God, I know I've caused everyone a lot of grief over the years."

"You haven't—"

"I have. C'mon, Lil. Zip lines? Or perhaps you might recall the shopping cart Olympics? Or the time I decided to excavate my own mine? I don't blame you for worrying. But it's been over two decades since I exploded anything. I'm going to be okay."

While his speech convinced Lily to change the subject away from Anime Midwest, Kyle's own words made him doubt his decision to stay away. He'd been brave, once upon a time. After that conversation with his father several months ago, he'd promised himself he'd find his fearlessness again. There was nothing valiant about backing out of a con.

Shit. He needed to make a decision, but even thinking about it tied his stomach in knots.

Kyle and Seth cleaned up after dinner, storing the leftovers in braille-identified containers in the fridge and then washing the dishes. Lily gave them each a quick hug when they were done. "I'm heading home."

"Stay," Kyle said. "We're just hanging out for a little while until Seth has to leave."

"Is your mom okay?" Lily asked Seth, sounding concerned.

"She has good days and bad. Lately the bad days have been coming more often. I'm just trying to spend as much time with her as I can."

"I bet you'll never regret any of that time." She sighed. "But anyway, I gotta go. I am out of clean clothes and food, and if I don't do something quick, I'm going to end up going to tomorrow's meeting in my Captain America pajamas."

Kyle walked her to the door, locking it when she was gone. Then he marched to where Seth waited, grasped his shoulders, and kissed him forcefully enough to back Seth into a wall.

"What was *that* for?" Seth wheezed when Kyle eventually broke off the kiss. He was hard and so was Kyle, their erections straining at each other through their layers of clothing.

"Riding to my rescue, oh fair knight."

Seth snorted. "Does that make Lily a dragon? And you a damsel in distress?"

"Something like that. Let's just say I find your lawyer voice very sexy." Kyle nipped at Seth's earlobe.

"Really? Well, then." Seth deepened his voice. "Hearsay is an out-of-court statement used to prove the truth of the matter asserted therein. And…. Oh, God, yeah, do more of that." *That* being Kyle firmly massaging the front of Seth's khaki shorts while simultaneously licking

Seth's neck. "A future interest m-must vest, if at all—Jesus, Kyle— within twenty-one years of a life in being at…. Mmmf."

More kissing, bright with the taste of chilies, and the soft thud of Seth's head against the wall.

They didn't make it to the bed that time. Not even the couch. Kyle ended up giving Seth a world-class blow job right there on the living room floor, making Seth cry out loud enough that Mrs. Zdunowski probably heard. Then Seth returned the favor. After, they lay in uncomfortable torpor on the hard floor, shorts and underwear around their knees, skin sticky with sweat.

"*That* was sort of adventurous," Kyle muttered.

"Huh?"

"Just thinking."

"IT'S ALREADY hot," Kyle complained as he and Seth did their prerun routine on his porch the next morning.

"I know. And the sun's barely up. This is as cool as it's going to get, unless you want to run in the middle of the night."

"Oh yeah, that'd be great. Let's run when neither of us can see a damned thing."

Seth laughed, then grunted.

"What on earth are you doing?" Kyle demanded.

"Bending over to touch my toes."

"Why?"

"Mrs. Zdunowski is watching through her front window, coffee in hand."

That made Kyle grin. "Giving her a thrill, are we?"

"You betcha. I try to get my charitable work in whenever I can."

They ran for just over three miles, sweat stinging Kyle's eyes and sticking his tank top to his skin. "I'm chafing," Seth complained as they ran.

"Where?"

"All the most uncomfortable places."

Kyle laughed. "You forgot to put on Body Glide, on a day like today?"

"You can't just kiss it better?" Seth was probably leering.

"When we get home. You want to cut it short today?"

"If you don't mind," Seth said. "God, I wish I was into swimming instead. Swimming sounds so good right now."

Kyle took a big swallow of his homemade exercise drink. "I used to be a pretty decent swimmer. I considered training for a triathlon, actually, but never did." He thought for a moment. "Do you think you could guide me through that? Or... I don't know. I'm not sure how the cycling part would work." He pictured himself riding at full speed into a crowd while Seth shouted, *Oops! I meant turn left, not right!*

"I bet there's a way to do it. Let's look into it."

"There is a blind triathlete at the Bridge. We could ask her." Kyle grinned. "Race you home."

They tried to up the pace, laughing as the other started to pull away, still tethered together. Kyle felt Seth start to falter due to the chafing, and they took the rest of the run at a slower pace than usual. Back in the house, they were happy to strip off their clothes. They took turns in the shower, which wasn't big enough for two, and then Kyle doctored Seth with some Neosporin and gratuitous groping. Clean and dressed, they headed downstairs, where Kyle made them some breakfast. They skipped coffee, opting for ice water instead.

"Long day at the office today?" Kyle asked while they were eating.

"Pretty much. I have these contracts to finalize on a new app we've been working on. How about you?"

"Starting a new book. No tennis or secret babies this time. Biker gangster with a heart of gold instead."

"Aww." Seth chewed and swallowed. "Hey, Kyle? Can I tell you something without pissing you off?"

Kyle's hackles immediately rose. "Depends."

"It's about Anime Midwest. But I *don't* mean to pressure you, okay? If you tell me to drop it, I will. I just thought... maybe you'd want to think about this."

In truth, Kyle had thought about the con all the previous night, tossing and turning when he should have been sleeping. One minute he'd firmly decide he wasn't going, and the next he'd conclude that he absolutely was. "What do you want to tell me?" he asked.

"Adam West."

"Um... what?"

"Adam West. He played Batman in the sixties TV series."

Kyle huffed impatiently. "I know who he is. I met him once."

"You met Adam West?" Seth sounded inordinately amazed, as if Kyle had just informed him he'd returned from a vacation on Mars.

"Sure, at a con. He does VO work. Nice guy."

"Jesus Christ. You know Adam West."

"We're not best buds or anything. But if you think his presence is going to lure me to Anime Midwest, you're out of luck. Been there, done that."

Seth scooted his chair closer. "Adam West is going to be at Anime Midwest?"

"Not that I know of."

"But you just said he was!"

"You're the one who brought him up, not me." Kyle rubbed his forehead, hoping to fend off an incipient headache. "Why are we talking about Adam West?" he asked plaintively.

"Because he's awesome and improves any conversation. And because of the analogy to you."

"You… think I should wear a cape?" Kyle ventured.

"No, although now that you mention it, well, it might be a good look on you. But here's the thing. He played Batman, what, fifty years ago?"

Kyle calculated. "Sounds about right."

"And he's never going to play him again. That batship sailed decades ago."

"Okay."

"Since then, there have been other Batmen." He chuckled. "Michael Keaton. Val Kilmer. George Clooney. Christian Bale. Ben Affleck! But it doesn't matter how many years pass or who else puts on that mask. It doesn't even matter that Adam West has done a lot of other work since then. He's Batman. I don't know how he feels about that. Maybe he's spent half a century cursing being typecast. But he still goes to cons— and fans still come to see him. I would."

By now Kyle had a pretty good idea of Seth's point, but he decided to play dumb. "So?" he asked, leaning back in his chair.

Seth poked Kyle's arm. "You're Ecos. Maybe you won't voice him again. Maybe somebody else will. But you'll always be him. Your fans will always love the work you've done. If you want to move on, that's fine—I wouldn't blame you. But if you want to go to a con now and then, sign a few autographs, fend off groupies with the Cane of Pain, that's legit." Seth took Kyle's hand. "Either way, I'm here."

For several minutes Kyle mulled over what Seth had said. It made sense. Even better, it helped him reach a decision. "I don't have to wear plastic nipples, do I?"

Seth hooted a laugh and leaned close to kiss Kyle's temple. "Nope. Although maybe I should give that a try myself. It'll help with the chafing issue."

CHAPTER SEVENTEEN

"I SHOULD have worn a costume," Seth muttered as they walked through the convention center lobby. Kyle had tucked his folded cane under one arm, and Seth guided him through the crowds. He kind of wished they'd brought their tether, even if it would have looked weird.

"Who would you dress up as?" Kyle asked. *Focus on Seth. Seth is safe. Ignore the crowds.* Easier thought than done, because the place echoed with hundreds of voices. And somebody nearby smelled like stinky feet.

"No idea," Seth said. "I don't really know anime characters."

"Robin," Kyle said firmly. "Not exactly anime, but if I'm Batman, you've gotta be Robin."

"The Boy Wonder? I'm not sure green is my color."

"Well, there's the beauty of it. Your costume could totally clash with your skin tone, and I'd never know."

"Tell you what. You show up at the next con in spandex and a cape, and I'll do the same."

Kyle chuckled. "I think I'll stick to jeans and a button-down, thanks."

"Just as well. I always thought that whole young-ward thing was a little creepy."

Snickering, Kyle walked with Seth through the crowds. He'd decided to attend the con as long as he could limit his appearances and keep Seth as his handler. Seth was fully on board with that, and Lily had been so pleased Kyle was going that she hadn't complained. Consequently, Kyle had to be present for only three events: a panel discussion on voice acting, an autograph signing—both today—and an *Ecos*-specific panel the following day. After that last event, he was going out to dinner with Daniel, Aero, Seth, Lily, and a few other people. Or at least, so Lily had informed him; Kyle wasn't privy to the details. He figured by then he'd be relieved to have the con over with, and he'd happily drink himself senseless with whatever booze the restaurant offered. He was hoping for something other than kombucha.

"Oh my God!" cried a young woman.

Seth came to a screeching halt, Kyle jostling against him.

"You're Kyle Green!" the woman said. "Oh my God! I got your autograph two years ago at Anime Expo, and we got a picture together too. I shared that photo on Tumblr and got, like, a bazillion reblogs."

"I'm glad to run into you again."

"Can I get another photo? I know it's not official photo op time, but it would be so cool and all my friends will be, like, insanely jealous."

"Sure." He smiled at her. "What's your name?"

She giggled. "Sasha. And thank you. Oh my God!"

Kyle let go of Seth's elbow. "Would you mind getting a shot of us together?"

"I'd be glad to."

Sasha was so excited she fumbled her phone twice before handing it over to Seth. At least with her constant nervous laughter, it was easy for Kyle to locate her. "I'm going to put my arm around your shoulder in a little hug, if that's okay," he said.

"Okay? Oh my God! I'll never wash this shirt again. It'll be, like, my official Kyle Green Hugged Me shirt. My friend Ella? Well, sometimes we fight a lot but usually she's my friend, and she was supposed to come here today but ended up going to some stupid baseball thing with her boyfriend instead. She is going to shoot herself when she sees this picture! I'm going to Snapchat it to her as soon as we're done."

While Sasha babbled, Kyle positioned himself beside her and carefully draped an arm over her shoulder. She was short and smelled vaguely like vanilla and peppermint, and her frizzy hair tickled his arm.

"Say cheese," Seth ordered.

"That's boring," Kyle countered. "How about if we say yaoi instead?"

Which they did while Seth took several shots, including one of Kyle kissing Sasha's head. That made her squee so loudly Kyle worried about his hearing.

"You're the best!" she enthused after Seth returned her camera. "You are so cool. You've, like, totally made my year. And your boyfriend is hot!" Still giggling, she disappeared into the crowds.

Seth offered his elbow to Kyle, and they resumed their journey. "Well, *that* was frigging adorable," Seth said.

"It's embarrassing."

"You should've seen her. That kid was glowing. You're a real celebrity."

"I'm—"

Seth stopped and set a hand on Kyle's shoulder. "She was thrilled. She probably already has those photos plastered all over her social media. And she didn't give a crap that you can't see or whether she's ever going to get more episodes of *Ecos* from you. You are the famous voice actor who was nice to her."

"It was a just a couple pictures."

"Yeah, but that was enough. Your fans are stoked by you, Kyle Green. They adore you just as you are."

"Even with no more Ecos?"

"Adam West, babe. Adam West."

THE PANEL discussion was fine. It was fun, actually. Kyle and the other actors talked about some of their favorite roles and most enjoyable scenes. Then the moderator took suggestions from the audience and had the four panelists do an improv bit about the animals of Noah's ark planning a mutiny. By the end, everyone was laughing so hard—including the panelists—that they had to stop. The audience applause shook the room.

Afterward, a crowd formed around the front table, but Seth fought his way through and took Kyle's hand. "That was awesome," he whispered into Kyle's ear. "You're awesome. You're so getting laid tonight."

Blushing, Kyle wondered if anyone could overhear.

Kyle introduced Seth to the moderator and his fellow panelists, and then, just when the crush of the crowd felt like too much, Seth cleared his throat. "Shit! We have to get to that thing, Kyle. We're late."

There was no *thing* to be late to, but Kyle gratefully allowed Seth to lead him out of the room, into a back hallway, and over to the hotel lobby. They'd decided to book a room for the night rather than fight traffic, and now Kyle was grateful they had a private retreat space. He slumped against the door as soon as it was closed. "So many people," he groaned.

Seth leaned against him, chest to chest. "I am so in the wrong business. Lawyers never get mobbed by fans."

"I'll mob you," Kyle said, grabbing Seth's ass.

"Perfect."

They made out for a while but didn't move past second base. The autograph session was drawing close, and Kyle didn't want to look too debauched for it. It was pleasant enough to kiss and engage in a little light petting, and then they lay atop the bed, fully clothed, resting.

"You know what?" Kyle said. "I know exactly what this room looks like even though I've never seen it. The furnishings are various shades of brown and tan."

"Got it."

"There's a little card somewhere telling us how to save the environment by reusing our towels. And another inviting us to join Hyatt's customer loyalty program."

Seth sat up, probably to look around. "Yep. What else?"

"Logoed pad of paper and matching pen by the bedside phone. Possibly another on the desk."

"Okay, hotshot. But what about the artwork?"

Kyle rubbed his chin. "Normally I'd say semiabstract cityscape featuring Willis Tower, Marina City, and/or the Bean. But since we're near O'Hare, I'm going out on a limb and saying the art involves airplanes."

"Ding-ding-ding-ding!" Seth rolled mostly on top of him. "Kyle Green, you're today's lucky winner. What do you want for your prize? Door number one or door number two?"

Suddenly quite serious, Kyle cradled Seth's face in his palms. "I've already claimed my prize."

"One lawyer, slightly used?"

"One incredible man who's guided me right into happiness."

"That's the corniest thing I've ever heard," Seth said. But then he kissed Kyle, soft and sweet.

THE AUTOGRAPH session went well. Seth made an excellent handler, snapping photos, guiding Kyle where to sign, fetching cups of water when Kyle's mouth went dry. A lot of the fans seemed to be aware that Seth and Kyle were a couple—how they knew, Kyle had no idea—which made the girls coo at them. Some people even wanted Seth in their pictures, much to Seth's amusement and delight. "Woo-hoo!" Seth said at one point. "Auxiliary fame!"

Seth's presence made everything more fun, but still Kyle was relieved when the session ended. Seth whisked him away to their room, where they ordered too much food from room service, ate until they were stuffed, and then crammed into a shower that was only slightly bigger than the one in Kyle's master bathroom. Clean and partially aroused, they lolled on the bed.

"Thanks for doing this with me," Kyle said.

"Thanks for letting me. I've been enjoying myself. It's really cool to see this side of your life, Kyle. I mean, I listen to your books and I've watched some of your shows, but this is… really cool. I never thought I'd watch my boyfriend sign a girl's tits!"

Kyle laughed. "I have no idea why anyone would want to walk around with *Kyle Green* scrawled on their boobs."

"Hmm." Seth guided Kyle's hand to Seth's chest. "Sign me."

Humoring him, Kyle traced out his signature with a finger, making Seth shiver lightly. "Sexy," Seth concluded.

"My finger's not a Sharpie."

"A Sharpie's not going to work on my chest unless I get waxed, and I'd rather not go there." Seth captured the idly moving finger and brought it to his lips for a kiss. "Seriously, though. I'm glad to be here with you."

"Ditto. I'm sorry Lily had to miss today, though." She usually loved this con, but some mysterious work catastrophe had pulled her away today. She'd promised to show up for the *Ecos* panel the following afternoon.

"She'll catch us tomorrow."

"She needs to relax. She's been distracted lately. You too, by the way."

Seth sighed. "Sorry. It's just—"

"I know. Work's busy and there's your mom. You don't have to apologize. I'm just saying, you deserve some downtime. Babysitting me at a con doesn't count."

"Babysitting? Is that what you think I'm doing?" Seth sounded on the edge of anger. He sat up, probably so he could glare down at Kyle. "I just told you I'm happy to be here. I'm having fun. It's a major goddamn thrill to see people lining up to talk to *my* boyfriend."

"Yeah, but you have to lead me around and—"

"Don't *have* to—want to." His tone softened. "And it's not exactly a chore. For one thing, it gives me an excuse to get touchy-feely with you in public. For another, after a lifetime of being single, it's a rush being so openly taken, you know? Especially when I'm taken by someone as awesome as you. And for another—we're up to three here, and I hope you're keeping track 'cause there will be a quiz—I *like* helping you. It's what partners do. You've spent hours and hours letting me cry on your shoulder over Mom, right?"

Kyle reached for Seth and managed to pull him down into a hug. "Okay. I get it," he said. "It's all good. I'll get over my insecurities eventually."

"You and me both," Seth said with a small chuckle.

"Someday we'll take a real vacation, though, okay? I'd love to show you Tokyo. Or Barcelona. I want to sit beside you in a vaporetto in Venice. I want to tromp through a Scottish castle with you, and drink port with you in Porto, and eat street food in Bangkok, and listen to Mozart in Vienna. I want you to drink Bosnian coffee with me in Sarajevo and smell the fish markets in Shanghai. I want to run with you on a trail through the Alps. I want to hear you scream your way down a zip line." As he said those things, a realization hit him: he would enjoy experiencing those places through Seth's eyes as much as if he were seeing them himself.

Seth made an odd little sound in his throat and nestled his face into Kyle's neck. "I want those things too." His voice was muffled, but Kyle understood.

"This is going to work," Kyle said confidently. "Seth Caplan, I'd like a future with you."

"Oh God, there's nothing I'd like more," Seth said before kissing Kyle's neck.

"Permanent?"

"Like… walking-down-the-aisle permanent?"

Kyle smiled widely. "Aren't you supposed to get down on one knee to propose?"

"You wouldn't see me anyway, so let's pretend I'm kneeling. I only… I think Mom would really, really like to see me married. Um, shit. Not that I want to pressure you."

"I would be very happy if you made an honest man of me," Kyle said, then kissed Seth's head. "I think my family would be equally thrilled. Is it okay if my sister is maid of honor?"

Seth was crying—Kyle felt the dampness of his tears. But damn if Kyle wasn't crying too, his sightless eyes overflowing with salt water. "Yes on the maid of honor if you'll wear a yarmulke."

"Done."

There was a long pause filled with sniffling. Then Seth spoke. "Oh God. I'm getting married!"

"What a coincidence. Me too."

CHAPTER EIGHTEEN

KYLE AND Seth did a five-mile run around the hotel in the morning, airplanes roaring close overhead. Then they showered, dressed, and checked out of their room. In hopes of eating without being interrupted by fans—a concept that still tickled Seth—they walked to a nearby hotel and had brunch at the restaurant there. But Kyle mostly picked at his food, and judging by the sound of things, Seth wasn't exactly ravenous either.

"Second thoughts about getting hitched?" Kyle finally asked him.

"No! Why? Are you having cold feet?"

"My feet are very warm." Under the table, Kyle tapped Seth's toe gently with his own. "But you're awfully jumpy today. Is the *Ecos* panel bugging you? You don't have to go."

"The entire Marine Corps couldn't keep me away from that panel. I'm just a little worried about this work thing I have coming up soon. Ignore my jitters."

"Is everything okay?"

"I think so. I'm pretty sure so. But it's a big deal and a lot's at stake, so I don't want to see this thing go belly-up. But let's talk about something else, okay?"

So they spoke instead about the possibility of running a half marathon in September, and when they should try that new brewpub, and whether it was time for both of them to get new running shoes. Then somehow the conversation turned to weddings, which quickly turned into a more complicated topic than either of them had anticipated. So many decisions.

"You know what we ought to do?" Seth asked.

"Elope?"

"Yeah, because that would go over so well with both our families. I think we ought to let Lily plan the whole thing for us."

"My sister?" Kyle squawked.

"Let's face it—she's going to be in the middle of everything anyway. Why not let her take over? Honestly, I don't care much about the details as long as it's not too fancy and you say *I do*."

Kyle smiled. "'I am my beloved's and my beloved is mine.' I think we should say that too."

"You know that line?"

"It was in a book I narrated. Gay Jewish vampires."

Seth snorted. "Is that why the cross freaks them out? Okay. We tell Lily we want to say that line. And that we want the ceremony simple. And soon?" His voice cracked a bit over the last word, an acknowledgment of the unspoken truth that they didn't have long if they wanted Ruth to be present.

After considering for a moment, Kyle nodded. "Okay. Lily is our wedding planner. Just be prepared for her to boss us around."

"As if she doesn't anyway." Which was true. Lily had apparently decided that Seth qualified as another baby brother and was therefore fair game for her orders.

Despite the upcoming ordeal, Kyle felt almost lighthearted by the time the brunch was over. Yes, he was going to have to inform Daniel and Aero that his days as Ecos were over—and he was probably going to have to face disappointment from his fans. But he'd survive all that, and when he got home, he'd have a fiancé to cuddle and a wedding to dream about. Huh. He'd never pictured himself as misty-eyed over tuxedos and three-tiered cakes. And of course he and Seth also had the truly important things to think about—all the wonderful, gory details of merging two lives.

They had barely reentered the convention center when Lily descended upon them. "Where have you guys *been*? The panel's in, like, fifteen minutes, and the room is standing room only, and Daniel and—"

"We were talking about our wedding," Kyle said.

That brought her to a screeching halt. For a full five seconds she was utterly silent. "Wedding?" she finally squeaked.

"Yeah. Want to help us plan it?"

"Oh my God!" She gave Kyle a hug that squeezed all the air from him, squished Seth hard enough to make him grunt, then turned back to Kyle for seconds. "Congratulations! I'm so excited! Jeez, Mom and Dad are going to be over the moon."

Kyle nodded. "Maybe we can call them tonight after dinner and tell them the news."

"Maybe," she answered, but there was something odd in her tone. Before Kyle could ask why, she bonked his arm. "But you have a panel to get to, remember?"

As she'd warned, a large crowd had already assembled in the meeting room. The conversations buzzed loudly, filling the space and echoing off the ceiling and walls. But with Lily and Seth as his honor guards, Kyle walked confidently to the front, where Daniel and Aero were there to greet him with handshakes and, he knew, bows.

"I am so happy you were able to come to Chicago, Aero-sensei," Kyle said in Japanese.

"I am honored to be here. And I am delighted to see you looking so well."

"I'm feeling well, thank you. I, um, just got engaged, actually." He urged Seth slightly closer, then conducted introductions in both languages.

"Congratulations, congratulations to you both. Such wonderful news!" Aero seemed genuinely pleased, as did Daniel.

Which made the next bit harder. Kyle swallowed. "I, um, need to talk to you about the show. You've been so kind about working around my blindness, but Ecos can't stay silent forever. And I'm afraid—"

Aero-sensei interrupted him in English. "Let us talk about this later, if you please."

"It's important."

"Very much so. We can give the subject the time and attention it deserves later."

Kyle had to admit that minutes before a panel, in front of hundreds of people, was not the best time or place for this conversation. He shouldn't have been such a coward; he should have called Aero and Daniel weeks ago. "Of course, Aero-sensei. Just… be careful what promises you make to the crowd, please."

Aero continued in his fluent English. "We will take care. But I think everyone will leave this room quite satisfied today."

Seth squeezed Kyle's hand—Seth's palm was sweaty—and left to take his seat. Kyle and his colleagues remained standing on the raised platform, each behind a chair at a long table. Once introduced, they would take a seat in front of individual microphones. He knew from Seth's hasty description that large posters behind them displayed images from the manga, and a table off to one side held a collection of *Ecos* memorabilia and stills from the anime. The moderator, a round-voiced man named Sam, had a podium of his own, slightly to one side.

"Ladies and gentlemen, welcome to the *Ecos* panel!" Sam boomed. "I'd like to thank our panelists for being here today, some all the way from Japan!"

The audience clapped wildly. After they'd calmed a bit, Sam introduced the panelists—more clapping and even some cheers—and gave a rundown of what would follow as the panel seated themselves. The plan was for him to let the panelists address a series of prompts, and then he'd open things up for questions from the audience.

The prompts were good. Some were more serious, like the real-life social problems that had inspired certain story lines. And some were fun, as when Sam asked which Disney heroes or heroines would be best suited as Ecos's sidekicks. Kyle enjoyed the friendly banter, and the audience ate it up voraciously, responding with enthusiasm to everything the panelists said.

After a laughter-filled discussion about the Striped Pirate, one of Ecos's chief nemeses—Daniel-san got a roar of approval over his suggestion that the pirate try therapy—Sam stepped out from behind his podium. "Okeydoke. It's time for you guys to ask questions. I'm taking my mic with me so we can all hear you. Don't be shy!"

Kyle steeled himself, wondering how long it would be before someone asked when Ecos would speak again.

"You, sir," Sam said. "What's your question?"

"Well, I'd like to ask Mr. Green whether he's planning any zip lines anytime soon."

As the audience waited in silent puzzlement, Kyle nearly swallowed his tongue. He recognized that voice. He ought to—God knew it had been raised at him often enough in his youth. "Colonel?" he choked out.

"I asked you a question, young man."

Kyle felt his face grow hot. "Sorry, folks. Apparently somebody let my father in here." Oh, he was *so* going to have it out with Lily later. For now, he just smiled weakly. "Yes, sir. There are definitely zip lines in my very near future."

"That's what I want to hear, son."

Everyone laughed, but it was clear they were confused about what was going on. Hell, no more confused than Kyle. But when Sam chose the next audience member for a question, Kyle wasn't especially shocked to recognize his mother's voice. "Hello, honey!" she called out.

He sighed. "Hi, Mom."

This time the audience roared. Kyle's mother waited for a lull before she continued. "I have a question for you too. How come you never visit us? And by the way, Seth is very handsome."

Kyle covered his face with his hands. "I am so sorry, everyone," he said when the room quieted enough so he could speak. "I had no idea my family was invading today. Aero-sensei, Daniel-san, please accept my embarrassed apologies."

Aero answered through his chuckles. "Not at all! This is quite wonderful."

"Maybe somebody has some real questions? Someone who's not related to me?" Kyle asked plaintively.

"Does fiancé count?" Seth shouted. Several moments of chaos ensued. Kyle couldn't tell exactly what was going on, but it sounded as though the audience was having a wonderful time—and his parents were going a little nuts over the news that their baby boy was getting married.

"There's nothing like a nice, quiet announcement," Kyle finally said.

"I'm a lawyer. I like to make a big impression. Anyway, I do have a question for you. A real one."

"What?" Kyle asked suspiciously.

"Well, as you know—but the rest of this crowd doesn't—I work for an app development company. We've been working on this new app that I'm really excited about. We've betaed it quite a bit already, so I'm confident it works. But would you please try it out for us?"

Shit. This was all clearly part of some huge setup, but Kyle had no idea what was really going on. "Now?"

"No time like the present."

"But… we're in the middle of a panel discussion."

"I think everyone might want to see this."

"Yes," Aero chimed in. "Please demonstrate."

Great—so he's in on it too.

And everyone clapped, so Kyle could hardly refuse.

He sighed into the mic. "Okay. I guess."

Seth must have hopped from his seat and dashed over, because he was immediately at Kyle's side. Sam joined him, and they spent a few seconds fussing over wires of some kind. "It's just an iPad," Seth explained quietly. "We're setting it up so it's displaying on a screen."

"Why are you doing this to me?" Kyle moaned in a whisper.

"Because I love you. Okay, here we go." Poking at the tablet, Seth stood close enough to lean against him. Kyle didn't know whether to hug him or strangle him. "The app's open. Hang on... okay. Can you see anything?"

Kyle stared at the blackness, squinting where he thought the iPad was. And after a moment, he could see something—a flash of vague movement, and then.... "It's a ticker. Like the one on TV for weather warnings."

Seth heaved a noisy breath of relief. "Exactly. That's where I got the idea. Remember that evening in the basement?"

Kyle's face flamed. "Uh, yeah." And the subtext must have been obvious, because the audience wolf-whistled, catcalled, and laughed uproariously. Oh God, his *mother* was there.

"Can you read the ticker?" Seth asked.

"There's...." Kyle shook his head. "No words. Just a bunch of weird symbols. Arrows and stars and stuff."

"Perfect! That's perfect! Now, just a sec." Seth prodded the tablet some more. "Now what do you see?"

Above the scrolling symbols, colors coalesced into shapes. Kyle realized he was looking at an episode of *Ecos*—was looking at Ecos himself, actually. Ecos was in the middle of an argument with the Striped Pirate. He could make out the shapes and their movement, but not the details of the faces. Then the sound kicked in—his voice in English, squabbling with the voice of the guy who did the pirate. "I remember this episode. The Striped Pirate tried to enslave the dolphins, but I—well, Ecos—scared him off with the help of some sharks and octopi."

"Good!" Seth sounded as excited as a little boy opening birthday presents. "Now watch this." The scene replayed, this time with the dialogue and black lines, circles, arcs, and other shapes above the words. The lines changed shape as the characters spoke. The room was silent except for the anime. After a bit, Kyle *did* notice something. "Every time

Ecos talks, I see the line moving in sync with the dialogue. Oh! When Ecos laughs, an arc widens and then narrows again."

"The app reads facial expressions and translates them into a code synchronized with the related word. You can't see the cartoon face grinning, but you can see the lines. It's only going to take you a little time to learn the code—you picked up braille fast—and then you'll have a way to read facial expressions."

Kyle was so stunned that the importance of this didn't sink in at first. "It's like one of those flip books...." He stopped. "Oh. Oh, God. I can do dub work again." He swallowed thickly, coughed, swallowed again. "Aero-sensei? If you give me a little time to learn this, I think I can voice Ecos again."

The room erupted into cheers and applause, but Kyle was too busy embracing Seth to care. The embrace was followed by handshakes and quiet congratulations from Daniel and Aero and by drive-by hugs from his parents, Lily, and even Sam the moderator. Everything was entirely surreal.

Eventually the room settled, and Sam took questions from audience members. Kyle even answered some of them. But he had almost no idea what he said, because he was far too infused with joy. Less than a year ago, he'd thought he'd lost everything. Yet here he was, his family at his side, having gained far more than he'd ever dreamed.

He'd return to being Ecos. He'd regained a sense of adventure. But even better, he'd have Seth running at his side.

Chapter Nineteen

"THIS IS insane. I can't believe we've been sitting in line for nearly ninety minutes already just to get to the red carpet." Kyle, Seth, Matt, and Gil were in the back of an SUV limousine on the road to the Academy Awards ceremony. Six weeks ago Matt's documentary short, "The Petroglyphs of Time," had been selected as one of the five finalists. Now it seemed like six weeks had passed since they got into the car. At a near standstill, the limo air-conditioning was having a hard time keeping up with the unusually hot temperatures for late February.

"This is worse than the Eisenhower Expressway at rush hour," Matt complained. There was a slight rustling.

Kyle snorted. "Matt, don't tug at your collar."

"How do you know he's tugging at his collar?" both Gil and Seth asked, almost in unison.

"He never liked wearing a tie and would tug at the collar all the time."

Gil laughed. "You have that right. When we went to the gala fundraiser for the hospital, you'd think I'd asked him to cut off his arm when he read the attire was black tie only."

Matt was usually calm in any situation, but Kyle could smell Matt's cologne as it got stronger with each fidget. Then Matt groaned. "At this rate we'll miss the opening ceremony and the seat fillers will be in our seats."

"This is so much more glamorous on TV," Seth said.

Kyle smiled at him. "Smoke and mirrors—the Hollywood illusion."

Seth tapped his phone. "We're about four blocks away. Do you want to get out and walk it? The temperature is beginning to drop... from ninety degrees to eighty-nine. And it's forty-five minutes before the show starts."

Matt flung open the door, escaping one of his two prisons. Unfortunately, Kyle thought, he still had to wear the bow tie.

The walk down to the Dolby Theater took about ten minutes. "Finally," Matt sighed. "Let's get through the gauntlet and get in and cool off."

They were the nobodies of the group, so they thought they would slip right past the interviewers. But there was a news crew from Japan covering the awards, and they called out Kyle's name. They pulled Kyle over to talk to him about Matt's Oscar-nominated documentary short. Kyle drew Matt into the conversation and acted as translator between him and the journalist. When the interview finished, the journalist noticed the wedding ring on Kyle's finger. The reporter squealed, and Kyle and Seth were cooed over and pictures were taken. Once finished, they had only ten minutes to get to their seats before the live telecast.

"Let's go!" Matt said, and the four of them ran down the red carpet, nearly taking down Dame Helen Mirren, who was finishing up her last interview.

They made it just under the time limit to be seated. They were all the way back on the main floor with all the other documentary nominees.

"That was a surprise, the way the reporter reacted to our wedding rings," Seth commented as the emcee was warming up the crowd before the cameras began to roll.

"Our wedding wasn't much of a secret, was it?" It had been a beautiful ceremony, filled with friends and family and joy. And midway through the reception, Lily had confided that she and Gary had recently begun considering their own wedding. Life would become more complicated for her, especially considering she'd become a stepmother, but she was excited about the challenge.

The audience in the Dolby Theater began to clap as the live telecast began. Matt put his hand on Kyle's shoulder. "Hey! We're on TV!"

Kyle just laughed and asked, "Do I look as good in person as I do on TV?" Matt laughed, and Kyle could feel the tension slough off his friend.

Seth leaned over. "I'm glad that we're leaving for our long-awaited honeymoon in a few days."

"You're sure you don't mind honeymooning with Daniel and Aero?" Since same-sex marriage was not performed in Japan, Aero and Daniel had decided to spend their Christmas and New Year's vacation on a trip back to Chicago. They got legally married in the Windy City, in a ceremony that was a combination of Shinto and Christian traditions. The publisher of *Ecos* had gifted both couples with luxury accommodations in Tokyo, a private cabin on the Sunrise Seto/Izumo train, and a few nights' stay at a gorgeous inn near the Izumo shrine.

"It'll be fun," Seth said. "And I'm looking forward to AnimeJapan."

The evening went on, and then finally came time for the documentary short award presentation.

"Holy shit! Look who's presenting the award!" Seth exclaimed. "Helen Mirren!"

Kyle laughed. "Yes. And she was so polite to us, even though we almost left shoe prints on her back in our mad dash to get to our seats."

"What a weird twist of fate that she's presenting the documentary short subject. I think she either winked or gave the evil eye when she looked at our section."

As it turned out, a documentary on the search for the mythical giant Brute was the winner of the short subject. But after the ceremony, at the governor's ball, Matt's disappointment eased when he was approached by many stars and producers. His nomination had garnered a lot of attention, and there were several big donors interested in helping out the project. Before the evening was over, Matt had been promised enough money to extend the project an additional five years and give him and his crew a nice pay raise.

As Seth and Kyle danced close together, Kyle gloried in the feeling of being in his husband's arms. No matter where in the world their travels took them, they'd always find home together.

Kyle whispered in Seth's ear, "Let's get out of here and start that honeymoon early."

Kyle didn't get a verbal response. Just a laugh, a tug on the arm, and out the door to begin a new adventure. No longer running blind.

KIM FIELDING is very pleased every time someone calls her eclectic. Her books have won Rainbow Awards and span a variety of genres. She has migrated back and forth across the western two-thirds of the United States and currently lives in California, where she long ago ran out of bookshelf space. She's a university professor who dreams of being able to travel and write full-time. She also dreams of having two perfectly behaved children, a husband who isn't obsessed with football, and a house that cleans itself. Some dreams are more easily obtained than others.

Blogs: kfieldingwrites.com and www.goodreads.com/author/ show/4105707.Kim_Fielding/blog
Facebook: www.facebook.com/KFieldingWrites
E-mail: kim@kfieldingwrites.com
Twitter: @KFieldingWrites

VENONA KEYES is a modern woman who believes in doing it all; if doing it all is only in her head. She amazes people that she can be wholly unorganized yet pack a perfect carry-on suitcase for a ten-day trip to Paris. Ms. Keyes is a believer in the just-in-time theory, and can be seen sprinting to the airport gate before the plane door closes.

Venona has experienced love and loss at the deepest level, and is thankful for writing and daydreaming, for it kept, and still keeps, her sane. Writing also introduced her to some of the most supportive and wonderful people, to which she will always be grateful.

Venona is a voracious reader, loves her feline boys, volunteers at an animal shelter, attempts to cook everything in her CSA boxes, is an accomplished speaker, is a seasoned triathlete, and enjoys swimming, biking, hiking, skipping, and her beloved overgrown garden.

You can find Venona Keyes:

Facebook: www.facebook.com/venona.keyes
Goodreads: www.goodreads.com/author/show/5255358.Venona_Keyes
Website: www.venonakeyes.com

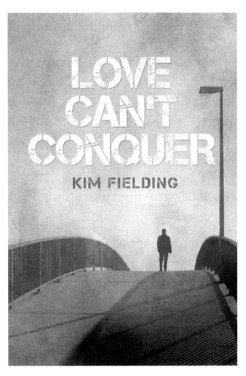

Bullied as a child in small-town Kansas, Jeremy Cox ultimately escaped to Portland, Oregon. Now in his forties, he's an urban park ranger who does his best to rescue runaways and other street people. His ex-boyfriend, Donny—lost to drinking and drugs six years earlier— appears on his doorstep and inadvertently drags Jeremy into danger. As if dealing with Donny's issues doesn't cause enough turmoil, Jeremy meets a fascinating but enigmatic man who carries more than his fair share of problems.

Qayin Hill has almost nothing but skeletons in his closet and demons in his head. A former addict who struggles with anxiety and depression, Qay doesn't know which of his secrets to reveal to Jeremy— or how to react when Jeremy wants to save him from himself.

Despite the pasts that continue to haunt them, Jeremy and Qay find passion, friendship, and a tentative hope for the future. Now they need to decide whether love is truly a powerful thing or if, despite the old adage, love can't conquer all.

www.dreamspinnerpress.com

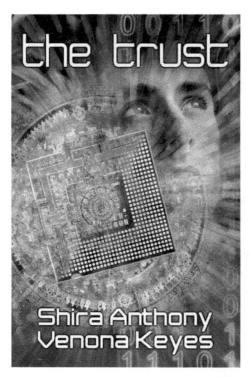

Eight years ago, Jake Anders was a college kid from the wrong side of the tracks. Then Trace Michelson recruited him into The Trust, a CIA-backed agency whose "executives" eliminate rogue biotechnology operations. Trace was everything Jake ever wanted in a man: powerful, brilliant, and gorgeous. But Jake never admitted his attraction to his mentor, and Trace always kept Jake at arm's length.

Now Trace is dead and Jake is one of The Trust's best operatives, highly skilled and loyal to the organization. But the secret agent has his own secret: six years ago, before he was assassinated, Trace designed a Sim chip containing his memories and experiences—and now that chip is part of Jake. It's just data, designed to augment Jake's knowledge, but when Sim becomes reality, Jake wonders if Trace is still alive or if Jake really is going crazy like everyone claims. He doesn't know if he can trust himself, let alone anyone else.

To learn the truth about Trace and the chip, Jake embarks on a dangerous mission—except he's not the only one looking for the information. Some of the answers are locked in his head, and unless he finds the key, he'll be killed for the technology that's become a part of him.

Now, more than ever, Jake wishes Trace were here to guide him. Too bad he's dead... right?

www.dreamspinnerpress.com